I0693828

"In *Promise in the Desert*, author Sheila Grinell paints a strong sense of place for this drama set in urban Phoenix. The themes of friendship, familial legacy, and loyalty weave throughout as the young Bee Wells must weigh her employer's hidden motives for a large swath of undeveloped land against her growing respect for the land's owner."

—Katrina Shawver, author of *Henry – A Polish Swimmer's True Story of Friendship from Auschwitz to America*

"Bee Wells arrives in Phoenix alone and naïve with a dream of creating a new way to live in the desert. She discovers a friendship that helps her succeed beyond her wildest dreams. This coming-of-age story combines adventure and romance with the ecosystem of this unique desert."

—Pam Hait, author of *Day Trips from Phoenix, Tucson & Flagstaff* (14th edition)

PRAISE FOR
Appetite, a Novel

"Grinell weaves a rich history of the Adler family, slowly revealing how Paul and Maggie grew apart and how Jenn became a free-spirited young woman. *Appetite* examines the different ways we seek satisfaction in our lives—some of us are hungry for power, others for love, and some find comfort in duty and tradition. This realistic and engrossing portrait of two generations is a promising first novel with wide appeal."

—*Booklist*

ALSO BY SHEILA GRINELL

Appetite
The Contract

Promise in the Desert

A Sonoran Stories Novel

SHEILA GRINELL

Sibylline Press

Copyright © 2025 by Sheila Grinell
All Rights Reserved.

Published in the United States by Sibylline Press,
an imprint of All Things Book LLC, California.

Sibylline Press is dedicated to publishing the
brilliant work of women authors ages 50 and older.
www.sibyllinepress.com

Sibylline Digital First Edition
eBook ISBN: 9798897409815
Print ISBN: 9798897409822
Library of Congress Control Number: 2025938499

Cover Design: Alicia Feltman
Book Production: Aaron Laughlin

To my sister, hoping she can read this

"We don't see things as they are, we see them as we are."
— attributed to Anaïs Nin

APRIL

average daytime high = 88° F

days of rain = 1

1

I parked in the driveway beneath forty-foot palms bordering a velvety lawn that didn't seem to belong in the desert. The house was too grand for one old lady to manage, so I expected to be greeted by a housekeeper when I rang the bell. Despite heavy shutters closed against the April sun, I could still hear a loud chime. Whoever lived here must be half deaf, and she paid a lot for help.

The door opened; a tiny woman in a scooter chair, white bob sprayed in place, stared at me.

"Mrs. Hammer? I'm Bee. We have an appointment?"

Had she forgotten? My boss had said she was over ninety, a legend in Phoenix, and still sharp as they come. I'd grumbled about why I got the weird assignments. He'd said it was because I'm good at improvising. I *have* always been willing to try new things, although that sometimes got me in trouble.

"Well, you're prompt." The woman pushed the little joystick beneath her right hand and the chair revolved one-eighty. She rolled into the house, and I followed. The Saltillo-tiled corridor led into a living room where a chintz-covered couch faced two matching wing chairs across a glass coffee table. Framed photographs, mostly black and white, crowded one wall. A larger-than-life painting of a toddler petting a dog hung opposite the picture window. Books and papers cluttered a desk crammed into a corner.

She scooted next to the couch and motioned me to sit. I did, tucking my bag behind my bare legs, waiting for her to speak.

"Tell me why you are here." She adjusted herself in her chair and stared at me with old eyes—brown irises rimmed in gray—surrounded by wrinkles.

"My boss sent me to find out if there's something you need or something I can do to help, since we're going to be neighbors. You and Continuity, I mean."

"To help me? I'm self-sufficient. Just a little problem with my hip." She nodded and raised one eyebrow. I do that too, when I'm skeptical.

She raised the other. "If he's so concerned, he should come see me himself."

I felt a blush coming on. Dammit, was I about to get slapped down?

"My boss would like you to know more about how our community is coming along. I'm here to explain." Actually, Nate wanted to know if she was going to oppose him. Most people dislike real estate development in their backyard. He'd told me to make a new best friend.

She leaned forward; voice lowered. "You mean *his* project. Or is it yours, Bee?"

"I just work for Mr. Hargrove. But I think his ideas are terrific." He'd warned me this could take a while. "Mrs. Hammer—"

"How old are you?"

"Almost twenty-three."

"Why don't you get something to drink? There's iced tea and water in the fridge in the kitchen."

"No, thank you." I didn't want to poke around her kitchen. Might be a musty-smelling, mess, like the old people's place back home. But Nate had sworn this assignment was vital, so, here I was.

"Come now, you must not be from Arizona. We natives know how important it is to stay hydrated."

"I had some water in the car. Happy to get you some, though." I got up to face the unavoidable.

The kitchen lay at the end of another long, tiled corridor; it was cool and light and tidy, evidence of a competent house-keeper. A glass-fronted cabinet in a corner held gold-rimmed cups and saucers. Family heirlooms probably, from a lifestyle lightyears from my own. I took two bottles of water from the fridge and returned to the living room, figuring it might grease the wheels to drink with her. I unscrewed the cap of her bottle and asked if she wanted a glass. She shook her head, so I handed over the bottle.

She took it in both shaky hands.

"Thank you. You seem like a respectful girl. Care to tell me about yourself?"

Okay, I thought, I'm making progress. "I grew up in Pennsylvania and came west when I was eighteen. I got an asso-ciate's degree, and when the economy tanked after Covid, I was lucky to land an entry-level job at Hargrove-Spence."

"Pennsylvania? So far away. Why did you leave home?"

I'd shoved that part of the story into the back of my brain, but it popped out under her scrutiny. I could feel the blush crawling up my neck, stinging my cheeks, and there was nothing I could do about it. "Oh, I wanted to see the country."

Mrs. Hammer squinted at me. "What about your family?"

"They're still back East."

Again, she raised penciled eyebrows. "Your parents let you go so far away alone?"

"They had no choice."

"Do you keep in touch?"

"With my little brother."

"I see." She folded her hands. "What do you do for Hargrove-Spence?"

"Promotions, mostly, and whatever else comes up. The company is innovative. It's doing Arizona a lot of good." I thought it was doing the whole *world* a lot of good, but didn't want to boast.

"So, you've been here four years and already you can make judgments about what's good for the state?" She crinkled a smile.

I guessed I'd overstepped in my enthusiasm. I needed a safer tack. "Mrs. Hammer, would you tell me about your ranch? I heard you also had a gold mine here on the property that your great-grandfather started."

"It was my grandfather. Silver, not gold, almost a hundred and fifty years ago. I'm ninety-two, you know." She drew herself upright, looking proud, and I didn't blame her. I'd like to make it to ninety-two with all my marbles and plenty of attitude.

"My great-grandfather came to Arizona because his daughter had tuberculosis. He bought the land that became the heart of the original ranch. My grandfather was a young man at the time, and he caught gold fever. Like most, he never succeeded. He found a silver vein on the family's property, but he didn't develop it properly. Except for my errant grandfather, my family has been ranchers, not prospectors, thank goodness."

"A hundred-fifty years. Wow."

She pointed to the wall of photos. "Go take a look."

There must have been two dozen photos on the wall. Men and women in nineteenth century dress. Men with wild facial hair. Men and a few women on horseback. A map of Maricopa County dated 1888 with a legend I couldn't decipher. Several pictures of cows with cacti in the background.

I heard the scooter whir behind me. Mrs. Hammer rolled up and pointed an arthritic hand—sporting a ring with three heavy diamonds on one bent finger—to a hill with a hole in it. Timbers shored up the top and sides of the hole. Ropes and odd-looking gear protruded from it.

"That's the original entrance to the mine. Not very hospitable, is it?"

I had to agree. But Nate wanted to know more about it.

She rolled to my right and pointed to another photo. "That's my great-aunt on horseback." A dark-haired young woman wearing leather chaps. "The one who had TB. She got better in the dry heat like so many others back then." She flicked her wrist. "As a teenager, she used to ride out at night when it was cooler, holding a blazing torch to burn thorns off the cacti so the cattle could eat them. It was really too dry here for the cattle they herded back then. Now we run a hybrid more suited to the territory." She screwed up her face. "I suppose I should say biome."

I couldn't help it: I burst out laughing. She looked so coy. I hadn't imagined that a rich old lady would care to impress me.

She waggled her forefinger at me. "Would you have done that job?"

"Sure. It sounds like fun. Only I don't know how to ride."

Her lips tweaked into a closed-lipped smile. Maybe I'd struck a vein myself. "Mrs. Hammer, are you still involved with the ranch?"

"Only with the finances. My son handles the rest. He's a dentist, really, but we have an excellent foreman. *His* family has lived on the land almost as long as ours." She did another one-eighty and rolled back beside the couch, talking as she rolled. "Now tell me what you want to know about the ranch."

I sat again, folding my legs over the bag that held the paperwork. Nate had told me to be straight with her, but cautious, which was good, because I'm allergic to lying. Despite the practice I'd had at home. Maybe because of it.

"Everything. I think maybe Hargrove-Spence wants to buy it." Oops, didn't mean to blurt like that.

She smiled. "Oh, I know that. What I don't know is why they've sent *you* to sweet-talk me."

She had me there. I didn't know either.

"Maybe because I like to learn things?" I thought for another nanosecond. "I've always wanted to go into a mine. My great-great grandparents were coal miners, but they closed the old mine where I'm from. Now they just dig coal from the surface. I've never walked into a hole in the ground. I bet it's impressive."

She harrumphed. "If you want to see it, I can show you photographs from the years it was in operation. It's dismal now, and dangerous."

I didn't want to see any more photographs; I wanted to get the feel of the place to report back to my boss. He'd said we needed first-hand knowledge of the White Bear Ranch, including the mine, sooner rather than later. "I'm really curious. I wouldn't disturb anything."

Her eyes glittered in their frame of wrinkles. "What about the snakes?"

Now, that was a challenge. Last week, walking in the Preserve, I'd come across a rattler on the trail right in front of me. I hadn't known what to do. They didn't teach about rattlers in school in Pennsylvania. Fortunately, it slithered away.

She must have seen me hesitate. She reached for my arm. Her touch was cool and light. "I shouldn't tease you. I understand curiosity. Even when it's motivated by commerce. I could have indulged mine more when I was your age, but I was too busy chasing cowboys. Then I married young. Too young." She pointed at my legs. "What do you have in the bag?"

"Drawings of the future community. A mission statement from Hargrove-Spence. And a burrito made by my roommate's mother. She's a good cook." Something told me not to rush her, so I didn't open the bag. "Would you like to see the drawings?"

"There'll be plenty of time for that. Tell me more about you. You have an unusual name for a young girl these days. How do you spell it?"

Every time I had to tell the story of my name, I felt my past tug at me. But there was no escaping her question without lying.

"Like the insect. My mother wanted me to have a Biblical name, and she picked Deborah, shortened to Dee. My father thought it would be funny to call me 'Bee' since our last name is Wells, and I sting." I clamped my mouth shut. I had never found the story funny.

She paused. "Do you want me to call you Deborah? We can use our proper names with each other. I can call you Deborah and you can call me Sydelle. That's my full name, although everyone for the last seventy-five years has called me Sy."

I liked that. "No, thanks, Mrs. Hammer. I'm fine with 'Bee.'"

Her little kindness loosened a kink inside me, and I began to think my assignment might work out. "May I have your permission to explore the ranch? I like to hike."

Her head shook slightly—was it a "no" or an old-age tremor? —and she patted my arm delicately. "In time, my dear, in time. First, we are going to get to know each other. You'll come visit me again. And when my hip is better, we'll see about going out to the ranch. With my son, of course. You'll have to meet him. He takes care of me, not that he needs to."

Jumped the gun after all. I hoped she couldn't see my discomfort. Old people didn't see well, but she seemed pretty aware of things.

She lifted her hand from my arm and placed it on the joystick. "Now you must go. I have a doctor's appointment to prepare for." The chair whirled around, and she headed toward the door. I picked up my bag and followed.

"Come see me next week," she said gesturing at the door. "I will have more time for you then." She scooted away as the door closed.

I followed the flagstone path, stepping onto the centers of the slabs like a little kid, to my car in the driveway. As Nate had said, this was going to take a while. She might be stringing me along just to have company. Maybe she thought I was stringing her along, which was sort of true. But she was interesting, and I had a goal. I'm good with goals.

I got in my car to head to central Phoenix, but I stopped at the intersection with Scottsdale Road. It would take forty-five minutes to get back to the office, or I could go north to check out Mrs. Hammer's ranch and take the Carefree Highway to I-17 South to go home from there. I turned north.

On the west side of the road north of Highway 101, vacant properties sat flat and colorless except for a saguaro here and there; the east side featured upscale malls and entrances to fancy developments with Spanish names like "Villa del Lago," although there was no lake in sight. Hargrove-Spence was building something lasting and beautiful in the foothills farther ahead.

I drove north and east, past a park, two towns, and the last of the golf courses, toward the gate of the White Bear Ranch. I'd meant to ask Mrs. Hammer if there had been an albino bear or if her family had invented a ghost story to keep the superstitious away. I would ask her next time. I pulled over on a gentle rise and got out for a three-sixty view. Hargrove-Spence owned land to the east and south. The mine lay to the north. I squinted to see if I could find the hill pictured on Mrs. Hammer's wall, but all the slopes looked the same: brown-green, with ocotillo spikes and creosote bushes, saguaro sprinkled in the sunniest spots. Saguaros, the trees of the Sonoran Desert, looked to me like giant, swollen phalluses, though everyone out here seemed to prize them. Perhaps because they symbolized The Wild West, which didn't really exist, although people pretended it did.

Two buzzards circled high overhead, and a lizard dashed across the gravel in front of me. I remembered the first time I saw a real roadrunner cross a road, just like in old-time cartoons on YouTube. But the coyotes didn't look like Wiley. They were more like long-legged, big-eared, skinny dogs, hungry, and evil. The desert was an alien landscape, for sure, but it was also magical, and people like Nate Hargrove were using the open space to experiment with how to live better. Nate was creating the world's first pandemic-proof, sustainable community. I was more than willing to babysit Sydelle Hammer to help him succeed.

A creosote bush sprouted in front of one of the ranch's gateposts. I rolled two of its tiny leaves between my fingers and sniffed. Nothing much, yet after a rain, creosote released an odor I found almost intoxicating. Even dry, the open desert smelled a lot better than my street in Phoenix's Sunnyslope neighborhood. I took one more deep breath and got back in my old car. I headed downhill toward the Carefree Highway and my forty-minute drive home. I hadn't thought about it before, but Carefree was also an aspirational name. Arizona was certainly a destination for dreamers.

2

Arms loaded with groceries, I opened my apartment door with my hip. My roommate Gabi hustled over and took one of the bags. As she led me to the kitchen, I glimpsed a bulging backpack on the floor in the hall. I laid my bag on our kitchen table. "I got the whole list except for yogurt. They only had the junky kind I don't like."

It was my turn to buy staples. We shopped separately for other stuff and cooked separately. Well, I didn't really cook, I assembled my meals. Gabi always shared the food her mother sent up from Ajo with whichever member of her family was driving north. We lived close to the I-17, within easy reach of her relatives. I sometimes bought beer to thank Gabi for the tamales I took from the freezer whenever I wanted to, which was pretty often. I'd developed a taste for Mrs. Martinez's cooking.

Gabi wagged her thumb like a hitchhiker toward our back door and ushered me out onto the concrete slab that served as our patio. We walked into the dusty alley behind our apartment complex. A couple of our neighbors were tending grills near their own back doors, sending the odors of lighter fluid and charcoal into the air. The cooks paid us no attention, and we ignored them back. In our low-rent neighborhood, you guarded whatever privacy was possible.

Gabi said, "My baby brother Aaron is crashing on our couch. Aaron moved out of my parents' and needs a place to stay. I think he'll be fine in the little room, if that's okay with you?"

The little room was actually a deep closet off the kitchen that was supposed to be a pantry but had served as a nursery for the previous tenants and still had blue teddy bears stenciled on the walls. I couldn't imagine a full-gown person living in it. "Too small, don't you think?"

"He only needs a bed. He'll be working and going to school. He won't have time to hang around."

"He'll need to eat and pee."

Gabi's eyes narrowed. "My parents want him to stay with me, at least for a while until he can get settled. I want to help him. He's a good kid. You'll like him."

Shit. Her parents. Even when their ideas were ridiculous, she still honored them. Gabi was a couple of years older than me, totally cool and hard-working. She didn't need parental guidance in anything, but she took it, which annoyed me. We disagreed about family. She said you owe them respect; I said only if they deserve it. I didn't communicate with my parents, and they didn't reach out to me. I *did* care about my little brother, and I texted him now and then. He didn't text back.

"Do you want Aaron to take over my room?" I felt I had to offer because Gabi had taken *me* in when I had nowhere to go four years ago. The apartment, the furniture, the freezer—all hers.

"No, no! Your room is your room. I promise this won't be for long."

I couldn't deny her. I nodded. She rushed at me and hugged, her softness molding around my bones, smelling like the fruit-flavored shampoo she favored. She rebounded and stepped into the kitchen to unpack the groceries.

I went into the living room and contemplated the figure stretched across the couch. Gabi was a thoroughly good person. It felt good to be around her because she was caring by nature and never asked for anything in return. But her brother, wrapped in a dirty hoodie, looked dubious.

I spoke his name, and he turned over. He was a masculine version of Gabi with the same broad cheekbones and deep-set eyes, but with a scraggly beard sculpted on the sides. His hair looked as if he rarely combed it, and I smelled cigarettes when he stood up. He was taller than Gabi, same height as me.

"You're Bee." Really low voice for a relatively short guy.

"Did your sister tell you this is a no-smoking apartment?"

He grinned. "Of course. She's the boss. I should quit anyway." He reached across the trunk we used as a coffee table for his phone. "I'll go put my things in my room."

His room? Evidently Gabi had already agreed to house him. "Just a minute. I have to empty it out. I have some stuff stored in there."

"I'll help." He rubbed his eyes, like a kid.

I turned on my heel. He followed me to the closet, which had no window and a utilitarian fluorescent fixture overhead. I imagined if he stretched his arms out sideways, they would almost touch the teddy bears on opposite walls. He'd have to organize his stuff vertically. Put up some shelves, all the way to the ceiling. I stopped myself; according to Gabi, he wasn't staying long enough to need shelves. I bent toward the cardboard cartons in the middle of the room that contained my stash and lifted one of them. Aaron picked up another and asked, "Where to?" I led him to my room down the hall.

"Put it under the window. You can stack another box on top." I thought I might turn the boxes under the window into a night table. Throw a cloth over the stack and put my speakers on it. The other boxes would have to sit behind my door until he split.

Aaron placed the carton where told. "What's in here that's so heavy?"

I was keeping the books and papers that had earned me my degree. They were my only valuables, paid for with student loans that I should start paying off as soon as I finish paying off my second-hand car. The books served as evidence of my ability to lead my own life far away from Pennsylvania. "Books." I didn't care to explain and launched a diversion: "So what brings you to Phoenix?"

He brushed hair back from his forehead and said, "I really want a cigarette. Come outside with me and we can talk?"

I detested smoking, but I wanted him out of my room—the pandemic had totally turned me off crowding—so I followed him onto the patio and watched him light up. The sun was low in a sky streaked with wispy clouds. Sunset would be gorgeous tonight, and I made a mental note to come out and look. The horizon would light up in bands of turquoise, pink, salmon, maybe even dark purple reflecting from the clouds against the fading blue. I never saw the sunset in Pennsylvania. Here, I never wanted to miss it.

"You know Ajo, where Gabi and I grew up?"

I shook my head. He lit a cigarette, holding it from the top like a gangster.

"Our grandparents went there from Mexico to work in the copper mine. It closed down when my dad was young. He became a mechanic. He's good with his hands." He tossed his head. "He wants me to join his business." He took a long drag on his smoke. "I'm not good with my hands."

"Can't you find something else?" I wanted to be polite for Gabi's sake.

"Not in Ajo." He smiled a crooked smile and took another drag. "I told my parents I'm going to get a job and go to school, like Gabi. They said okay if I stayed with her. They trust her because she works hard, and they feel guilty."

"What do you mean 'guilty'?"

His face lightened up. "Oh, you don't know. Sorry." He dropped the cigarette and crushed it underfoot. His sneakers looked expensive; they were untied, like a gangster's.

Gabi had told me that her mother, who was from Sonoyta across the border in Mexico, went to visit family in her ninth month, and Gabi was born there. She was the only one of the siblings who wasn't an American citizen. But she had a green card, so I didn't worry. Of course, I wasn't going to ask him to explain his comment. If there was more to know, Gabi would tell me. We shared everything. She was the only one who knew why I'd come west when I did, and I trusted her to keep my secret. No one else needed to know about my father's criminal behavior and how I got involved.

Aaron leaned close to me and said, "No more cigarettes, I swear."

I turned away from him. "There's another box. I'm going to get it."

"I'll get it." He held the back door open for me and followed me inside.

I went to my room to look for the shawl Gabi had given me to use as a tablecloth, and after a minute Aaron reappeared in my doorway with the last of the boxes. I pointed behind the door, and he put it down. I expected him to leave, but he stood there, an odd look on his face.

"My sister says your real name is Deborah. My name is biblical, too. My parents named me after my uncle and my grandfather, but they expect me to be like Aaron in the Bible and do great things. They've set me up to fail. What about you?"

An interesting thought: your name as fate. I wonder where that would leave me. "My parents don't care what I do."

"Then you're lucky." He extended his hand for a shake.

I shook it: warm and strong. He walked out of my room bouncing on his toes like a teenage boy. Who was this kid?

In all the time I'd roomed with Gabi, she'd never infringed on my space, although she had a right to since I wasn't paying half. We'd met at community college when I first enrolled. She had been assigned to mentor me and we hit it off. When her roommate left to have a baby with her boyfriend, Gabi invited me in. She knew I had no money, so she gave me a super deal. I made an okay salary now—well, I was still waiting for the promotion Nate had promised when I signed on, explaining that he couldn't pay me more because I didn't have credentials or seniority, but I could work my way up—but Gabi wouldn't change the deal. She said she'd gotten promoted to supervisor at her call center, and I was family. I guess that made me Aaron's cousin or something in her mind.

I shut the door and pulled my laptop out of the courier bag on the floor under the table. I sat on the floor and powered up. Gabi had given me the table to use as a desk, but I kept my printer on it instead. I didn't have the desk habit; there were no desks in the house where I grew up, and when I studied in college, I sat on a couch in a corner of the student center, books in my lap. I could use a desk at the Hargrove-Spence office, of course, but I felt odd sitting at it, as if I were pretending to be someone else, someone who assumed the universe came with desks.

I pulled out my phone to scan my email. Two messages from Hargrove-Spence, but I was too hungry to tackle them. I got up to go assemble my meal.

Gabi was in the kitchen putting a pot of water to boil. She invited me to have spaghetti with her and Aaron. I teased her about cooking for an invisible brother. She said he should be comfortable his first night in our apartment, *mi guerita*. Gabi called me "her little blonde" because I have blue eyes and mousy brown hair that she helps me highlight once in a while. When we go out, she makes me up, and then I don't look so plain.

There's nothing she can do about my twisted front teeth, of course. At least she doesn't call me "her little rabbit."

"No, thanks," I muttered. "I've got leftovers to put in a salad."

"My spaghetti is better than your salad."

Undoubtedly. I could sit with them and eat something warm and filling, or eat cold food alone. I'm not big on cutting off your nose to spite your face. I offered to turn my veggies into a side salad for everyone. Gabi radiated a smile.

I took my veggies out of the fridge and carried them to the sink, watching Gabi out of the corner of my eye. She chopped onions, then tomatoes. While the onions sautéed, she crushed garlic and took baggies of spices from El Super out of the cabinet. Maybe because she used Mexican oregano instead of the regular kind, her sauces always had a southwest flavor. She sang to herself as she worked, a sure sign of her pleasure. As I tore lettuce into pieces, I realized I needed more info. "Why do you call Aaron 'baby brother'? How old is he anyway?"

"He's your age, almost. He's the youngest and the only boy. He's everyone's baby."

Ah, ha! She wanted to mother him! Gabi once told me she'd gotten a scholarship to Northern Arizona University, but her mother hadn't wanted her to live "so far away." Give me a break! Flagstaff was only a five-hour drive from Ajo. She was close to her mom—they still talked on the phone every day— and she'd let her mother dictate where she went to school. The idea of her turning into a surrogate mom, like I'd been for my little brother, boiled my blood.

Gabi said, "I feel sorry for him. He was a senior when the pandemic hit. He stayed home in the lockdown, and then didn't leave, so he's a little behind."

I didn't feel sorry for him. I would never have gotten stuck at home, pandemic or no. Once before coming West, I had almost escaped. This amazing biology teacher in high school challenged me to think about my future, and when I told her I might want to help people like my mom, she convinced me to apply to a five-year nursing program at a community college two towns over. She helped me write the application essay, and I got in. My dad said he couldn't pay, and I couldn't swing it on my own. Well, I'd found a way to help people live better lives anyway.

My phone dinged. Another message from Hargrove-Spence. Thinking of my job, what did three emails sent at the end of the day signify? I finished assembling the salad and went to check.

3

Must be someone important that Nate wanted me to meet because he'd repeated himself. So, I got up early, filled my gas tank, and drove north to the construction site. I arrived at nine on the dot dressed up in black jeans, wedges with a little heel, a loose blouse with short sleeves, and studs in my ears. My work disguise, bought second-hand at the Buffalo Exchange. Plain me preferred cut-offs, tank tops, and hiking boots. Work me and plain me both liked my little leather purse that doubled as a backpack, perfect for carrying tools.

I parked beside the main gate and walked to the double-wide Hargrove-Spence used as a field office. The trailer and a row of port-a-potties were the only structures on ground that had been cleared for the central plat. Contractors in hard-hats passed in and out of the trailer. They normally started at seven to beat the heat, but because there were no neighbors to disturb at this site, they began here at the crack of dawn. None of the workers stopped to talk to me. I didn't mind. I liked hanging out on site, watching progress happen. I liked smelling the stacks of raw wood and the dug-out earth. I also liked the aroma of concrete drying.

I had fallen in love with the odor when Nate first assigned me to a project shortly after I started working for him; the smell seemed too strong at first, but as the foundation pour dried, my nose signaled better things to come. In the early years of the pandemic, real estate was thriving in Arizona. Low interest rates were good for buyers, and low inventory was good for sellers, so money was made by those who already had plenty. I, on the other hand, just needed a job.

Turned out, I grew to love that job. Not the social media part, which was supposed to be my principal role, but rather the promise. Nate made sense. He had begun planning Continuity when he saw how deeply the pandemic had shocked people. He realized that they would be in the market for change, so he asked a survey research firm to ask potential home buyers in two age groups about what would make them feel safe. Then he commissioned a couple of architects and engineers to expand on the focus group suggestions. Then he massaged what they produced and began selling the concept to the city planners. He told me he went around channeling Steve Jobs. Nobody knew they needed an iPhone until they held it in their hands. Same, he would tell people, about a residential community that conforms to your lifetime needs and is a model for planetary stewardship. I didn't follow the lingo, but Continuity felt like an antidote to the moral poison I'd left behind. It lit me up inside to think I could play a role in creating it.

Nate's Lexus pulled up to the trailer. He got out and walked around the car to open the door for his passenger. A pair of legs stretched out wearing white, tipped by sandals with rhinestone-encrusted straps. Nate offered a hand and she stood, an artificial blonde well into her middle years. I straightened my tall-girl slouch and prepared to greet them.

Nate said, "Bee, I'd like you to meet Katherine Morrison. Katie, this is the young woman I spoke about."

I spotted the diamonds on her finger. "How do you do Mrs. Morrison?" I expected her to flick eyes over me and swivel to the head honcho, like the other VIPs Nate ushered around. I was wrong. She stared at me and nodded.

Nate faced me. "Katie is one of the organizers of the Friends of White Bear Ranch. They're a group of volunteers interested in preserving history. She's come to see what we're doing here. I'd like you to get to know her. If I have to miss a Friends meeting, you'll fill in for me, so I'd like you to be prepared." He turned to her. "Are you okay in those sandals? Would you like to borrow boots?"

"I'm used to rough terrain. Do I need a hard hat?"

Nate said, "We won't get close to active construction." He motioned to the company jeep next to the trailer. "We're going to drive." He opened the door for her. I got in the back.

So, he was making an exception to the hard hat rule. I went on high alert.

I had never heard of Friends of White Bear Ranch. Nate had this way of throwing me into situations and explaining later. Even then he didn't tell me much. I guess he expected me to figure things out on my own, which I usually did. Sometimes, though, Nate told me things more appropriate for his wife or golf partner, like who got drunk at a business meeting or whose kids hated him. I didn't get it, but I forgave him for being eccentric because Continuity made me happy.

Nate drove uphill to the end of the property next to Mrs. Hammer's ranch. We climbed out of the jeep and faced southeast so we could see the extent of the construction. The site was still in the prep stage, laying down roads and sewers. It looked like Mars: no vegetation, channels and ridges cut into the bare, red earth. Scoops and tractors were crawling along, looking like toys from this distance. I turned around to see if I could spot the entrance to Mrs. Hammer's mine from this angle. No luck.

Nate began his pitch. I watched Mrs. Morrison's face. She and Nate made a handsome couple, both blondish, wearing clothes from Banana Republic or someplace more expensive.

"As you can see," Nate told her, "the structures will be centralized down below. Primary access is from the road on the east side."

He waited a minute as she shaded her forehead with her hand and took in the vista.

Then he continued. "The key ingredient here is flexibility. We're not offering the typical product mix, no single-family houses, or condo towers or multi-family rentals. We're creating flexible structures that accommodate the needs of the people who commit to them. The structures will change configuration depending on collective decisions. For example, if the residents of a particular compound want to segregate by age, we move walls around and arrange a senior living section, move day-care to another space. Everyone can have a home office however they like it organized, and video intranet. Everyone in the community can work from home simultaneously without interference, if they want to."

Nate paused for a reaction, but Mrs. Morrison stared straight ahead. He did not show any sign of impatience, and I admired his cool.

"If there's an emergency or a new virus, people in the community can stay socially connected to each other but physically isolated from essential services, which are located over there," he pointed, "off the highway and highly automated. We have our own solar power alternative and our own first responders; of course, we coordinate with the county and DPS."

He waited. Still no questions. He lowered his voice conspiratorially. "Our technology is top notch. Glass walls that darken as the sun shifts with no draperies or crevices to harbor germs. We have our own hygienic water supply and a full-service clinic that can convert every room to negative pressure at the touch of a switch. The buildings will use natural ventilation and sunlight as much as possible, and that's quite a lot if you do it right.

We've built in climate-resilience, so when the architects and engineers come up with additional safeguards, we'll add them."

At this point in the pitch, people usually either became excited, shook their heads in disbelief, or looked down their noses in disgust. Nothing registered on Mrs. Morrison's face. She brushed off the fly that had landed on her shoulder. I wondered if she were a lawyer or a cop, trained not to respond. I pulled out my phone and videoed the panorama to post later.

Nate continued. "The big idea here is not technology, it's conscious community. People making informed decisions together. We're committed to supporting our residents for a lifetime."

Still no reaction.

"Most people ask me if I've been drinking when I lay out our plan. But I'm no Paolo Soleri, and this is no fantasy. The secret is: it's not for everybody. It's for people who learned the lessons of the pandemic, who understand how connected we all are, and who want their public spaces to be part of their life plan."

He lowered his voice. "I'm staking everything on the idea of permanent flexibility."

I loved listening to his pitch. My chest puffed with pride every time he laid out the vision. It beamed with Arizona sunshine versus Pennsylvania murk. Back home, the best planners could do was to rename an old coal-mining town after a Native American Olympic champion from Oklahoma whose widow needed money. Mauch Chunk became the town of Jim Thorpe overnight, but nothing really ever changed there.

Nate leaned toward Mrs. Morrison. "I'm happy to tell you that we're almost twenty-five percent subscribed. The first structure will break ground in September."

She nodded. Finally. "Congratulations. Tell me, what have you planned for phase two?"

"Whoa, we're not planning an expansion. First things first."

"I trust you're not thinking about infringing on White Bear?"

Nate looked at me and I figured it was my turn to talk. He always said two voices were more persuasive than one.

"Mrs. Morrison, do you know that the name of this development is 'Continuity'? The idea is that we don't want to break with the past, we want to build on it and carry its values into the future. If people are rooted to the place and its history, then they'll care for it going forward."

A flicker of something passed through her eyes. I went on.

"There have always been pioneers in this region, people making new lives in the desert, people taking a chance." I was channeling my boss. "Like the people who built the White Bear Ranch. We're continuing their tradition."

"You're not going to raise cattle, are you?"

Nate laughed. I felt my color rising. Clearly, fine words didn't sound as good coming from my mouth as from Nate's. "Oh, no, I didn't mean to imply going backwards. We just want to share the history. We want to be good neighbors with White Bear Ranch, and there could be opportunities for joint activities."

"Such as?" She leaned back and folded arms across her chest.

"Well, the mine for example; maybe we could reopen it as an education center."

"Are you planning to build a *ghost town*?" She spat out the words.

Nate stepped in. "Katie, this is the kind of thing I'd like to bring up with you and the Friends, if and when you think it's appropriate. We're still adjusting the concept, and I'm very grateful to you for being willing to take this in," he swept his arm across the vista, "at this point."

She uncrossed her arms. "I appreciate the heads up. I have the paperwork you filed with the county, and I would also like to see your drawings. Not today, though; I have another engagement." She turned to the jeep.

Nate hustled to open her door, and I climbed into the back seat. I wasn't sure I'd earned my keep this trip, but I'd done the best I could with no preparation. I hoped Nate had the situation under control.

When we reached the trailer, Mrs. Morrison asked to use the "loo" and disappeared inside. Nate took me around the corner, out of earshot.

"I got a tip that a Friends group was forming, and I wanted to establish a relationship now. Find out what they're up to." He looked toward the door into which Mrs. Morrison had disappeared. "I'm going to need you to handle the Friends solo for the next little while. And don't tell Sydelle Hammer about it. You're my secret weapon."

"What does her group want anyway?"

"Ostensibly, to preserve the White Bear Ranch. This is something people do around here. A bunch of women started a movement to save the Phoenix Mountains in the 1970s. Another woman went after the McDowells in the 1990s."

"Isn't that a good thing?"

"Yeah, if that's *all* they want. This bunch might be angling for more acreage, which could wipe us out."

"How? Hargrove-Spence owns the land!"

"Not all of phase two and not all the rights of way. We're still negotiating. We need real friends, not vigilantes."

"What makes you think they're vigilantes?"

"She's got our paperwork. No other reason to visit with the county."

"Are we really starting to build in September?"

"Lord willing and the creek don't rise."

Whenever he got folksy, that meant end of conversation. My boss was a complicated guy, but I didn't have to understand him to work for him. I'd asked myself, is it okay to support an opaque person leading a noble cause, or would it be better to find a transparent boss whose ideas might be boring? I'd decided I could hack working with Nate, and whoever else he brought along, as long as our goals got accomplished.

4

Being April, it was still cool enough to walk the local trails, and Gabi wanted to show her brother the turf. She said she wasn't much of an outdoors person, so she needed me to guide them. I thought it was a trick—she wanted me to get to know her baby bro—but it was Saturday, and I was free, so I planned a gentle hike. The Dreamy Draw trailhead was fifteen minutes east of our apartment in Sunnyslope. Sunnyslope used to be a town—actually, a refuge for sick people—until it got gobbled up by Phoenix, like so many other towns in the last century. It butted up to the Phoenix Mountains Preserve, where you could hike for miles and miles. I planned something shorter.

The three of us got into my gassed-up car. I drove under the highway and along an emergency spillway to the Draw, a pass between hills in the Preserve. I found a parking space in the crowded lot near the trailhead. Crowded because I wasn't the only one around here who liked to hike. I locked the car, put my water bottle in my day-hike pack, and offered to carry the others' water. Gabi handed her bottle over, but Aaron refused. He didn't have a pack, so I suspected he was being macho, but okay.

We climbed up to the mouth of the main trail, a four-foot wide, dusty pathway that rose steadily for half-a-mile to a saddle between peaks. From there it dropped east across the valley. As we walked upward, hills on both sides of us, our feet crunched the chopped-up rocks the Parks Department had dumped in the trail bed to keep it from eroding. The smell of rocks in the hot sun perked me up. Scraggly palo verde trees and creosote bushes edged the trail, pale green-brown accents in the tan-gray landscape. It had taken me a while to adjust to the Sonoran Desert's muted palate, but now I found the desert beautiful. Plus, without trees to block the view, you could easily see the contour of the land as you climbed.

We passed other people going up and down but made no contact because the pandemic had taught us not to breathe around strangers. Gabi puffed a little but still chatted nonstop. She broke into Spanish every once in a while, her voice high with excitement. Aaron walked next to her, his fancy sneakers getting dirtier with every step. He kept stubbing his toes but did not complain. It was still only around eighty degrees, and I filled my lungs with chaparral-scented air. This particular trail was like a friend to me, always welcoming when I showed up.

We reached the crest of the saddle. My fellow hikers paused to breathe and look eastward at the landscape of the Preserve now visible: more hills, washes, mountains in the distance, and housing off to the north, a reminder of our mid-city location. If you didn't look north, though, you saw just what the early settlers would have seen in the 1850s, or what the prehistoric tribes who first irrigated the area a thousand years earlier must have seen: a wide, wild land, tough to live on but full of possibility.

Aaron wiped sweat from his forehead and said he wouldn't mind a cigarette. Gabi looked daggers at him. He told her he was kidding, that he was okay to keep going. I led them onto a side trail that looked like a rut made by animals, or more likely mountain bikes. Gabi asked where I was taking them. I told her I had something special to show her.

We followed a series of ruts in single file down into a wash, then up a hillside and along a ridge. On the ridge, Gabi started looking left and right, anxious about the fact that the ground fell away on both sides. I slowed down. Aaron noticed his sister's agitation and stepped close to her, saying he would catch her if she slipped. She gasped. I told him to be quiet and tried to distract her with a story I'd run across at work.

"You know why they call this place Dreamy Draw? People say it's because they used to mine cinnabar here, which is an ore of mercury. They say miners walked out of the pass in a dreamy state from the mercury. It's probably not true, but I like the sound of it."

Aaron said, "I believe it." He sounded snarky.

"Do you know something about cinnabar?"

"No. But I know about mining. The owners don't give a damn about anything but profits. My grandfathers had it rough."

Gabi said, "No politics today, okay?"

Aaron snorted.

I stepped ahead and led them off the ridge, onto a hillside where I left the path and climbed a little hill to what looked like a hole in the rock face. They trudged up beside me. I pointed to the ground.

"Look closely. I think this used to be an old turquoise mine. I found it on one of my rambles. They mined a lot of things here, not just cinnabar." I shot a look at Aaron.

Gabi squatted and began to sift the rocky soil between her fingers. She jumped up, "Look how pretty!" She showed us the mottled, greenish pebbles in her hand. Then she pocketed two of them and squatted down to look for more.

"She's a sucker for pretty," Aaron said to me. He pulled his phone out of his pocket and tapped. I asked if he was searching turquoise mining, and he turned away from me.

I watched Gabi's soft, round cheeks widen into a smile as she focused on the bits of earth under her fingers. Her pleasure made me warm inside. Aaron pocketed his phone and stooped over his sister to watch. He straightened after a minute, evidently not interested in prospecting. He looked around and settled on a rock ledge a few yards away.

I watched Gabi pick up pebbles one at a time, turn them over with care, then replace them on the ground. Every so often she pocketed one. I supposed her finds would wind up in the basket of odds-and-ends overflowing on her dresser, next to the old lipsticks and unused hairbands, and she'd forget about them, but so what. Most of the time Gabi went around looking like she'd just stepped out of the shower: stringy hair, no make-up. But at party time, she would dig through her piles of assorted cosmetics and ornaments to doll up. Then she looked shockingly pretty. That, plus being so nice, I could understand why guys hung around her. They didn't hang around me, for obvious reasons.

I handed her my water bottle. "Pour water on them and you'll see the colors better."

She removed the pebbles from her pocket and arranged them in a row. She let water trickle over them, smoothing their surfaces with her thumb and exclaiming, "Oh, wow! I'm going to find the prettiest one."

She sat on the ground and focused on her finds. She had once told me the college nurse told her she might have ADHD, which meant that although her attention drifted a lot, she could also focus with hyper-intensity. I'd seen her do this a couple of times. Maybe it was happening now, which was okay with me.

I turned away and found myself a seat on the ledge near Aaron. A fine film of grit lay on the warm rock. I hugged my knees to my chest, which is the best way to sit on a rock, in my opinion. I could have spent the next half an hour just sitting, fingering the dust and staring at cacti in the distance while Gabi hunted for turquoise, but I thought I should make an effort toward poor, bored Aaron.

"How are you doing?" I asked.

"Are you into mines?"

"Not really." What an odd question! I didn't know what to say next.

"You brought us to the right place. My sister likes shiny things." He picked up a bit of rock and examined it cursorily. He tossed it off to the side. "They already took the good stuff. Gabi's getting crumbs." He looked at me. "She likes shiny people, too. You must have met some of them."

"Hmmm."

"Who's she dating now?"

"You should ask her."

He shook his head. "I love my sister, but she screws up. She picks jerks, then she makes excuses when they don't treat her right."

This was news to me. Gabi didn't complain about the guys she dated. She'd had a boyfriend for a while whom she worried about when he lost his job, but she hadn't said anything about mistreatment. She seemed to be getting along with her new guy. I shut my mouth.

"Sorry, that was out of line. Forget I asked."

I stood and called out, "Gabi, let's go before it gets hot."

Gabi looked at her treasures and pocketed a selected few. Then she stood and brushed the dirt off her bottom. "Thank you!" She grabbed me for a hug. "You knew I'd like it."

I led sister and brother back the way we'd come. No one spoke as we walked single file along the ridge, but I could tell Gabi was holding her breath. We made it to the saddle on the main trail and paused to rest. I told everyone to drink water because it was, in fact, getting hot. Gabi took her bottle and stepped in front of me.

"I know the way from here. You two start talking." She snapped a shot of the two of us, no doubt looking puzzled. She turned and began to descend, picking her way steadily down the rock-filled trail.

Aaron grinned. "That's my sister. She wants everyone she loves to love everyone else she loves."

I was not about to love Aaron, even for Gabi's sake. But I offered to pack his water, and this time he agreed. We walked two abreast at my normal pace, Aaron kept up without stubbing toes. I guess he'd adjusted to Dreamy Draw.

The sun was high, and I felt a tell-tale tingle on the back of my neck that meant cover or else. People with my complexion didn't belong in Arizona. But I'd landed well for a girl from a small town back East with no connections. I asked Aaron to hold up for a minute while I dug a bandana out of the bottom of my pack.

Aaron said, "Wet the cloth first."

"You're a hiker?" I asked as I doused my bandana.

"I like seeing mountains in the distance. I like the faded colors."

"So do I. I hike all the time except when I'm working or it's too hot. Clears my head."

"Gabi says you work for a developer?"

"Yup."

"Isn't that a contradiction? For someone who likes open space?"

Uh, oh, I thought, here it comes. "People need to live some-where, and we're giving them a good place. The best, actually. Everyone who buys into Continuity, that's our development, will be a good citizen in every sense. They'll respect each other, and the common areas, and the land." I was channeling Nate again.

Once, in junior high, I had invented a social studies pro-ject that made me happier than anything. My little brother and his friends used to play soccer in the street. It wasn't safe—a woman was run over by a pizza delivery truck right in front of her house—and I couldn't make the boys stop. So I started a GoFundMe to build them a real pitch in a vacant field. When I asked my dad for a contribution, he told me I was too stupid to make it work. He made me take down the site and apologize to my social studies teacher. The first time I heard Nate talk about a responsive community where good ideas could come from anybody, my heart zinged. Imagine growing up where they listened to you! Every time I heard Nate lay out the plan for Continuity, my heart lifted.

"Somebody's swallowed a line," Aaron said grinning.

"I know a good idea when I hear one."

"You can't be that clueless."

"Clueless would be ignoring how your community shapes the way you live. Schools, parks, neighbors with or without fences, it's all there. What have you got against innovation?"

He looked pained. "It's horseshit."

"There's no 'shit' in Continuity."

"I bet there are gates to keep my relatives out, except to mow the lawn and change the diapers. Do you know your fancy development is a polluter? Twenty-five percent of the world's carbon dioxide comes from the building industry." He shook his head. "No offense, but we don't need it."

I didn't want to antagonize Gabi's baby brother, but he sounded ridiculous. I controlled my temper. "Aaron, you should read our brochure before you jump to conclusions. The next generation of environmentalists is going to grow up at Continuity."

He shook his head again. "I will read your brochure. But the next generation is coming from the streets. From people who lived in crummy neighborhoods and then got evicted by the pandemic anyway."

"What are you talking about?" I looked at him and stubbed my toe on a rock protruding mid-trail. He reached out and caught my elbow. I righted myself and he let go.

"I did a lot of research when I was at home. I started following things that interested me. It was better than high school. High school doesn't teach you about the necessity for protest."

"High school doesn't teach you what you need to get a job. You need two things: skills and a positive attitude."

He laughed. "Are you going to big sister me, too?"

I felt blood creep into my cheeks because he'd caught me being condescending. I hoped he'd take my pinkness as a sign of exertion. "We should go." I headed downhill.

Aaron walked beside me. "I grew up in Ajo. I see things differently. No offense?"

I hadn't done the usual stuff in high school either. I wasn't the spoiled white girl he assumed I was. Aaron and I had more in common than he knew.

"No more free job advice. You'll have to pay next time," I said, trying to keep it light.

"To pay for your advice, I'd have to get a job to get the money, but then I wouldn't need the advice."

He was keeping it light, too.

We walked in silence. I hadn't hiked with anyone else for a while, and I was aware of his sweaty body breathing beside me. Pretty soon we reached the place where the trail intersected a bike path. Gabi was waiting, standing in a fringe of shade cast by a palo verde.

"Hey," Gabi said, "Are you two friends now?"

5

I peered through the plate glass at AJ's bakery counter and pondered whether to opt for strawberry shortcake, my favorite, or an apple "galette" that might be more to Mrs. Hammer's elevated taste—she had invited me for tea and instructed me to bring cake—although the crust looked chewy. Then it occurred to me: one of each, and I'd eat whichever she rejected. I bought one slice of shortcake and one galette for an outrageous sum and went out to my car in AJ's lot.

Even after living here for four years, I couldn't get used to the splendor of Phoenix's supermarkets. AJ's was the upscale chain, but even the Safeways and Krogers seemed palatial. In the neighborhood where I grew up, the old grocery had narrow aisles with stuff piled ceiling-high. Here, as I walked the wide, clean aisles, I had to question how many different kinds of chips the world really needed. I sympathized with people who criticized excess, but protesting didn't appeal to me. I had better things to do.

Mrs. Hammer was waiting when I arrived, seated in her scooter and dressed in a fluffy white sweater despite the season—of course, it *was* cool inside—with a big smile. She welcomed me and gestured toward the kitchen. She'd had her hair and nails done, and, I could tell by the way she waved her hand around, that she was proud of it. Old women earned the right to be vain just by making it to old age. She twirled the joystick on the scooter arm with red-tipped fingers like spiky ocotillo blooms and sped into the living room. I made my way into the kitchen to plate our goodies.

"I'll have the apple," she said when we had settled around the coffee table bearing the tea tray. "I'm allergic to strawberries."

"Do you have other allergies I should know about?" I asked as I poured the tea into our cups. I offered her sugar, but she waved it off.

"Yes, latex. Evidently strawberries and latex are related. My allergist says I have nothing else to fear. My son thinks I have plenty of things to fear. He sees quacks and opportunists around every corner." She sighed and took a tiny bite. "This is delicious. You did well."

"Do you have many children?" I really wanted to get to know her.

"I had another son. I lost him in an accident."

"I'm sorry."

"It was a long time ago." She pursed her lips for a moment. "Now, tell me why you work for Hargrove-Spence. It seems an odd choice for a girl from back East." She took another lady-like bite.

I didn't want to tell her it wasn't a choice, just plain luck. I flashed back to my interview at Hargrove-Spence. I'd mistaken Nate for a foreman because he was a big guy dressed like a middle-aged trucker: blond hair slicked back, construction boots. He'd explained he'd just come from "the site" and invited me to sit in an upholstered chair.

I remember how he'd fidgeted with a magnetic toy while he talked.

"I'm building the world's first pandemic-proof, climate-smart community. I have the best people thinking this through." He paused. "Why do you want to work here?"

"I need a job." What a stupid thing to say!

He laughed. "At least you're honest."

"I mean, it sounds interesting." I could feel my cheeks redden. "I don't understand how you can make a community pandemic-proof."

He proceeded to tell me how, and I was dazzled. Of course, I knew zilch about real estate, but his ideas sounded forward-looking and honorable. I particularly liked the honorable part.

I blurted, "Maybe I can help you communicate to the younger generations." I handed him a copy of my résumé, which I'd printed on quality paper with my communications degree at the top in big type. I wasn't a natural creator, but I'd taken a couple of social media marketing classes and was willing to try anything to get out of debt.

He glanced at it and then looked me in the eye. "Maybe you can."

The next morning, I showed up at the office with my hair slicked back, ready for anything.

Mrs. Hammer cleared her throat. Raising my teacup, I snuggled my bottom into the seat of the chair. "When I got my associates degree, I saw a parttime data-entry job posted at the college. It was pandemic time, and the alternative was a McDonald's drive-through. I figured I'd work hard, and they'd promote me eventually, which is what happened. I'm lucky!" I shoveled a fork-full of shortcake into my mouth. It was as good as it looked. Thank you, AJ's.

"Lucky? Why do you say that?"

"Because I never thought it would be possible for me to do something important in the world." I could feel the red bloom in my cheeks. I must sound like an idealistic idiot to a ninety-two-year-old. I hoped she wouldn't press me to explain because I couldn't. She wouldn't understand desperately needing a paycheck either.

"What did you study in college?"

"Only two years. I liked biology but I settled on communications. The course blurb promised to teach me how to interview for a job, and I wanted a good one. It worked out. I love my job."

"So you say. Is it your job or your boss you love?" She lifted those imperial eyebrows.

"My job! I love my job, not my boss."

"Are you sleeping with him?"

"No! Mrs. Hammer!"

"Sy."

"Sy, I wouldn't dream of it." The thought of screwing Nate made me nauseous, and I swallowed hard.

"Many young women sleep with their bosses these days."

What was she getting at? "Not me." I loved Nate's vision, but I didn't lust after a married man with two kids and a pot belly.

She smiled and took another tiny bite.

I put my plate down, no longer hungry. Why couldn't people believe that a girl like me can fall in love with an idea?

Sy said, "I'm not a prude, you know." A crumb slipped between her lips. "You can talk to me about sex. I have a vibrator."

I choked up imagining her going at it. "I'm not sleeping with Nate Hargrove."

"Good. Then I can trust your judgment." She reached for a cashew in a crystal bowl on the tea tray and placed it on her plate next to the nibbled galette. "I don't want you to make unnecessary mistakes."

What could I say to that?

"It's important for women in business to have the right ideas about men. I had the wrong ideas for years."

I didn't understand where she was going but knew I should shut up and listen. I folded my hands in my lap and tried not to feel patronized.

"I married the handsomest of the ranch hands at twenty. My husband ingratiated himself with my father while I had babies. He took over the business after my father's stroke, and I helped him run it. I knew just as much as he did about cattle and the land, and I was better at numbers. I did the books, and he wore his big white hat and hobnobbed with the Cattle Growers Association. Everyone thought he was running the place, and I thought so, too, because that's what he told me, and that's what I expected. My generation, you know."

I felt sorry for Sy's younger self and that relaxed me. "But you figured it out at some point?"

She raised an eyebrow. "My husband went to Washington to lobby our congressional delegation with the other big white hats. They misbehaved. He kept it up when they got home. When I found out, there was trouble."

"Did you divorce?"

"Of course not. I had children to raise and a business to run, and you did not divorce in my family. But it opened my eyes." She sat straighter.

I could imagine her feckless husband coming home and she icily announcing she had fed the kids and was going upstairs to run a bath; he could look for something to eat in the fridge.

I couldn't imagine running a business all icy. "How did you keep working together?" "I thought it was important to make money. I didn't have an education. There was nothing else I could do." She took another dainty bite of galette. "You have choices I didn't have. Don't throw yourself away on Nate Hargrove."

"I just want Continuity to succeed. Have you read the brochure I sent?"

"The manifesto? I read it. More interesting than its author."

Nate had told me that I might hear other developers talk smack about him because he broke with the ranks. He said all developers sniped at one another. He sniped at people often enough, and not just developers: bankers, lawyers, and especially politicians. But I didn't expect Sydelle Hammer to snipe at him. I had to ask.

"Is there something you want to tell me about my boss?"

She paused. "I think not. In this case, what you don't know won't hurt you."

I was glad she didn't want to gossip. I didn't want to get between her and Nate, and I needed to stay in her good graces. "Okay."

"Eat your cake or throw it away. No strawberries in my house." She wagged a friendly finger at me. "You have an honest face. We are going to be friends."

I finished my cake and gathered the tea things onto the tray. She told me to leave it in the kitchen for the housekeeper. On the way back from the kitchen, I stopped in front of the photo of Mrs. Hammer's aunt on horseback. The dark-haired girl in leather chaps sat upright in the saddle and stared, unsmiling, at the camera. She and Mrs. Hammer—Sy—may have lacked opportunity as young women, but they'd grown strong anyway. I would, too.

"I see you're interested in my family history," she said when I got back to the living room. "I may have a project for you that no one else around here will do. You will have to pay close attention, and it will be worth your while. We'll talk about it in the future when I'm ready."

She scooted over to her desk and began fussing with papers, a sign that I should disappear. But I had another base to cover.

"Sy, before I leave, can I ask you about something?"

She looked at me over the top of her readers.

"Have you talked to your son about taking me to see the old mine?"

"I don't know why you want to go there. There's nothing to see."

"But there is, for a coal-miner's great-great granddaughter."

"Well, all right." She flicked one thin wrist. "I haven't had time to discuss it with Thomas."

Okay! My cheeks bunched up. I straightened my face and thanked her for the tea. As I shouldered my bag and walked to the foyer, she called out, "Don't be a stranger." She shouldn't worry; Nate wanted me to haunt her, and I actually enjoyed her company.

I drove south, then took Indian School Road across town toward the office. Halfway there, on the spur of the moment, I pulled into the parking lot where the City of Phoenix had turned an old hydroelectric plant on the Arizona Canal into a park. Mrs. Hammer's conversation had been playing in my head, and I could think better outdoors. Back home, when I couldn't stand to watch my mom say nothing as my dad belittled her, I would storm out of the house and stomp around the block. I got in the walking habit. Here, I hiked the Preserve so often that Gabi gave me an REI gift card for my birthday to buy boots. Never had hiking boots before. Was it ridiculous to love an object, a symbol of my new life?

I climbed a ramp to the concrete dam containing the power plant and a series of locks. I took a pathway across the canal to inspect the waterworks from the far bank, where a staircase descended to a platform perched a few feet above the water. I climbed down to the platform; on this side of the dam, the water level was twenty feet lower than up top. I leaned against a guardrail and watched water spill from a ledge in the dam and from sluices on either side, forming three curtains of foam, a triple waterfall. Scum created by the force of the falls floated westward along the canal. The spray smelled earthy, as if it contained souvenirs of its journey from the mountains. Without this water diverted from the Salt River, the city would not have developed. Who knows where I would be now?

I backed off the guardrail and sat on a metal bench beneath the sluice, listening to the water splash and gurgle. I cleared my mind to focus in on what had happened in Sydelle Hammer's living room. When she'd questioned my feelings for Nate, I'd flashed back to a conversation Gabi and I once had. She'd asked how come I never had a partner, and if it had anything to do with my boss, whom I talked about constantly. I'd told her no, I didn't have a crush on Nate, which was true.

But I must admit that Nate had a quality the guys I dated couldn't match: his sense of purpose. A purpose he let me share.

6

I stood at the curb outside my apartment complex at six-fifteen. Nate's Lexus pulled up five minutes later, and I climbed in. He grunted a greeting and twisted the steering wheel for a U-turn as I attached my seatbelt. He was wearing a tie for the kick-off meeting of the Friends of White Bear Ranch, which Katie Morrison was about to hold. His sport jacket hung from a hook in the back. I settled into the cool leather seat for the long drive. The lowering sun flashed in the passenger side mirror as I groped around inside my bag.

"I borrowed my roommate's digital recorder in case you want the whole thing and my phone dies. Otherwise, I'll just take notes on my phone." I waved the device at him.

"Don't need to record. Just get names and affiliations. Your job is to make friends. No pun intended." He drummed his fingers on the console.

After a beat, he looked at me. "Remember, everyone here will have a different agenda. Try to figure them out. I'll introduce you, then they're all yours. Do-gooders are more your type."

I didn't know what he meant. It seemed to me he was doing as much good as anyone.

"How's it going with Sydelle Hammer?" he asked.

"Really well, I think. She asked me to come over every Friday for tea and cake. I buy the cake. She's interesting."

Nate grunted. "Keep it up. Get Maria to reimburse you."

We didn't talk for the next twenty minutes.

We pulled up next to a sizable house behind a wide driveway that looped from the street to the front door, and back to the street. Several cars were parked along the curve, half-a-dozen others on the street in front of the house, which was not new but upscale. Nate pulled in behind an SUV with national park stickers plastered across the rear. He checked his watch and made a face. "We're right on time," he said, "although it appears we're among the last to arrive." When we got out of the car, he put on the sport jacket.

I followed him into the foyer and through a living room to where eight people sat around a polished dining table, Mrs. Morrison at its head. Several others sat in a row of folding chairs along a wall. We took seats beside them. Mrs. M glanced our way and nodded. She was dressed in black with a long, silver Navajo necklace and perfect make-up, looking regal in a middle-aged way. I spotted a big dog under the table at her feet. She turned to an outdoorsy-looking man in a khaki uniform on her left and handed him a sheaf of papers.

"We're all here now, so let's get started. Please take one and pass the rest."

I took one of the papers when the sheaf reached me. Nate waved it away. He studied the room, and I followed his gaze. Mostly white, middle-aged folks and one young brown man looking out of place. Nate bent toward me. Whispered, "The rangy-looking guy? Works in the county planning office. He's supposed to be neutral. The well-dressed woman is a lawyer for a real estate investment trust with commercial property in Scottsdale. Could be here for altruistic reasons or a legal angle? Over there, woman with glasses? She's from the Sierra Club. The others could be neighbors or perpetual activists. Find out if any of them are connected to Sydelle Hammer."

Katie Morrison introduced herself—she had an impressive background in conservation—and asked the rest of us to do the same. The young Hispanic-looking guy who said he was her intern punched the keys of his laptop all the while. When it was our turn, Nate spoke for both of us, and the intern stopped typing to check me out. I smiled back. He and I appeared to be the only under-thirties in the room.

A half-hour of excited talk followed about the benefits of open space for both people and wildlife, as well as the significance of the Ranch for the county over the last century. When the discussion ended, Nate turned to me, whispering he had distilled the meaning of it all into two propositions. "Katie *says* 'Let's preserve the history and beauty of the place as well as the ecological services it provides,' but she *means* 'Let's buy up the surrounding property and stop growth.'" He grumbled, "If anyone grabs land around the Ranch, it's gonna be me."

He stood to address the room. "If I may add something?" Faces turned to him. "As I've said, I represent the community developing next door. We share your values. Our entire community is being built to the highest environmental standards. The kind of people who will move in will want to join this group. Or at least they'll donate." He paused for the expected chuckle. A few heads nodded.

"I'm inviting you all to visit the site. Call Bee for a date," gesturing to me. "I welcome your input. There may be opportunities for our two groups to collaborate on stewardship and educational activities. We could do a lot of good together."

Murmurs emanated from around the table. I looked at my boss and started to rise, but he shook his head slightly and I sank back onto my chair. Nate placed a stack of Continuity brochures on the table. "Our contact information. Thanks for your attention."

After a few more hems and haws, Mrs. M adjourned the meeting and invited everyone to the living room for refreshments. Everyone got up; the dog emerged from under the table and led the way. Nate stood at the living room threshold and gestured for me to go forward. I figured he wanted to avoid the calories, but I was hungry. I piled chips and guac on one of Mrs. Morrison's lacey-edged plates and looked around for a place to sit. French doors opened onto a flagstone patio, and I took my plate and a beer out to a wrought-iron table. The guac was garlicky, not as good as Gabi's.

I heard someone say, "May I join you?" Before I could answer, the intern pulled out a chair beside me. He had a skinny face with a shadowy beard, wore glasses, and held a beer in his left hand. I nodded, pointing to my mouth full of chips.

"Are you a teacher?"

I swallowed. "No, why?"

"Your boss mentioned 'educational activities'."

"Oh, I did some research. It wasn't hard to think up some fun field trips." I nibbled the chip in my hand.

"I thought you might be studying STEM ed or something.

"I wish."

"I'm Luis, by the way. Are you a captive, like me?" He smiled and his glasses inched up his nose.

"This is part of my job. What about you?"

"I'm working on my doctorate in applied math at ASU. The internship is a favor to my advisor. A compulsory favor." He raised his beer. "Salut."

I clinked bottles with him, wondering if he was hitting on me or just making "friendly" conversation?

"I don't know what applied math is. What do you do?"

"I write algorithms for wrestling gigabytes of climate data. Mostly, I hang out with other nerds. I'm hoping for a better conversation with you."

Definitely a hit. I liked it. "I'll do my best."

Nate showed up on the patio. "There you are. Sorry to interrupt, but we need to get going."

I got up, intending to bus my plate and bottle, but Nate said to leave everything. I excused myself to Luis and followed Nate inside. Katie Morrison was standing in her front hallway, saying goodbye to departing guests. She surveyed Nate as we approached.

"I hope you appreciate the enthusiasm you saw here tonight. It's a good group."

"Thanks for the invitation. Bee and I will be happy to participate." He grinned. "Mostly Bee, but you'll find her a better volunteer than I am."

"I'll be grateful for her help." Mrs. M faced me. "I send an email every week. Be sure to whitelist me, okay?"

Nate took my elbow as we walked to the door. His lips were closed so tightly you couldn't see them. A breeze swept us along the now empty driveway. I started to talk but Nate hushed me and pointed to his car. We got in, the engine purred into life, and he headed west. There was no traffic, and the moon rising in the east behind us made the desert sparkle.

"Did you notice what was missing?" He kept his eyes on the road.

I thought for a beat. "What?"

"No one represented the local tribes. Katie's squash blossom necklace was compensation. No one mentioned the Hammers. Makes me question their capability."

"What do you mean?"

"I mean you need to stay close to Sydelle Hammer. Keep us in the front of her mind. And one more thing."

I waited.

"When you get a chance, I want you to go to her mine and look around, see if anything unusual catches your eye. Any evidence of what people did there in the past. I might have to get soil samples."

"What for?"

"We need to know if it's contaminated. If it is, whatever we do in the area could cost double." He glanced my way as if to see if I followed his explanation. He turned up the ramp to the 101.

"Shouldn't you ask one of the engineers? I didn't take geology."

He laughed. "Bee, you don't need geology to snoop. Just use your good common sense."

"Okay." Whatever.

"Don't tell Sydelle Hammer; just do it while you're still friends. She's mercurial."

"She seems pretty steady to me."

"Yeah, but she has whims. Take my word for it."

"Okay." I settled deeper into my seat. Nate must have realized I was confused because he lowered his voice.

"Listen, I have a plan that's going to unfold in the next few months. Do not tell Sydelle Hammer about anything you hear in the office, and do not tell her about the Friends. I don't want her talking to Katie Morrison."

"But Continuity isn't a secret. Aren't we getting ready to advertise?"

"Those two women could cripple us. I don't want you accidently provoking them. Get intel, don't give it. Okay?"

7

I tried not to slam the Lexus' door—unlike my car, you didn't need to shove to make it latch—but my brain was cranking, and the door slammed anyway. I waved an apology as Nate drove off. No one was outside the complex, and I slipped into my room quietly to think. The idea that Sydelle Hammer or Katie Morrison could threaten our work, or would even want to, chilled me. Was Nate being paranoid or was something lurking in the background that he hadn't shared? I hated being manipulated. It had happened big time once before.

It was the week before I'd graduated high school. My father had told me to come to his office in a dress, no make-up, flat shoes. When I showed up hoping to talk about a job, he scooted me into the bathroom. He stooped over a bassinet and picked up a baby swaddled in a blue blanket.

Dad said, "I'm going to take you into my office. There's a couple waiting to adopt. Hand the child over, and, if they ask you anything, just thank them for taking care of your son. Then turn around and walk away. No talking. Got it, Deborah?"

He *never* used my full name. I took hold of the baby carefully, and my heart said *something is wrong*.

He made the shush sign with finger to lips and took me by the elbow. In the office, a middle-aged couple sat next to my father's lawyer pal, Artie. The woman held out her arms, and I handed over the baby. She clutched him to her chest and started to cry. The man teared up, too. I turned around and Dad escorted me out of the room.

"What just happened? I whispered in the hallway.

"You made those people very happy."

"Why did you ask me to hand over the baby? You could have done it."

"They wanted to be sure the mother approved. Artie's taking care of the legal end."

"Why did you pretend I was the mother?"

"You don't need any more information."

"What are you and Artie up to?" Dad had said Artie made piles of money, none of which I ever saw. I planted my flat-soled feet. "I'm not moving."

Dad frowned, his eyes darting to the open office door and back to me. He pursed his lips. "Okay. The mother is black, and we didn't want them to get cold feet. Now just leave quietly."

I left the building, growing nauseous as my brain processed the situation. My father and his crony had probably just sold a baby, and even worse, under false pretenses. I was disgusted. I felt sick.

As I tromped toward home, disgust turned into anger, then anger turned into fear. What if the couple found out and made a stink? How would I hold onto a job? I needed a job to escape my rotten home. The day after graduation, I stuffed some things into my little brother's duffel, took the money I had stashed, and left a note for my poor mom. I put most of my cash on the counter at the bus terminal and asked for a ticket as far west as possible, which turned out to be Phoenix. I would have preferred California, where people go to reinvent themselves, but Arizona would have to do. And, later, it did.

At least, I thought it did.

As I took off my meeting clothes, I replayed every word of Nate's conversation. Maybe I was being oversensitive; my allergy to half-truths could make me jump to conclusions. There could be a good reason for telling me to hold my tongue around Sy and Katie Morrison. If so, I needed to know it, and soon. I went to brush my teeth. The guacamole taste had lingered.

8

I sat in my corner at the office waiting for a meeting with a graphic designer about a TV ad. I'd asked Nate if I could attend to learn more about branding, and he'd grunted his approval. He was on the phone, and the designer wasn't due for twenty minutes, so I busied myself Googling Katie Morrison now that she and I were going to be buds. Plenty of articles popped up. I learned that she'd moved to Phoenix with her husband thirty years ago; he'd died young, and she went into business decorating houses and flipping them. Then one day, she told an interviewer, her neighborhood at the foot of a mountain had been threatened by a developer, and she decided to fight back. I guess she got good at it: in a photo, she was leading a squadron of moms with their kids and dogs down a sidewalk. An article from a Chamber of Commerce magazine cited her for "preserving community values."

I wondered exactly which values she'd preserved, and if she'd ever been to my community in Sunnyslope.

I clicked on a video featuring the mayor of a nearby town handing Mrs. M an award and praising her leadership. She looked very blonde and happy as he sang her praises. I Googled her home address and found the estimated sale price; she wasn't rich. I checked the Friends' Facebook page. Someone—Luis? —was posting a ten-part series about life on the White Bear Ranch between the World Wars. The page had a couple hundred followers—not bad for a newbie—and a button to subscribe. I clicked it.

So, Mrs. M and Sy were both widows. Maybe being a widow made you stronger? To become a widow, I'd have to first get married. Not likely! Not now and maybe never. I didn't want to end up like my mother, who let herself be dominated by her husband, and let her husband bully her children. She was nothing like Sy, who seemed to have it all together despite having a shitty husband. Some women have grit.

The doorbell rang and I closed the computer. I ushered the famous Becca Howard into the conference room, the only space where we could display site plans, architects' renderings, and maps too big to share onscreen. Nate entered and took a seat at the head of the conference table. I offered the designer coffee. The woman was tall and big and dressed in a caftan, not exactly Nate's style. She proceeded to show us her concept for the ad. She projected a big C on the wall; then the little letters *onservation* emerged beside it, followed by *onnection*, and *ommunity* in turn; then *Continuity* appeared at the bottom. Conservation, connection, community, Continuity. Simple, like the Nike swoosh. I liked it. Nate hated it and practically bolted out of the room, telling me to get the woman her check. So rude, in my humble opinion. I escorted Becca Howard to the door wondering what exactly had ticked Nate off. Back in the conference room, I unplugged the coffee pot that had begun to smell stale.

I trotted over to the comptroller's cubby to process the designer's payment. Maria had the corporate checkbook spread open on her desk. Hargrove-Spence still did some stuff the old-fashioned way. I explained what happened with the TV ad concept, and Maria said she'd send a check that afternoon. I was about to go back to my corner when a thought struck me. "Have you noticed how touchy Nate is today? Is something going on?"

Maria took off her reading glasses. "Honey, he could care less about TV. We have a loan repayment coming due that he's having trouble with. I warned him about those people, but as you know, sometimes the boss doesn't listen." She sat back. "I've worked for developers for thirty years and they're all the same. Living on the edge, land rich but cash poor. Always hustling." She leaned forward and put her glasses back on. "Do you spell 'Howard' the normal way?"

I left her searching through her files and retreated to my corner to pack up my stuff. On the drive home, all the way up Seventh Street, Maria's comment twisted in my brain. Until now, I hadn't given Continuity's financial condition a thought. Nate always seemed cool, and I didn't know about loans and finance. Maria didn't seem terribly worried, maybe because she dealt in six or seven figures all the time. She'd worked for Nate for ages and was entitled to criticize him. I couldn't help wondering, though, if *my* job was secure. I *needed* my paycheck, what with my student loans and car payments, and I shuddered to think Continuity might go belly up. Not just for me, but for the world. Continuity ought to be built, and good people ought to be able to live there.

I parked in an uncovered space outside the apartment complex, but I didn't go in. I walked up to the second-floor landing and looked north and west across Sunnyslope to the foothills. Close by, dumpy cottages and thirty-two-unit apartment complexes tried, and failed, to be middle class. In the distance, multimillion dollar homes clung to the slopes. In between, a couple of hills that looked like giant mounds of dirt sprouted houses on top. On the closest, a house with a glassed-in porch looked like the prow of a ship. Probably built by a rich cigar smoker who wanted to look down on people. This was what diversity meant in my neighborhood: rich people on hilltops looking down at poor folks on the flat.

Continuity would do better. We wouldn't look down on anyone.

Gabi's car pulled up to the building. Both front doors opened, and I recognized José, her latest boyfriend. I hurried down the stairs to greet them. Gabi asked if I wanted to share a pizza. We went inside and José got a pitcher of iced tea from the fridge. He offered me a glass. He ignored Aaron, who was watching TV in the living room. I went to my room to change out of office clothes. I was hungry and pizza sounded good. At the moment, I could afford to pay my share.

After dinner, I tried to watch TV with Gabi and José, but my brain kept sliding back to the office. Did Nate have money trouble? What had Maria meant about him always hustling? I got up, feeling itchy all over. I didn't want to have to spy on my boss, but if my paycheck were threatened, I might have to. The problem was how.

~ ~

The next morning, I went to the office and sidled up to Maria's desk. Her computer was open, and a steaming Starbucks cup sat beside it, so she must have just stepped away. There were dozens of file icons on her desktop. I tried to read the names, but they made no sense. If I figured out which file to choose, would I have had the guts to open it? Fortunately, Maria came back to her cubby and wiped criminal thoughts from my brain. I told her I wanted to follow up on the Howard payment, and something else. She motioned for me to sit.

"Yesterday I realized something is going on here that I don't understand money-wise."

"You know, I don't know all the details myself, although I should. The only one Nate talks to is his wife."

"Are we going to be okay?"

"He always manages to pull a rabbit out of a hat. I'll give you a heads-up if you need to worry." She picked up the

Starbucks cup and waved me away with her other hand. "The designer's check is in the mail."

I went back to my corner. Clearly, she wasn't going to say more. She and Sy both had information about my boss that they wouldn't share. Sy said I was better off not knowing. Maria acted like it was no big deal. I honestly didn't know what to think, so I decided not to.

9

On my way to Sy's for Friday tea, I stopped and bought a lemon pound cake. In the weeks we'd been having tea together, I'd brought classic pastries, so today I'd decided to branch out. The bakery special, a red devil cupcake, had looked tasty, but I didn't think Sy could handle two inches of icing. The pound cake was big, but whatever we didn't eat the housekeeper could freeze for later. I had come to love my dates with Sy for reasons that went beyond the goodies. History had never interested me in school, but hearing her reminisce about life on the Ranch was like living it. And she made me feel good about the prospect of growing old. My mom wouldn't be as lucky.

I parked against Sy's fence and gathered my stuff: the cake and my tool for spying, a.k.a. my phone, on which I sometimes took notes. Sy and I rarely talked about Continuity, so there was never much to write. When I stepped into the living room, I stopped in my tracks. A white-haired man was bending over Sy, easing her into her scooter chair. She clung to him with skinny arms, and there was an expression on her face I hadn't seen before, maybe fear? Or just concentration? The man helped her smooth out her skirt and straighten the reading glasses on the chain around her neck. He stood and glanced in my direction.

"Ma, you have company. I'm going to go over your prescriptions with Leticia." He stepped into the corridor that led to the kitchen.

I was taken aback. I hadn't realized Sy couldn't get into her scooter by herself because she always appeared so strong.

"What have you brought today?" Sy asked, rolling close to the coffee table that bore the tea tray.

"Lemon pound cake." I displayed the open box.

She pointed a bent, red-tipped finger at the cake. "One of my favorites. My son, Thomas, likes it, too. He may have some with us."

I sat across from her and sliced the cake, laying down a plate where I thought each of the three of us would sit. I had just finished pouring tea for Sy and me when her son returned.

"You're all set for the week. I need to pick up the new hypertension scrip. You remember Dr. Gordon made a change?" He spoke to his mother in a weary tone, as if he were the parent and she the child. It didn't seem to me that Sy needed parenting.

"Yes, of course. Sit down and have a cup of tea. Bee brought lemon pound cake, the clever girl."

"Ma ..." He shook his head.

"Thomas, this is Bee Wells. She works for Hargrove-Spence and she visits me every Friday."

He sighed and sat. Then he looked me in the eye, and I felt like a bug under a microscope. I remembered she said he used to be a dentist and wondered if he'd noticed my unfortunate bite. He broke off a piece of cake and stuffed it into his mouth. His hands were big and smooth, and he looked like he might have been handsome in his youth. He wore jeans and a plaid shirt, an altogether different style from his put-together mother. A beige cowboy hat lay on a side table.

"This is good," he said, breaking off another piece.

"AJ's," I said, not wanting credit I didn't deserve.

Sy said, "We've been talking about the early years of the Ranch. Bee is fascinated by the nineteenth century."

Heat crawled up my neck and into my cheeks. "It's so different from where I grew up. I like imagining your grandaunt on horseback at night carrying a flaming torch."

He laughed. "Ranch life isn't romantic. Cows stink, and you patrol endless miles of fence looking for breaks. That was my job as a kid. Which is why I went to dental school." He wiped his fingers on one of Sy's embroidered napkins.

Sy said, "But you understand the business."

"I had a good teacher." He reached a long arm over the table and patted her knee. "I'll be back with the new prescription."

Sy said, "You don't need to check up on me. Leticia and I can monitor my blood pressure."

"Yes, I do." He stood and turned to me. "Thanks for the cake." He left the room.

"Well," Sy said, "You've met my son. He always departs hastily, so don't take it personally. He thinks he needs to hover over me, but he doesn't enjoy caregiving. I can't convince him to stop doing something he doesn't enjoy." She leaned toward me. "He'll get his comeuppance eventually when my grandson hovers over him." She leaned back. "Tell me how you are getting on."

"Fine. Work is fine."

"Do you have a sweetheart?"

I thought I'd gotten used to Sy's bluntness, but the question threw me.

"No," I said slowly. "I have friends. I hang out with my roommate."

"Hanging out is not sufficient. You also need intimacy. Sex without intimacy is unacceptable, although intimacy without sex is possible. But I don't recommend it."

My face must have shown my embarrassment because Sy changed her tone.

"My dear, there's more to life than work. Surely you have dreams?"

No one had ever asked me about dreams. I scanned my brain, but I couldn't find any. All I'd pined for was to escape from my family and prove I wasn't the dummy my father accused me of being. I knew I could do better, but I had no idea what better meant until I heard Nate talk. I didn't know what my peers dreamed about—you can't trust what you see on social media—and I didn't care. So I side-stepped: "Would you be surprised if I said I want to make money?"

"Money is definitely desirable." She nodded once. "What else do you need to feel fulfilled?"

"Well, you know that my job ..."

"What are you going to tell your grandchildren you loved to do?"

"I don't dream about grandchildren."

She pushed the joystick and whirled away. "Come with me."

I laid my cake plate on the table and followed her out the French doors onto the patio—a genuine patio, not a slab of cracked concrete—bordered with bushes and topped with a ramada. She rolled across the flagstones, passing through stripes of shade cast by the beams overhead, and stopped near the property wall. I stood beside her.

"Do you see the red flowers over there?" She pointed shakily. "They bloom once a year. You're just in time."

In full sun, against the block wall, a pair of blood-red, trumpet-shaped flowers topped a stalk protruding from a cluster of dark green leaves shaped like tongues. The velvety blooms were as big as my hand, with a yellow stamen in the center. If I were a bird or a bee, I'd visit in a heartbeat.

Sy said, "Amaryllis. Tricky to grow in colder climates, but easy here, if you know how to tend them."

"They're amazing."

"I have always had a garden. Even when I was running the business and raising children, I made time to prune and weed. It kept me connected to the land." She cocked one thin wrist. "Refugio does the work now, but these are my amaryllis, planted in the good soil by my hands."

She looked at her hands. "I grew roses around the ranch house, all colors. I had vegetables and herbs in the back, but the roses were my special pleasure. My husband and the boys didn't appreciate them. I cut a few for the table every day when they were in flower."

"Did you grow any native plants?" I could talk intelligently about cactus and chaparral.

"Of course not. They were everywhere. I loved the hillsides where we ran the cattle, *and* I loved my garden. That's my point. There are many things in this life that have value. You, my dear, should find yourself an amaryllis to cultivate."

She spun one-eighty and rolled back toward the house, me tiptoeing behind the scooter where she couldn't see. I'm not good with symbols—give me facts any day—but I knew she hadn't meant "amaryllis" literally. My heart shrank. I didn't have a sweetheart or a garden; I didn't dream about grandchildren. I wasn't really Sy's cup of tea.

As Sy reached the living room threshold, the front door opened, and Thomas Hammer walked in with a Walgreen's bag in his hand. Leticia took it and asked if she should give the pill now. He said no, but he needed to take Sy's blood pressure. Something made him look up and notice us poised at the French doors. Sy reached for my hand and whispered, "The helicopter has landed. I'm afraid our conversation will have to wait until next week. I look forward to it." She let my hand go and pushed the joystick ahead.

"Still here?" Sy's son said to me when I followed her into the room. "You'll have to excuse us. Medical business."

"Of course." I picked up my bag from the couch. "Nice to meet you," I remembered to say as I stepped out the door.

The steering wheel was hot because I'd neglected to put up the sunshield again. I cranked the AC, and, driving with forefinger and thumb of each hand, I turned into the first east-west street I came to. My brain felt cloudy; I barely noticed the buildings and cars on either side. What should I have said when she asked about dreams? If Sy knew the mess I'd left behind, she'd understand why I'm not social. But if she knew I'd helped my dad sell a baby, would she still respect me?

Hot shame spread through my body. If Sy had been in my place, she'd have called him out and stopped the fraud. Just when I'd most needed it, my power had deserted me. I thought of myself as such a fighter. Maybe I wasn't really tough.

I reached home in ten minutes and parked across the driveway from the carport in an uncovered spot. I sat for a minute. Gabi would love to hear about Sy's amaryllis and immediately Google the flower, but I felt too raw to talk about it. Then I bucked up and went inside. Gabi was on the couch, on the phone, spewing Spanish, and in tears. I plopped down next to her and drew a question mark in the air. She paused, told me she needed a minute, and resumed sobbing in Spanish. I got up and went to the bathroom to wash. Someone was making my friend cry. Must be her family or maybe Aaron because she was crying in Spanish. Gabi tried so hard to help people, especially her super-demanding family. I wanted to defend her, and I was prepared to take them on. That's what friends did for friends, help them solve their problems even when they didn't understand the problems themselves.

MAY

average daytime high = 96° F

days of rain = 1

10

The Friends' second meeting started on time. The same people I saw at the kick-off had gathered in Katie Morrison's dining room, except for Nate. The same dog sat under the table. I expected to listen carefully and say nothing meaningful, as befitted my status as a corporate spy.

Mrs. M called the meeting to order and passed out agendas. As the group approved the minutes of the first meeting, a young couple entered and took seats in the rank of chairs against the wall. He looked like a college guy; she looked like a ho, dressed in spandex, as little as possible. The guy waved at Mrs. M, who seemed surprised to see him. The dog got up, threaded through chairs, and poked its snout at the guy, who petted it. I made a mental note to find out who those two were. I prided myself on being thorough, whatever the task.

Mrs. M handed out folders containing a long list of people whom she'd judged could become Friends. The people around the table pounced on the list: they added some names, subtracted a few, and agreed to contact at least three prospects of their own. Heads nodded when Mrs. M talked about needing to coordinate their contacts to maximize outreach. She asked them to send their suggestions to Luis, who would build a master list. I looked at Luis as Mrs. M spoke. Nothing showed on his face. Then she called on him to speak.

Luis stood slowly. He picked up his tablet and consulted his notes. He told us the ranch had been in business for a hundred fifty years and had once included a silver mining operation. The herd had shrunk in the last few decades under the management of a gentleman farmer, son of the owner. People murmured: *I didn't know about the mining; my grandfather worked there for a time; we gotta keep that wildlife corridor open.*

Luis continued. "The Ranch uses well water, and they've had to keep drilling deeper. The towns in the area gave up on wells decades ago. They tap into the Central Arizona Project canal and have their own water treatment plants." He raised his voice. "You realize, I'm sure, that as the climate worsens, the water table will continue to recede. The Ranch may have a significant water problem."

"Tell me something new," the city planner said. He was a tired-looking man in a short-sleeved shirt with a pocket protector. "Those towns have been fighting with each other over water for years, and the developers are scrambling."

Mrs. M jumped in. "What can you tell us about development in the area, Jim?"

"I see announcements all the time."

"Can you show Luis where to find that information?"

The city planner fished a card out of the protected pocket and tossed it to Luis. "Come to my office. Call first."

Mrs. M said, "Is there anything going on now that would affect the Ranch?"

"Yeah, I remember seeing something a little while ago about a water deal. I'll show him," pointing to Luis.

I guessed Luis had to clean up after Mrs. M like I cleaned up after Nate. I wondered how he felt about it.

The Friends chatted amongst themselves a bit. Then Mrs. M adjourned the meeting and invited them into her living room for wine and nibbles. People got up and shuffled toward the food. I hung back, making notes in my phone. Luis appeared next to me. I decided to enlist him in my espionage. "Who are the two who came in late?"

"Katie's son. And I guess he brought a girlfriend."

So, Mrs. M's son dates a rebel. "Is he a conservationist, too?"

"Not that I know of. By the way, conservationists are not the same as preservationists, and they get irate if you confuse them. Conservationists believe in helping nature out; preservationists want to keep things as wild as possible."

"Thanks for the tip. I'll be careful not to call anybody anything."

"All of them need to learn about mitigating climate change. I sow my seeds without prejudice."

I was about to ask him to explain about his seeds when Mrs. M approached.

"I'm glad you're still here," she said to me. "I'd like to ask you something, in confidence."

Luis backed away. "See you soon."

I hope so, I thought. A decent-looking guy with a brain.

Mrs. M led me to a corner and gave me a thousand-watt smile. "It's so nice to see young people among the Friends. We need your point of view!" She paused. "I was wondering if you'd like to come to my place for a little gathering of your generation? Not a focus group, just a casual discussion about our shared struggle?"

"I'd be delighted." Not really, but it was my job.

"Wonderful. I'll send an evite tomorrow."

I turned to go, but she stopped me.

"There's one more thing." She took a breath. "I heard that you visit Sydelle Hammer."

I tried not to show my surprise at Mrs. M's intel. I nodded.

"What do you tell her about the Friends?"

"We don't talk about it."

"What do you tell her about Continuity?"

I looked straight into her eyes. "She's read our stuff."

She paused, as if waiting for me to say more. I kept my mouth shut.

"I'd like you to do me a favor. We're going to discuss the Hammer family in future meetings. I want to avoid any possible misunderstandings, so please don't tell Sydelle about what you hear. Is that okay?"

"Sure. I'll keep your secrets. Goodnight." I slipped out of the room without looking back. I had promised not to blab to Sy, but Nate was going to get an earful.

~ ~

I burst into Nate's office the next morning eager to tell him that Katie Morrison had been spying on *us,* but he wasn't alone. His wife was sitting on the arm of the VIP chair, holding a straw sunhat in one hand. She wore black leggings and a white V-necked top—definitely not office mode—and gave me a big hello. Nate had a sour smile on his face. "Excuse me," I said. "I'll come back later."

"No, stay. It's nice to see you." Dana Hargrove swiveled to face me. "Nate and I were just talking about vacations. You're not a workaholic too, are you?"

"Not at all. I like weekends." Now that was dumb.

She picked up her purse and turned to her husband. "May I have your passport? I'll renew it along with mine in case we *do* decide to go somewhere."

Nate opened the top drawer of his desk and groped around. He pulled out something blue and handed it over. She slid it into her purse and stood. "Thank you." Turning to me, "I hope to see you at our house for dinner some evening. Is there anything you particularly like to eat?"

Wow. An invitation from the boss's wife. I must have done something right. "I eat everything."

She laughed. "I can't promise you everything, but I can promise a good, healthy meal. Our daughter, Madison, will enjoy talking with you." She swished out the door. Nate watched her rear recede.

"Dana's been bugging me to have you over. Sorry I haven't gotten around to it."

He leaned back in his fancy, lumbar-supported, five-legged chair. "Sorry I was brusque the other day with Becca Howard. Got a lot on my mind."

Had Maria said something to him? I thought he should apologize to the designer rather than to me, but I liked him knowing that I have feelings, too, and I softened inside.

"What's up?" he said, picking up a pencil.

I summarized what I'd learned at the Friends' meeting. He lowered the pencil. After a moment, he told me to remember not to tell either of my dangerous women about the other. Then he swiveled away from me and faced his desk. Okay, I thought, back to normal. Whatever was bugging him wasn't my affair.

I walked into the conference room to contemplate dinner at Nate's house. I couldn't pick up food with my fingers, my preferred way to eat. Gabi had tried to teach me table manners, which she had learned in her supervisor training at the call center. She was supposed to model proper behavior for the other employees at company picnics, et cetera. The company assumed the poor people who worked the phones had never been taught etiquette. Safe assumption, I benefitted from it.

On the wall in front of me, the Continuity site plan was mounted next to a six-by-four-foot blowup of a satellite image of the surrounding land. I stared at the mural, idly examining the roads, which ran mostly in straight lines, and the residual waterways that curled and converged like the veins on the back of a leaf. I stepped closer, and with one finger outlined the White Bear Ranch and potential preserve on the hillsides to the east.

Superimposed on the image of the mostly light brown desert was GIS data in bright colors: municipal parks and state lands in green; developments in brown or blue depending on their stage of completion; landmarks among the specks that were houses labeled in white. Looking at the literal big picture made me anxious. All that color screamed competition for the land. No wonder Nate sometimes acted paranoid. A wave of pride flowed through me: I would play a role in helping him rise above the other developers and define a better future.

11

"I'm glad you're early," Sy said as I entered. "I may have been a little ... insistent last week. But here you are."

I handed the marzipan candies I'd picked up at See's to Leticia. The tea tray lay on the coffee table complete with the usual cashews in a cut-glass bowl and petit fours on a paper doily. Places were set for three. I wondered if her son was coming. She anticipated my question.

"We will be joined by Katie Morrison, an environmental activist. You can tell me afterwards what you think." She tapped her temple with her forefinger. "I appreciate a second opinion."

Shit. I couldn't pretend not to know Mrs. M. No lying to Sy, no matter what Nate warned against. "I know her. My boss asked me to attend her meetings."

Sy's mouth fell open a tad. Then she smiled. "How devious of him. How fortunate for me. Let's carry on. It's almost two."

We settled into our usual places. I noticed Sy looked extra nice, in a knit suit and string of pearls. In addition to lipstick, she wore a hint of blush on her cheeks. Leticia had done a good job. I felt underdressed in my customary T-shirt and shorts. I reached into my all-purpose bag to find that tube of tinted Chapstick, the closest thing I had to make-up.

The bell rang, and Leticia let Katie Morrison in. She was dressed up, too, in a loose-fitting shift and sandals with little heels. Her diamonds sparkled as much as Sy's. If she was surprised to see me as she took a seat on the sofa, she didn't show it. We all greeted each other. I picked up my teacup and leaned back to watch the dangerous women in action.

"You have a lovely home, Mrs. Hammer," Mrs. M said.

"Thank you." Sy nodded. "I prefer my ranch house, but it's too big and too far away from my doctors and such." Her teacup hovered over its saucer, trembling slightly.

"This is a beautiful tea service."

"I like to make use of my Spode. Why not?" She took a sip. "Now, why are you here?"

"As I explained on the phone, it's about the Friends of White Bear Ranch."

Sy waved one hand. "Yes, but what is it you want?"

Mrs. M readjusted herself in her seat. "We think the story of the Ranch deserves to be known more widely. Your family represents a way of life that made this region what it is."

Sy said, "I'm not sure what you mean."

Mrs. M took a breath. "Your family tamed the desert. You gave jobs to generations of immigrants who came looking for a decent living. You respected the indigenous people who lived here before. We think it's important to share your story with future generations."

"Frankly, I am not interested in future generations. They need to go to work and work hard. Nothing good comes from hand-outs," Sy said with a little smile.

What a tease!

"That's what I mean," Mrs. M said, clasping her hands in her lap. "Your story will inspire young people to work hard to help keep this property intact. For your great-grandchildren's sake."

"I don't make decisions for my great-grandchildren. I have four at last count, by the way. There could be a great-great soon, if Eleanor's not careful."

I stifled a snicker. I'd heard about the infamous Eleanor. When I'd asked Sy about a photo lying on the coffee table a few weeks ago, I'd learned a new word: "vixen."

Mrs. M said, "Congratulations! I'm sure you want all of them to enjoy the landscape you grew up in."

"My dear, you must not have grandchildren, or you'd know they live in a different world than you do. I have no designs on their future."

"But surely you want them to live in a naturally beautiful place with clean water and air?"

"Certainly."

"That could be the White Bear Ranch."

The older woman shrugged her bent shoulders. "I have no control over what my son will do with the Ranch after I'm gone. He runs it now, you know. He doesn't particularly care for the cattle business. He may well carve it up into 'ranchettes' or whatever you call them these days."

"I'm sorry to hear it." She leaned forward. "Perhaps my group can help you prevent that outcome."

"Why would I want to?"

"To keep your beautiful place as wild as possible so people and animals can enjoy it forever. As your legacy, a gift to the people of Arizona."

Sy snorted. "I have no intention of leaving anything to the State of Arizona. Run by cowards by and large who can't make decisions."

"Oh, I didn't mean to imply the government."

"Now, now, Mrs. Morrison. I read between the lines of what you sent me." She placed her cup and saucer on the table and pointed a gnarled, bejeweled finger at Katie. "You want to make a park. That would come under government jurisdiction."

"Not a park. A preserve that includes your ranch and the surrounding property with a slope of ten degrees or more, about two hundred acres in all. We'd run the preserve with volunteers. There's precedent in Phoenix and Scottsdale for that."

"So you'll need money to buy land? Are you a charity?"

"Nonprofit but not tax exempt."

"I will not make a donation."

"Mrs. Hammer, I wouldn't dream of asking you for money. I simply came to ask your permission to tell your family's story to the Friends group ... and their friends." She folded her hands in her lap and leaned forward over them.

Sy's eyebrows arched into crescents. I shot her an encouraging look, but she didn't catch it.

Mrs. M said, "We'd like to include a brief history of the Ranch and the determination it took to make it prosper. Tell the story in a brochure and on our website." She didn't blink or move a muscle.

Sy frowned. "Well, it depends on the story."

"We have the publicly available material, but I'd like to interview you to get more detail."

"I don't want you poking around in my past looking for something sensational."

"Of course not. We'll ask you to approve whatever we write. We just want a few anecdotes that capture the spirit of the place."

Sy paused, as if consulting a mental calendar. "Very well. But not today. I have another appointment. You should come back after I've talked to my son."

"Wonderful! I'll contact you next week." She unfolded her body and rose quickly. "Thank you for the tea and your time. I'll see myself out." She nodded at me and scurried away.

As soon as the door shut behind Mrs. M, Sy turned to me. "Well? You were quiet."

"She didn't want to hear from me. She wanted your sign-on. She needs to tell the world she represents White Bear Ranch. No one else in her Friends group does."

"I see." She bent forward to pick up her cup. "Katie Morrison was foolish to leave you out of the conversation." She took a sip of cold tea. "Will you continue to attend her meetings?

"It's part of my job."

"Good. Then you can keep me informed. I don't trust that woman. There's something fishy about her. Now, pass me the petit four with the chocolate on top."

~ ~

On the way home I stopped at Arizona Falls again to collect my thoughts. I parked in the spindly shade of an acacia and crossed the dam to the north side of the canal to walk along the bank. It was ninety-two degrees, still cool enough. Stones crunched under my sandals as I strolled eastward on the packed dirt path that paralleled the waterway. Hardly any breeze, so I could smell its musty, muddy odor. It was quieter on this side of the canal, which bordered backyards rather than traffic. A lone jogger trotted by. On the opposite bank, three men on electric bikes, packs strapped to their backs, whizzed along. A drake and a duck paddled upstream on the water's gray-blue surface.

As of today, all three of my elders had asked me either to spy on or to keep secrets from the others. How had I wound up here, in the middle, them circling? Could I satisfy all of them? Should I? I owed loyalty to Nate—no, to Continuity—but I liked Sy, and her motives seemed pure. She didn't want to grab other people's stuff, as Katie Morrison and Nate seemed to. Which of them would wind up controlling the White Bear Ranch? Maybe neither. Maybe it would be Thomas Hammer; I knew nothing about him except that he took good care of his mom. I could support that if he really were a good guy. From the outside, my dad appeared to be a regular guy, but he wasn't. Next time I met Sy's son, I'd try to figure him out.

I reached the place where another canal intersected the one I was walking along and turned around to head back to my now undoubtedly greenhouse-hot car. The walk had not done its magic. I was still confused, which made me feel low as well as hot and prickly. I kicked a pebble so it bounced forward, caught up with it, kicked it again, and then again. A bird flying close by made me look up. Ahead, in a lot north of the dam, I saw a forest of power poles, each topped by a mean-looking transformer. Of course! A power station to channel the electricity made by the churn at the dam. Power and water churning together. The gringos who created the waterworks around here understood that conquering the desert would be a question of water *and* power. All sorts of power, including the kind Nate and Mrs. M were jockeying for. I didn't want to be a pawn in a power play, not anyone's.

12

I puttered in my bedroom, getting ready to go to Mrs. M's not-a-focus-group party. I packed my phone in the cute little purse Gabi lent me. I was wearing my best yellow dress and sandals with heels. Gabi said not many *gringas* could pull off that shade of yellow, which pumped me. I wondered who else would be at the party, hoping one person in particular would show up.

When I entered Mrs. M's living room two minutes late, Luis was not present.

Mrs. M looked grand in a silky, ivory onesie that matched her hair and the drapes—color-coordinated deliberately? —and she was serving wine to her son, his girlfriend, and another guy who looked a little older than me seated around the coffee table. The big dog lay at her son's feet. He wore shorts, and the girlfriend, yoga pants. Evidently, I had guessed wrong about attire. Mrs. M said she had invited Luis, but he had a lab problem or some such keeping him away. Which didn't matter, she said, because he was a little older than the rest of us and his ideas were probably irrelevant anyway, coming from New York. I wanted to point out my ideas came from Pennsylvania, so should I leave? But I didn't. I settled myself on a chair and accepted a glass of red wine from the guy who wasn't Mrs. M's son.

The guy introduced himself as Oscar, an old friend of Eddie, Jr.'s. He said he'd worked as a trainer in a gym before the pandemic shut it down but now he worked in the bank with "EJ." I gathered he still hit the gym regularly because his muscles bulged out of his clothes. He asked what I did, and when I said

I worked for Hargrove-Spence, his eyes lit up. He opened his mouth to say something, but Eddie, Jr. interrupted to introduce the girl—woman? I couldn't guess her age—sitting beside him wearing a floppy top that showed her breasts when she moved. He said her name was Corinne and she taught yoga. She didn't say a word.

Mrs. M placed a tray of snacks on the coffee table, the kind of finger food Hargrove-Spence served at investor parties: bruschetta on a wooden plank, and multicolored macarons on a glass plate. Corinne took one of the bruschetta and raised it to Eddie Jr.'s mouth. He bit through and gave her the other half. I glanced at Mrs. M, who had chosen a chair near me. Her lips were pursed, fingers tapping on her knee. I could sense the steam building up inside her. The dog got up and came to her, tail swishing over the food on the coffee table. She stroked its head without glancing at it. She sat straighter.

"Now that you've all met, I hope we can begin," she said. "Everyone should speak up. Your opinions are important to the Friends." She looked around the room. Her eyes seemed to rest on Corinne a nanosecond longer than on the others. "Remember, we want to know how you really feel about the growth of our city."

She proceeded to ask questions about what we valued in the environment. She went around the room starting with her son. He repeated stuff I'd heard her say at the Friends meeting. Corinne passed. I went big on responsibility for our shared commons, and Oscar countered with an appeal for individual liberty. He got agitated, praising Arizona for upholding freedom despite the corruption coming from the coasts. I reminded him that without the investment from D.C. in the Roosevelt Dam, there would have been no prosperity in Arizona. He spouted some nonsense, and I countered with data. He shouted at me, and I couldn't help myself: I shouted back. He stood, red-faced and bristling. The dog barked. Mrs. M stepped between us. She told Oscar to sit and asked me to accompany her to the kitchen. I was glad to. I felt ashamed of sinking to Oscar's level. The dog followed.

In the kitchen, she took a tray from a cupboard and placed it on the marble-topped island. She turned to me.

I spoke before she could. "I'm sorry. I just wanted him to admit that other people's perspectives are worth listening to." Not that it was my job to correct every wrong person on the planet.

"He knows that. Oscar is redeemable when handled properly." She took another bottle of wine from a cabinet. "I've known him since he went to high school with my son. He was trying to impress you, and it got out of hand."

"I'm sorry for ruining your party."

"Oh, you haven't ruined it. You are showing us how you think. The others would do well to emulate you. Did you notice Corinne didn't comment?" She fished around in a drawer and brought out a corkscrew. She placed bottle and corkscrew on the tray and picked it up, testing the balance. "I'm going to ask Oscar to open the wine. It will soothe his ego, and we'll be able to resume." She stepped toward the threshold. "Coming?"

I followed her back to the living room. I had to, otherwise there wouldn't be enough people for her to gather opinions from, and I wouldn't be doing my job. The dog followed us. I took my seat and told myself to speak only when spoken to. Oscar apologized for being "hot-headed." I apologized for shouting at him. Mrs. M handed him the bottle and corkscrew. He opened it and poured another round, looking calm as predicted. Corinne refused a second glass of wine, saying she had to leave soon to pick up her son. EJ puffed himself up and said Jackson was the world's smartest four-year old. He couldn't wait for us to meet him. I watched Mrs. M straighten the stack of cocktail napkins, and I imagined her biting her tongue. The dog slunk away, settling down on a doggy bed across the room.

The questioning resumed for half an hour or so. Bored, I excused myself to go to the bathroom, which Mrs. M said was down the hall to the left. Halfway down the hall, I noticed what looked like an office on the right and poked my nose inside. Dark wood paneling with built-in shelves up to the ceiling and a black leather chair behind a big desk: a man's room. Maybe it was her late husband's? Clearly, she'd taken over. Arranged neatly on top of the desk were file folders, some fat, some skinny. I glanced at the labels and stopped short. Mrs. M had a file on the Hammer family. I opened it carefully. Thomas Hammer in his cowboy hat stared back from a photo in a magazine story about restoring antique cars. Sy hadn't mentioned anything about cars, and I hadn't seen any at the Ranch. Thomas Hammer's hobbies were none of my business. I closed the file and tiptoed out of the room. At the far end of the hallway, the dog's big hairy head stared at me. I made the shush sign, and the head withdrew. Whew.

When I returned from the bathroom, Oscar and EJ were talking about bank stuff, and Corinne was looking at her phone. After a minute, she rose and announced it was time to go. EJ jumped up, said good night, and escorted her out the door. Oscar took his leave right after them. I stayed behind to help Mrs. M clean up and to learn whatever I could about what she intended to do with the contents of her folders.

Mrs. M and I carried the uneaten food to the kitchen. She packed the leftovers into plastic containers and put the glassware and plates into the dishwasher, talking to me over her shoulder all the while.

"I was impressed with your comments. Did you learn about city planning in school?"

"No. My boss gives me books to read, and I get tips from the staff. Everyone at Hargrove-Spence is friendly."

"That's wonderful. You wouldn't get very far if you had to rely on Nate Hargrove alone." She reached under the sink for dishwasher powder. "I don't suppose you know how he made his bones?"

"I don't understand."

"His grandfather operated a water company that got bought out by the City of Phoenix ages ago. He left his fortune to Nate. Made the rest of the family resentful. Your boss is not the entrepreneur he touts himself to be."

I digested the information. Where Nate got his money didn't matter to me. Continuity was my prize. I pursued my agenda. "How did you get involved with the White Bear Ranch in the first place?"

"Oh, a friend lives nearby. She saw construction signs going up and called me. When I saw how important the property was, I decided to save it. You know I have experience in that arena."

"Are you a friend of the Hammer family?"

"Not yet." Mrs. M started the dishwasher and straightened up. "Well, that does it. Thank you for your participation tonight. You were a great help."

"My pleasure." A white lie.

"May I say something? You tend to cover your mouth with your hand, but you don't need to. No one's bite is perfect, and you have so much to contribute to the conversation. Unlike my son's latest."

I nodded and got out of the lion's den as fast as I could. Mrs. M had my head spinning. She didn't like Nate. She didn't like my teeth. She liked her son's girlfriend least of all. Suddenly it occurred to me that maybe she didn't care about Gen Z's opinions. Maybe the whole not-a-focus-group thing had been a set-up to embarrass Corinne. If so, it hadn't worked. Corinne obviously didn't give a shit, and Eddie, Jr. hustled right out of his mama's house after her.

I drove home slowly, a metallic taste on my tongue. Could be the red wine, could be a reaction to Mrs. M. I hate being manipulated. My insides clam up, as if I had an allergy. The battle lines Nate had warned me about appeared in full color in my mind's eye. I should prepare to defend myself among the Friends.

Turning onto Northern Avenue, I imagined describing my evening to Gabi. I'd been telling her what a fantastic idea the Friends had, preserving green space for everyone's use, not just rich folk. I had also thought Continuity's future residents would love hiking in their "backyard" and seeing wildlife flourishing in the hills. But the Friends' army was under the command of a sneaky general. Damned if I knew what that meant for its future. It made me sad to think that Mrs. M might spoil a truly good thing.

13

On Monday, Gabi asked if she could come to Sy's for tea with me that week. It hadn't occurred to me to introduce the two because the only thing they had in common was me. Sy said "sure" when I asked if I could bring my roommate. Then Gabi changed her mind. The next morning, she again asked if she could come with me on Friday, but reversed herself that evening. I finally told her Sy was waiting for the visit, and would she please make up her mind. She said yes.

She wanted to bring the Mexican wedding cookies her mother had recently sent up from Ajo with an uncle. I didn't know if Sy liked Mexican country cooking, but clearly Gabi had gone to a lot of trouble to get the cookies. I had no idea why she wanted to use half her day off to have tea with an elderly gringa rancher, but I picked her up at one o'clock to drive to Sy's.

We rang the doorbell, Gabi holding the cookies in a box wrapped in plastic and shifting from foot to foot while we waited. Leticia opened the door with a big smile and offered to take the cookies. She said she'd serve them on one of Sy's fine plates. Gabi seemed reluctant to let the box go, but I nudged her. I figured Leticia wanted to help Gabi make a good impression out of solidarity with the next generation of Latinas. Or maybe she was just very good at her job. In any event, my car had been cool enough to keep the powdery, white cookies in good shape.

The house smelled faintly like the vinegar Leticia cleaned with. Sy was sitting in her customary place behind the tea service in the living room. She wasn't dressed up, for which I was glad because neither was I. Gabi had made an effort, though. She wore one of her Sunday church dresses and a little make-up. She walked right up to Sy and reached for her hand. Sy arched those eyebrows, but Gabi forged ahead.

"I'm happy to meet you. I've heard so much about you. You're like a grandmother to Bee."

No, I thought, not like my dour grandmother. More like the biology teacher I had back in high school, the one who cared. An adult you could trust to take your side.

Sy said, "My dear, have a seat. We'll have tea, and then we'll talk."

I took my usual place and Gabi sat opposite me, an expectant look on her face. I could tell she was nervous, and I think Sy could, too, by the way she folded her hands and smiled. Leticia came into the living room with the cookies mounded symmetrically on a glass platter and placed them on the coffee table.

"Are those wedding cookies?" Sy said. Leticia put a cookie on a cake plate and handed it to Sy. She winked at me as she withdrew.

Sy took a nibble. "There was an empty building on the Ranch that we would lend out to the hands for weddings and funerals and such. I always went when invited." She flicked the cookie, scattering powdered sugar. "These were my favorite. I didn't much care for the other pastries." She took another nibble. "This is delicious."

"My mother made it for you. She got the recipe from my grandmother." Gabi almost whispered, "I don't bake."

"You should treasure the recipe nonetheless." Sy lowered the cookie to the plate.

I realized I'd never seen her really eat. Nibble, yes, but never a whole pastry. I gathered she didn't have an appetite for food anymore, only for mischief.

Sy said, "Tell me about your grandmother."

A smile bloomed on Gabi's face. "She lives in Ajo, in the house my grandfather built so he could bring his family from Mexico. They had six kids, only one girl. My abuela worked as a maid to learn English, and she cooked for everyone, including her children's families. I was her oldest grandchild, so I got spoiled."

"How so, in such a busy household?"

Gabi thought for an instant. "She made me feel like nothing was more important to her than my happiness. She was the only one who approved of me going to Phoenix to get educated. My mom wanted me to stay home with her."

"Your grandmother didn't spoil you. She honored your right to think for yourself."

"Thank you for saying that. I do still worry about my mom with no daughters at home."

Sy lowered her plate to the table with a shaky hand. "She will make do; she's a mother. Now, tell me why you came to see me."

Gabi's face registered surprise, although I'd warned her about Sy's no-nonsense manner. "I came because Bee listens to you. She's mad at me for letting my little brother stay in our apartment. Bee thinks I'm being taken advantage of. She's fuming underneath, and it's driving me crazy. I don't need more tension in my life. Just because her family was ... unfortunate doesn't mean I should abandon my brother."

Sy stared at Gabi. "In other words, you girls have a disagreement, and you want me to settle it?" She shook her head ever so slightly.

I could feel my cheeks reddening. Gabi had no business laying her so-called problem on Sy. It was a mistake to bring her here.

Gabi said, "Every time we talk about it, she won't open her mind even a crack. You have family. You know you need to take care of them, even when they mess up." She appeared on the verge of tears.

Sy reached and patted Gabi's arm. "I see how upset you are, but I won't intervene. You girls should talk it out. Take your time. Rome wasn't built in a day, as they say."

I gritted my teeth. "I didn't know why Gabi wanted to come today. I apologize for the intrusion."

Sy shook her head. "No need." She pointed a bent finger. "You two are not adversaries, are you?"

Gabi said, "No, we're not. But she has such a hard head!"

"I would agree, but that's her character."

Gabi looked at her hands in her lap.

"Ms. Martinez, I'll have you know that Bee and I have a substantial disagreement. She believes her boss to be a humanitarian, and I believe him to be an opportunist. Yet that doesn't impede our friendship."

Her words caught me up short. I'd conveniently forgotten her dissing Nate. Not actually forgotten, more like shoved to the back of my brain. I resented her bringing it up with Gabi. I said to Sy, "I don't see any evidence that Nate's misbehaving."

Sy's eyebrows arched. "Keep your mind open as well as your eyes." She nodded at Gabi.

My dander was up, and even though I had a few doubts about Nate myself, out of my mouth came, "He's accomplishing what he said he would. The brochure is coming true."

"In the short run, perhaps. Do you know it took seventy years for that infamous central canal to deliver water to the most distant customer? Your boss will not sustain the work."

How could she be so sure? I bit my tongue.

Moving slowly, Sy placed the cookie plate on the table. "I detect a lack of kindness in your boss that will doom his work." Sy turned to Gabi. "As you see, Bee and I are agreeing to disagree, as they say."

Gabi shrank back. "I'm sorry I wasted your time, Mrs. Hammer."

"Nonsense. Your cookies brought back wonderful memories." She sighed. "We hosted so many weddings over the years. At first, I kept track of the children they produced, but many of the hands moved on, and I stopped corresponding. The Ranch still sends Christmas greetings, and I receive photos of children and grandchildren in reply." She paused. "In the old days, some of the hands would go to Mexico for the holiday, and we would throw a New Year's party when they returned. I don't celebrate the holidays anymore. Too many doctors' and lawyers' appointments. Please thank your mother for the delicious cookies."

My cheeks had cooled off some and my temper eased a notch. Gabi appeared subdued, too, sitting quietly. Sy was right about our needing to talk it out, but not here.

Leticia appeared in the living room with the house phone in her hand, and I took advantage of the interruption to say we had to leave. Sy said nice meeting you and come again. Not on my watch! We got in my car and buckled up in silence. I meant to let Gabi talk first, but as I headed for the highway, the words spilled out.

"Why didn't you tell me I made you anxious?"

"Are you going downtown? I'm meeting Aaron near the airport. He agreed to go for job counseling. You can leave me off wherever, and I'll get an Uber." She pulled her phone out of her purse and tapped.

I was not going to leave her off, and I was not going to let her off the hook. "I'll take you, but you have to explain yourself."

Gabi put the phone away. "I'm sorry I embarrassed you. I didn't know what else to do."

"Why not talk to me?"

"Because it doesn't work. I'm so worried about Aaron, and every time I talk about him, you contradict me. You want me to show tough love, but you don't understand, and it makes me feel awful." She looked out the window. "Can we not do this now? Please?"

I tried to remember our last conversation about Aaron. I hadn't pushed my ideas on her. True, I'd criticized her attitude. Maybe she felt scorned. Or maybe she was jealous of all the attention I paid Sy. My eyes widened at the thought.

We reached the approach to the airport, and Gabi told me to take the exit ramp for the rental car center. I left her in front of the garage looking altogether blue, and I was sorry.

I pointed my car north. I thought I should stop at the office to sort through today's site pics, but I didn't want to encounter Nate in my current frame of mind. For want of a better idea, I headed home. I decided against using the highway and drove west toward Seventh Street to take the slow route back to Sunnyslope, which would be even slower now that the Friday rush hour had begun. I cranked the fan to fight the late afternoon heat and turned onto the two-way lane that was now supposedly reserved for cars going in my direction. I'd take my chance that an idiot driver going the wrong way didn't hit me head-on.

For the first time in our acquaintance, Sy had pissed me off. Slamming Nate and my ability to evaluate the work. I *did* see what's going on, and it was grand and elegant even if Nate revolted her. I needed to find a way to show her she was wrong. I punched the button for the classic rock station and turned up the volume. The old stuff had a beat that could penetrate any mood.

What did she mean about "a lack of kindness" dooming the work? I'd never heard anyone mention kindness in the context of business. Nate wasn't particularly kind, but he wasn't particularly unkind. Sy should realize that Nate wouldn't be her biggest problem. The person to watch out for was Katie Morrison, the do-gooder who hated on everyone and who had intel about Thomas Hammer spread out on her big fat desk. I wished I hadn't promised to keep the Friends' secrets. If any of them turned out to be toxic, I'd break that promise in a heartbeat.

14

Aaron pounded on my bedroom door. It was four in the afternoon on Sunday, and I was drying my hair, realizing that I didn't know Luis's last name. He'd been on my mind since Mrs. M's so-called focus group party. I pulled on my jeans and let Aaron in. His face was flushed and his voice panicky. He said Gabi was in trouble at the border. I knew she'd gone to a cousin's *quinceañera* in Sonoyta, across the border, and was due back today.

Aaron blurted, "She couldn't find her wallet with her ID. Some asshole must have stolen it at the party. There's a Gabriela Martinez on the deported list, so the Border Patrol detained her. Then they checked her fingerprints and found out she's legal, but she has to pay a fine." He shook his head. "She needs me to bail her out, but my credit card is maxed. I need your help."

"How long does it take to drive to the border?"

"Three hours."

Six hours round trip, seven if we had to wait for bureaucracy. It would be a long night, and I had a big meeting in the morning. Nate had connected with Thomas Hammer, and he wanted me there. "Don't your parents live close to the border?"

He snapped. "You don't understand our parents. Or the border. Gabi needs help. *Our* help."

I decided to overlook his nasty for Gabi's sake. "Okay, I'll go."

"I'm coming with you."

"Not necessary."

"I know the way. Google Maps doesn't work down there." He looked like he might cry. "She's my sister."

"Okay. We'll go in five minutes." If I didn't finish styling my hair now, I'd be a mess for tomorrow. I told Aaron to make a couple of sandwiches for the road and fill the cooler. He headed for the kitchen. At least he could take orders.

If Gabi was in trouble, how come she called Aaron and not me? She had that blood thicker than water thing going, but we were sisters in our hearts. I confessed to feeling a little hurt, especially since he'd need to borrow my car anyway. Maybe she wasn't thinking straight.

And what about José, her boyfriend? I remembered she'd said he was in some kind of training program in Tempe. Still, you'd think she'd call him before her brother. Maybe he really was the loser Aaron said he was, and she knew it deep down. I would find out once she was home safe.

We piled into the car, Aaron lugging the cooler. I had a full tank of gas, so we wouldn't have to stop. Twilight lasts long in May; I thought we'd reach the border before dark. I took the ramp onto the highway. Aaron sprawled in the passenger seat and plugged into his phone. Tiny squeals wound out of his earbuds. I wanted to understand the situation better, so I reached over and pulled the bud out of his left ear. He took out the other and stared at me.

"Tell me about the border. Have you ever been held there?"

"No. I'm an American. My passport is in my pack, just in case." He pointed his phone at the back seat. "My mom was held once. She couldn't find her papers. She was so upset and remorseful the agent took pity on her and let her in without a fine. It's up to them whether to block you or not. Gabi must have pissed the guy off."

Didn't sound like Gabi. But maybe she'd cursed in Spanish, which she tended to do when aggravated. I'd noticed that some of the other students at my community college had a different personality when they spoke Spanish.

"I don't even have a passport."

"Don't worry. You won't have to prove anything." He plugged himself back in.

I told myself to count to ten, then another ten, and then I unplugged his left ear. "Hey. You and I are taking a drive together to pick up your sister, my friend. Be nice."

He looked surprised. "I *am* nice. Gabi would kick me out if I misbehaved toward you." He smirked. "Her words."

I felt a surge of satisfaction. I liked being Gabi's priority. "Okay. I'll keep my hands to myself."

He plugged back in.

I took the ramp off the interstate onto the state route that would take us through Ajo to the border. Being Sunday, traffic was light. I turned the radio on and scanned for an FM channel that would come in clear all the way to Mexico. I skipped over the Bible stations and the pop and country, looking for rock. Near the top of the spectrum, there were a couple of Spanish-language stations in a row. I stopped the scan and tapped Aaron on the shoulder.

"Is this a good station?"

He unplugged. For two seconds he listened to a man croon about his *corazon.* "That's my mother's music. Miguel Bose."

"Is there a better station?"

"You can't get good music on the radio. Too commercial." He stared at me. "You and Gabi are pretty tight."

"She's my best friend."

"You're lucky."

So is she, you boob, I thought. I concentrated on the road ahead.

We rolled through flat farmland stretching to a line of craggy little hills. I hadn't been to Buckeye before. People at the office said the biggest new projects were coming online here. I was curious about the area but decided not to ask Aaron what he knew about it to spare myself an anti-development rant. The road took us through the hills, then onto flatland leading to another range of craggy hills. All the way into Mexico, we would be crossing flats followed by mountains, followed by flats and so on, like God-sized corduroy. I thought about Gabi driving this route on weekends to help her folks. They were lucky she was so loving.

Gabi was the best friend I'd ever had. She was the only person I had entrusted with the truth about my father. It happened after we'd both gotten vaccinated and decided to celebrate. We went to a wine bar with an outside patio that was packed to bursting with half-naked girls and Axe-scented boys. It was such fun to bump into people and shout over the noise after a year of quiet. I told her I felt free again, as free as I'd felt when I first landed in Phoenix and left all that shit behind. She asked what shit, and for some unknown reason and a lot of alcohol, I told her that my father sold babies, and I was his accomplice.

"What I did may have been legal, I don't know, but it was immoral," I whispered at the end of my story.

Gabi's lips had knit as if she couldn't believe I could be involved with anything so slimy. She thought for a moment. "What about your mom?"

"I don't think she knew." I began to sob. "And she wasn't going to leave my dad. She couldn't work. She could barely cook." The sobs kept coming. I had bottled up my shame for so long.

Gabi put her arms around me. I leaned into her.

"I'm sorry you had to suffer, guerita." She held me and stroked my hair. "It wasn't your fault."

I could have refused. "I could have reported them instead of slinking off."

"You did what you thought was best. No one could ask for more."

Such a simple sentiment. I wanted to believe her, but I didn't. She never said another word about it, and I didn't volunteer any.

I hadn't confessed that my trouble went way beyond the baby sale. Before my brother, Danny, was born, my mom had held it together, and my father had been practically invisible, but we were okay. After Danny, she crashed. We never went to church after that, and groceries got delivered. When I was twelve, my mother told me to look up "menstruation" online. I trekked to Walgreen's alone for whatever I needed. Around that time, my father began to bark at me, calling me stupid and hopeless, and I barked back. I grew so tired of losing every argument and being angry all the time. I tried being bad—not awful, just delinquent, minor drug use—but that didn't get me anywhere either. When he wouldn't let me go to nursing school, I was crushed. But he crossed a line selling that kid; that day I realized it was either him or me. One of us was crazy and I had to find out which. Gabi couldn't possibly imagine the poison in the air at my house. Not sure even I totally understood.

~ ~

The road narrowed to two lanes passing through dusty, barren fields bounded by barbed wire. Aaron slouched with eyes closed except when he ate a couple of sandwiches. We reached the outskirts of a town where stores were advertising "Mexico insurance," and one entire building was painted to look like the Mexican flag. A "whaddaya know" burst out of me. Aaron perked up and said welcome to Ajo. We stopped for the red light—it was a one-stoplight town—at the central plaza, a grassy park surrounded on three sides by fake-adobe buildings fronted by an arched colonnade. When I said the place had charm,

Aaron snorted and said wait five minutes. I could understand his snort. Back in Pennsylvania, they tried to rehabilitate my town's so-called downtown. It was a cosmetic effort to attract bougie tourists, and it didn't change the fact that the locals were mostly poor folk. I guessed Aaron and I had another thing in common.

Five minutes later, we'd left the buildings behind, and the road passed between two flat-topped mountains of rock, one dirty white, the other gray streaked with yellow. Tall mountains with straight sides, obviously man-made and ugly.

Aaron said, "This is what's left over after the mining company extracts copper from the rock they dig out of a pit. The town was built to work the mine. There was nothing here but desert a hundred years ago."

"They dig coal out of a pit where I grew up. They used to dig tunnels into the ground, but that's not profitable anymore. They're supposed to plant trees on top of the pits, but it doesn't really restore the landscape."

"Remediation is not required by law in Arizona, so it won't happen here." He turned his face away.

I could understand why Aaron bristled about the ugliness, but I didn't see him giving up electronics to save the world from copper mining. I decided to try to draw him out on a neutral subject.

"Made any progress on your job search?"

"What did Gabi tell you?"

"Just that you're going to get your associate's while you work. Like she did."

Aaron burrowed further down into the seat. He looked smaller than when standing.

"What are you going to major in?"

"Don't know. It's not important."

"It is! It'll help you get a job."

"Like yours? Sorry, I won't work for greed. I might work with the hackers who keep the internet safe. They're volunteers. No money in it."

"Aaron, I'm serious."

He sat up and looked at me. "My family has no ideas beyond their little Ajo-Sonoyta circle. Gabi had to push them to let her go as far as Phoenix. I want to go farther."

"What's stopping you?"

He rolled his eyes.

I remembered my own struggle when I landed in Arizona before the pandemic. It might be harder now to find a placement. I should cut him some slack. I turned on the radio. Too much static. I turned it off and Aaron and I sat in what I assumed was friendly silence.

I was wrong.

"You have no right to judge me," he said. "You mooch off my sister as much as I do. You think your bullshit job makes you noble, but your precious Continuity is just rules and walls to protect rich people from what they don't want to see."

I was stunned. I slowed down. "Aaron, that's not true. Continuity is for people who respect the environment. You won't need to be rich to buy in."

"Take your blinders off. Who really has a fucking chance in this state?"

I could feel the heat coming off him. I was hot, too, and reminded myself to watch the road. What he said about Continuity didn't get to me, just Aaron being Aaron. But Gabi … she'd given me cheap rent, free food, even help with my wardrobe for years. And I took it all, blithely unaware of how it mounted up. Did *she* think I mooched? I bit my lower lip. I was *not* callous; I would fix the situation ASAP.

~ ~

When we entered the Organ Pipe Cactus National Monument, the road got smoother and the scenery better: cholla as big as Christmas trees, chaparral and saguaro that hadn't ever been cut down to make way for crops. I couldn't help exclaiming how lush the desert looked down here. I expected Aaron to say something snide, but he stared straight ahead. In ten minutes, we reached the border at the Lukeville Port of Entry, a modest pink structure straddling the two-lane road. It was relatively easy to find Gabi, and not too hard to spring her since it only cost $595, and my credit was good. Aaron did have to show his passport to the border officer. Eyes downcast, he mumbled that he was born in Ajo. Then he shut up, halleluiah.

Gabi looked so relieved to see us. I could tell she was holding back tears. She did some more paperwork, and then we walked her into the parking lot where they had kept her car. She gushed thanks at me and promised to pay me back. Aaron gave her a long hug.

He released her and his face got serious. "Do I know the S.O.B. who stole your wallet?"

She laughed. "Probably. You know everyone who was there. But you're not going to do anything about it, right?"

He kicked the gravel.

She faced me. "I'm a little shaky. I'm going to spend the night with my parents. I'll see you tomorrow after work, okay?" She turned to her brother. "Coming?"

Aaron said, "I'm going back with Bee. You're safe."

What was that all about? He and I hadn't exchanged an unofficial word since his outburst.

Gabi pleaded, "They haven't seen you in months. Come on, just one night."

He shook his head.

Gabi flicked his shoulder. "I'll give everyone your love." She hugged me again and unlocked her car. She waved as she drove off.

We both watched Gabi's car disappear around a bend. Then we got back in my car and headed north. Clearly, Aaron didn't want to see his parents without having a job to brag about. I was glad for the company driving through the desert at night, though, even if he became hostile again. But he seemed more relaxed, lounging in his seat without earbuds. I guess I relaxed, too, because my thoughts turned to the next day's meeting with Sy's son. I hadn't been told what my role would be, but I'd be ready for whatever.

On a dark stretch of road just north of the town of Why— the sign said Why, although I couldn't see why, there being almost nothing there—I hit a bump, and the car careened to a stop on the left frontage. We got out. Front right tire was twisted half off the rim; twisted hub cap lay twenty yards back. It was a flat, the first I'd ever had in this car. In the trunk, we found one of those funny little wheels that are meant to let you creep into Discount Tire. To my surprise, Aaron acted the gentleman and put the wheel on. As I climbed back into the driver's seat, he said we should spend the night with his parents in Ajo, and they'd find us a real spare tire in the morning, one that would make it to Phoenix for sure.

I thought about his suggestion. I didn't want to be stranded in the desert without cell coverage in the middle of the night if I happened to hit a javelina and that puny wheel gave way. There'd been plenty of roadkill on the way down. Much as I wanted to make that meeting in the morning, I had to agree with him. I told him to text Gabi to expect us.

It was ten o'clock when we reached Ajo, at the edge of polite, but I decided to phone Nate anyway to tell him I'd be late tomorrow. When I called from the car, he exploded.

"Why the hell did you go to Mexico on a Sunday night?"

"My best friend needed rescue. I'd be home already if the road hadn't eaten my tire."

"Not good enough. Your priorities are out of whack."

How could he say such a thing! "Can't you handle the meeting without me? I barely know Thomas Hammer."

"You're the key to his mother's mind. You've been working her for weeks."

I resented the way he described my visits with Sy. I wasn't "working her." I respected and admired her.

Nate said, "I'm disappointed in you. Come into the office when you get back and we'll discuss how to make up the ground. I can't talk now." He hung up.

His criticism stung, unjustified though it was. Or was it? Was it wrong to prioritize your best friend's rescue over your boss's schedule?

Nate had never acted nasty toward *me* before. When I first started at Hargrove-Spence, I looked forward to conversations with Nate because he was friendly and animated. He used to compliment me on learning quickly, and he assigned me more and tougher tasks. He'd seemed happy with my work back then. He didn't seem happy with me these days. Or I with him, come to think of it.

We got out of the car and two figures silhouetted against the lit-up house came to greet us. An older man I assumed was Gabi's dad and a younger guy with the same shape beard as Aaron. I made my face look cheery and prepared to greet the Martinez clan. I hoped my high school Spanish would hold up. The young guy came over and said he was Gabi's cousin's son and thanked me for rescuing her. We walked up the steps into the house, and Gabi's mom pulled me into the kitchen, which smelled fantastic. Mrs. Martinez piled up plates for Aaron and me, and her husband brought beers. I could see where Gabi got the hospitality gene. They were speaking English for my benefit, and they kept singing my praises. Aaron was quiet.

After we'd eaten, Gabi told the family to let us go to bed since we'd have to rise early. Aaron went off with the cousin's son and Gabi took me to her room to share her bed, which was a double, fortunately. I was about to ask about the bathroom when Mrs. Martinez walked in with a bowl of vinca blooms from her garden. She placed it on the one empty corner of Gabi's dresser and came to me for a long, silent hug. I hugged back and, to my surprise, ached inside. It might be nice to grow up wrapped in a mother's protective arms. When her mother left, Gabi said I was a hit because I asked for seconds of the pozole. She said her cousin would fix me up with a tire in the morning because she was going to leave early and take Aaron. It was obvious he needed big sister time. I agreed, grateful to be spared his company on the drive home. I had other things to worry about. Namely, a boss pissed off for no good reason as far as I could see.

It was almost midnight by the time we settled down. As I drifted toward sleep, my stomach comfortably full of food and drink, my brain sorted images of the evening spent with Gabi's big family—a couple of other relatives had come over to meet "the roommate"—and I'd done my best to join in. We'd joked around some in Spanglish, except for Gabi's dad, who seemed standoffish. But he didn't strike me as malicious, more old-fashioned, like Pennsylvania people. Gabi obviously adored him, asking for his opinions and refilling his glass. Yet she'd defied him and gone north to work. Being female was complicated wherever you came from.

15

The Friday after my unplanned trip to Mexico, I imagined telling Sy about it, but I was still too mad at Nate, and I didn't want it to show. Sy liked hearing about my adventures—she said she was tired of her own stories—and I appreciated her interest in me. I felt comfortable at her place. Sy could be funny, too. I figured she'd already checked all her boxes, so now she could laugh at herself. She never laughed at me.

This particular Friday, we were tucking into blueberry scones—well, I gobbled, she nibbled—when I noticed a newspaper on the end of the table folded to the obituary page. Sy caught me checking it out.

"I read three papers every morning. I take the *Republic* for the obituaries," she said.

As I cleared my throat to ask why, I choked on a crumb.

Sy said, "You'd be surprised what you can learn about your community from the obituaries."

"Anything I should know that relates to Continuity?"

"'All work and no play,' Bee. What have you been doing after work hours?"

Leticia came into the room to say Sy's son had arrived. My face must have registered disappointment because Sy lowered her teacup and patted my hand.

"Don't worry, he won't interrupt. He telephoned just before you came. We have a little business to do."

Thomas Hammer, wearing Levi's and his beige cowboy hat, appeared on the living room threshold. He walked past me and leaned over to peck his mother's cheek. He removed the hat and sat across from her, telling the housekeeper not to bring another tea service.

Sy said, "Thomas, you remember my friend Deborah Wells, who calls herself Bee, I'll have you know."

I felt that damn blush coming. Named after an insect.

Sy faced me. "We have a problem at the ranch, and Thomas has solved it."

"I hope it isn't serious."

"The drought has lasted so long that we've run out of grass. Thomas has found a place in Texas to ship the cattle for pasture." She looked proud of her clever son. Guess some mothers take pride in their sons even in old age.

He said, "We'll be fine unless Texas floods or freezes again. No trusting the weather these days." He pulled a folded document out of his shirt pocket and spread it out on the table in front of his mother. My cue to scoot.

"I'll look at the photos in the hall. Take your time."

I found myself peering again at Sy's grandaunt. I tried to gauge her feelings about being photographed on her horse, cowboy hat shadowing her face. She hadn't smiled for the camera, although that may have been the style in the day. I looked at the photo of the mine entrance. Maybe Thomas Hammer could help me find it. I decided to risk being a pest and ask him outright.

When I returned to the living room, the document was back in his pocket and Sy was sipping her tea. I took my seat next to her while they chatted. At the first opening I said, "Dr. Hammer, can you tell me where exactly the old mine was located? The photo is intriguing."

He frowned slightly. "There were a couple of mines. The big one spread underground in several directions. We had to watch out for the air vents. They didn't seal up shafts and tunnels in the old days. It was dangerous. You could be walking along and suddenly the ground would open beneath you. We were lucky we didn't lose cattle."

"Or cowboys," Sy piped up.

"Or cowgirls?" I asked, recalling those unsmiling eyes in the hall.

They both laughed, smile wrinkles forming around their eyes.

Sy leaned toward her son. "My young friend is out to make her fortune, like all Easterners. I'm afraid she's looking for gold."

"I'm just curious."

She wagged a finger at me. "I don't want you poking around there. It will come to no good."

"I'm also curious about how a modern ranch works."

He said, "Mostly we follow government regulations. USDA, BLM, FDA, EPA. The *federales* think they're protecting the nation's beef supply."

"Shouldn't they?"

"I had more freedom in my dental practice. Even during a pandemic."

Sy said, "Can you take her along on your next inspection? Otherwise she'll pepper me with questions I can't answer."

"Sure thing." He got up and pecked his mother's cheek again. "I'll see you Sunday." He saluted me. "Nice seeing you again." He left quietly on rubber soles. I had half expected cowboy boots.

"Thank you for that," I said after the front door closed. "Should I wait for him to call me or just call him myself?"

"Yes, yes." Her head trembled slightly. "What an eager beaver you are. My kind of girl. But stay out of trouble." She adjusted the pillow behind her back. "Now, what have you been doing?"

I decided to tell her but leave out the part about Nate scolding me. "Driving to the border to pick up Gabi who had car trouble. Then *I* had car trouble and spent the night at her parents' house in Ajo."

"Do you think it's wise for a young woman to drive to Mexico alone?"

"Her brother came with me."

"Ah, I knew I could trust your judgment." She picked up her cup and saucer. "I gather that you and that nice young woman have settled your differences?"

"We're fine, thank you. I'm glad you think she's nice."

"It took courage for her to appeal to a stranger about a family matter. You don't do that in her culture." She lowered the saucer to the table and sank back against the pillow, closing her eyes.

She must have been really tired or else she would have grilled me about the trip. I had to remind myself that she was really old. I swallowed the last of my tea. "Nothing else to report. Should I leave now?"

"Yes, that's right." She sighed. "Before you go, what can you tell me about Katie Morrison? She contacted my son."

I shrugged. "I go to all the Friends meetings. She hasn't mentioned him."

"That woman is humorless. I don't like her." She opened her eyes. "You keep me informed."

"Will do." I pecked her cheek and picked up my bag. If Sy wanted intel on Mrs. M, I would be happy to provide. She and Nate had a mutual interest after all.

~ ~

Nate called back when he got the message that I'd been invited to inspect the Ranch with Thomas Hammer. I figured he couldn't cold shoulder me at *that* piece of news. I could hear the charge in his voice crackle across the ether.

"When is this inspection gonna happen?"

"I have to call him to set it up. I just wanted to let you know right away."

"Can you meet us at Wright's? Manheim is in town."

"When?"

"Now." He hung up.

Five o'clock, full-on rush hour. I'd take Camelback across the city. Should make it there on the half-gallon of gas remaining in my tank. I climbed into my dusty car and steered westward. Arnold Manheim was an architect Nate worked with. I'd had little contact with him. Nate was throwing me into the water again, trusting me to swim. Or maybe he didn't care whether I did. He'd been distant since I missed that meeting. How could he begrudge me one morning out of so many when I'd dropped everything to do his bidding? I wasn't sorry I'd rescued my roommate, and I think he knew it.

I was approaching Wright's, a restaurant with a fancy bar in the Biltmore Hotel Nate used for meetings. He once told me the hotel was an example of a developer's dream that had stood up over time. So, I had Googled the Biltmore. Opened in 1929, with a disputed history: Frank Lloyd Wright consulted with the local architect, who really designed it, but Wright claimed credit, and successive owners played up the Wright angle every time they renovated. Whenever we met there, I was tempted to ask Nate if he identified with Wright or the local guy. But I resisted the urge to shoot my mouth off.

I found a parking spot on the fourth floor of the garage the hotel had built supposedly in the Wright style—not that I could tell—and headed for the entrance to the main building. I must admit that I loved the old lobby. Even though there'd been no luxury hotels in my past, I could tell this one was special: tall walls made of concrete blocks shaped in the angular Wright fashion, discreet lighting, a hush emanating from sofas on area rugs near the picture windows. If I ever had any extra money, I'd rent a room and feel rich for twenty-four hours.

Nate, his wife, and his architect friend were seated around an end table; a waiter was delivering their drinks. Mrs. Hargrove gave me a welcoming smile. Nate waved at an empty chair across from Mr. Manheim, and I sat and ordered my usual ginger ale. My first time at Wright's I'd chugged a margarita and discovered that I couldn't work and drink at the same time.

"Tell us about Thomas Hammer." Blurting that meant Nate must have been on his second or third drink.

"I don't really know him. I think he loves his mother. He doesn't like the federal government. He dresses like a cowboy except with rubber-soled shoes. He was a dentist before he retired."

Mr. Manheim laughed. "A cowboy dentist. I accept the challenge!"

Nate looked at me. "We've been talking about phase two. Arnold's looking for inspiration."

"I think the Hammer family likes history. Mrs. Hammer has photos on the wall going back a hundred and fifty years."

Manheim said, "I need copies of those photographs. I will sketch something for the cowboy dentist. Although he is a contradiction."

"What do you mean?" I couldn't help asking, although I'd intended to just listen.

"A cowboy likes wide open spaces. A dentist likes tiny, crowded spaces. A cowboy respects nature, a dentist wants to fix it." He swept his arm across his chest, pleased with his pronouncement.

Frowning, Nate said, "You're getting ahead of yourself." Turning to me, "I got the impression Thomas Hammer doesn't care about the property. He doesn't say he's 'in it for his children's children,' like other ranchers. What's he in it for?"

"I don't know. Maybe I'll find out when he takes me on tour."

Nate's wife leaned toward me. She said, "You should be flattered, you know. The Hammers are private people."

Manheim addressed me. "Can you get me copies of those photos? I want to work up something for the dentist."

"I would have to ask permission to take photos of the photos. They'd want to know why."

Nate leaned way back and crossed his legs. "Arnold, that's unnecessary. We need the matriarch. She's the ultimate decision-maker."

You're darn right, I thought.

Nate got that vacant look in his eyes that meant he had gone inside his head. Manheim didn't seem to notice. I studied the architect: pink skin, Einstein hair, flashy clothing, big hands moving constantly. But he'd given Continuity a clean, almost delicate style. I didn't understand the artistic personality. I'd leave that to my boss.

"Premature," Nate said finally to Manheim. To me, "Go ahead with your plan. I will rein in my colleague. He has other things to do."

Mrs. Hargrove said, "I hope you're enjoying your visits with Sydelle Hammer. I met her years ago. A remarkable woman."

"I think so, too." Why had Nate sent me to chat with Sy, I wondered, when his wife already knew her? One puzzle after another.

She said, "Would you like to stay and have dinner with us? We'll be seated soon."

I glanced at Nate's blank face. "No, thanks. My roommate is expecting me." No, she wasn't, but I could tell I didn't belong in that company. I took a final gulp of the ginger ale which tickled the inside of my nose.

"Thank you for the good work," Nate said and raised his glass.

All the way home, I pondered whether or not I had a plan. I was still angry that Nate had begrudged me that one morning, but he seemed to want my help, and he'd just praised me in public, which was gratifying. True, he'd made me drive across town for a five-minute interview with his drinking buddy, and I wouldn't have been invited to dinner if not for Mrs. Hargrove. But then there was Continuity, and Nate had let me in on it.

So, what was my plan? Beyond inspecting that mine?

It was still rush hour, and I was slightly nervous about running out of gas on State Route 51. I got off the highway at Northern and pulled into a Quik Trip, a gas station with fourteen pumps and a convenience store the size of a Pennsylvania grocery. I loved the spaciousness of the West. If I had to choose between the cowboy and the dentist, I'd choose the cowboy in a nanosecond. I pulled up to the east side of pump number fourteen and turned off the engine. As I got out, I noticed two rapid-charging stations for electric vehicles at the side of the store. I guessed Quik Trip was hedging its bets. I guessed Nate was hedging his bets, too, making me spy on a retired dentist and his mother while waiting for who knows what.

It occurred to me that I'd wasted time waiting for word from on high before. When I was little, I thought my father's distance was a product of his authority, and I was in awe. After my brother was born and my mother fell apart, I needed help taking care of the baby, but he didn't offer any. He called me dumb, worthless, because I complained. I got frustrated, which hunched my shoulders and made my chest tight. The memory of that old tightness welled up, and I hated it. There was no point in comparing my father to Nate, though, because their motives were opposite. My father wanted to scam the system; Nate wanted to fix it in a big, bright way.

When I parked in front of our building, I saw Aaron on the steps, smoking. He turned away. I entered the apartment to see Gabi stomping around the kitchen, pulling pots from the cabinet and banging them down on the stove. I did *not* want to know what they'd fought about, but expected I soon would.

I decided to preempt more pot banging. "What's going on with Aaron?"

She turned away and went to the fridge. From inside the fridge, she mumbled something and then emerged clutching onions and peppers to her chest. She marched over to the sink and let the produce tumble into the basin. She looked me in the eye.

"I told our parents he's not working and he's not going to school. He yelled at me for telling them."

Nobody likes a snitch, I thought. Then I realized it was a good thing I hadn't been home when the fireworks began because I might have started yelling at Aaron, too. Our fight on the way to Mexico still stung.

"Then he told me he couldn't register because he didn't have a high school diploma. I could scream!"

"Why not?" I didn't really want to get involved, but what's a friend for?

"The pandemic hit his junior year. He was supposed to study from home, but he didn't. He told me he screwed around on the internet for eighteen months and lied to my mom about the graduation ceremony, which was virtual and in English, so she didn't go. I don't know what to do."

"Make him get a GED."

"How do I do that? He thinks he can learn what he needs on his own." She made air quotes. "He's smarter than the teachers." Again: "The technology in schools is obsolete."

"Threaten to send him back to Ajo." As soon as the words left my mouth, I knew they'd land wrong. Why did I have to keep relearning that you can't speak truth when someone doesn't want to hear it?

She pursed her lips and turned back to the sink. She began cutting the peppers and washing out their seeds.

I slunk off to my room. The last thing I needed right now was to fight with my best friend. Over anything, let alone her flesh and blood. Aaron could live in our closet forever if that's what she wanted. She already knew my opinion, and I wasn't going to repeat myself. I just wanted some quiet time to ponder my so-called plan.

16

Saturday morning, I got up at seven to hike while it was still coolish. To reach the top of North Mountain in actual cool, you have to get up at five-thirty, too early for this girl who likes to scroll in the quiet hours around midnight. I drove to the base of the more difficult of the two trails, so I'd have to concentrate on the footing and get out of my brain. The first quarter mile was pretty easy, a straightforward climb to a little ridge that overlooked some housing to the west, mostly creosote and sandstone along the way. Then the trail grew steep, and I scrambled over ledges and up steps cut into rockface, using my hands here and there to keep my balance. Whoever had cut this trail— might have been the Civilian Conservation Corps a hundred years ago, like on South Mountain—had plenty of ambition. The city fathers here let you climb and risk breaking your neck. Back East, they fenced off anything that might lead to a lawsuit.

The trail leveled out a quarter mile from the top, and I passed a family climbing up. An adolescent boy wearing flip-flops—danger! —was helping a woman who looked like his mom across a steep bit. They could have walked up a paved service road from the other end of the park, but they chose the hard way. Then a shirtless guy with huge calves, earbuds in place, passed me at speed. He was chugging air as much as I was—no one climbs North Mountain without puffing—but he muscled on. His shorts, shoes, and watch looked expensive. North was the poor man's mountain compared to Piestewa and Camelback; I figured the guy could be a stock boy at a sports organization, trying to keep up. Fantasizing about other people makes you forget the pain of the climb.

At the top, finally, I sat on a rock with my back to the microwave towers and watched the world below. Being the Sonoran Desert, no trees blocked the view. I could see the flat plain of the city glittering in the sunshine, rimmed by mountains as craggy and shadeless as this one. Tiny airplanes approached Sky Harbor to the east. Somehow, being above it all literally made me feel part of it all, connected to the tiny people in their speeding cars and to the cacti hanging onto slopes in the heat. After a few more minutes of awe, I stood and got ready to go back. Downhill took almost as much time as uphill because of the grade, although it didn't wind me. It took thirty-five minutes to reach my car. I'd walked a mile and a half and climbed seven hundred feet up and down: I felt revived. And hungry.

When I opened our apartment door, the welcome rush of cool air smelled like frying garlic. I spotted Gabi in the kitchen and José and his buddy, Red, a gangly white kid he played *futbol* with, in the living room hunched over the TV.

"Hola, guerita," José said without stopping what he was doing. He and Red appeared to be operating on the TV set. Cables and open boxes lay on the floor beside them. I muttered "hi" and headed for the shower. José had been coming over a lot lately. He usually had a smile for me, and I usually smiled back, but I was too sweaty dirty at the moment to interact. The shower felt delicious. Afterwards, I ran a comb through wet hair, sending droplets down the back of my fresh T-shirt, and went to the kitchen in search of calories.

"I don't need help." Gabi said. She was stirring sauce in a frying pan. "Brunch is almost ready."

"What's happening in the living room?"

"José is installing a video game he and Red bought. I told him they could play here after soccer practice. Maybe Aaron will join them."

"At soccer or video?"

"Hah! Go knock on his door, please, and tell him brunch in five minutes."

I knocked on the closet door. No answer. I went to watch the living room crew while my stomach rumbled. José was a stocky guy with close-cropped hair and a broad face. He'd be way taller than me if his legs didn't bow. As he moved the TV back into place, muscles bunched in his naked arms—I'd seen him pick up our couch by himself and carry it around until Gabi made up her mind where she wanted it—and I shuddered to think what he could do in anger. Not that I'd seen any sign of the bad behavior Aaron had hinted at. Gabi had told me José was studying to join the police force, which seemed like a good choice for him; he was tough enough, and Gabi would make sure he was nice enough. I didn't know anything about pale, skinny Red, not even his real name.

"Hey, you wanna check it out?" José brandished a controller at me. He and Red stood in front of the TV, testing their progress.

I shook my head. "No, thanks."

"Come on, I'll show you. A little aggression does everybody good." He grinned and stuck the controller in my hand.

"No thanks." José never took no for an answer, so I expected to struggle a little to avoid playing. I pushed the controller away, trying to hide my distaste.

"Come on. Don't be so serious all the time. Have some fun." He waggled the controller at me again.

I was about to open my smart-ass mouth and tell him cops had to be dead serious all the time or else they'd just be dead when Gabi called us to come and get it. I was first in the kitchen, heaping eggs and beans and *chilaquiles* on my plate.

The four of us carried our food into the living room. I sat on the floor, Gabi on the couch between the men. José praised Gabi's cooking—rightfully, brunch was soooo good—and she squirmed with pleasure. The sauce was milder than usual, maybe for Red's sake? Gabi took care of everyone in her turf. José had just started describing the morning's match when the closet door squeaked open. Aaron emerged, looking sleep-scruffy.

"There's plenty more in the kitchen," Gabi said. "Join us."

Aaron headed down the hall to the bathroom. I heard the toilet flush over the sound of José cursing his goalie for a big mistake. In another minute, Aaron re-appeared with a plateful of brunch and sat on the floor beside me. He ate silently as José bragged about the goal he'd managed to score in the last few minutes of the second half. Gabi wiped her lips with a napkin and pecked José's cheek. Red turned his head away. I imagined that he'd seen more displays of Gabi's affection than he'd wanted to.

José lowered his empty glass and leaned forward to reach into his back pocket. "Almost forgot. I have a present for you." He handed something yellow to Gabi.

"My wallet! How did you find it? I'm so happy!" She fingered the wallet's various compartments. "It's all there."

"When I was in Sonoyta last week, I checked with your cousin."

"You knew last week? Why didn't you tell me?"

Aaron said. "Because he wanted to make a big show in public. He probably stole it in the first place."

"*¡Pendejo!* José stood and growled something about "*tu madre.*" His fists were like big, hard balls; energy radiated from his arms.

Gabi sprang up in front of him. "No, no, no."

José said, "I'm tired of his bullshit. Stop acting like he's a baby. He needs to learn what happens when a man insults a man."

"Not here, not now." She stepped to her brother. Aaron rose to meet her.

"No more disrespect." She punched his shoulder. "Leave your plate in the sink and disappear." She turned her back and pulled José onto the couch to sit next to her.

Red and I both scrambled from our seats and followed Aaron across the living room into the kitchen. Red left the apartment, and I followed Aaron onto the patio. I was surprised to see how hard he'd taken Gabi's reprimand. I had expected him to say he was teasing, not to slink away without a word. I waited a bit, but he just stood there, leaning against the back wall.

I felt sorry for him.

"You look awful," I said to break the ice. "What did José say to you?"

"He said if I wasn't Gabi's brother, he'd smash me up."

"I wouldn't take him literally if I were you."

"I don't give a damn about him." He looked down. "It's Gabi."

"What about her?"

He looked up at me with a crooked half-smile. "You don't get it. She picked him over me. She kicked me out of the family."

"She took one side in an argument, that's all."

He shook his head. "It's bigger than that. She knew what she was doing." He pushed off the wall. "I'm going for a smoke." He walked toward the back gate of the apartment complex.

I went inside to get out of the broiling sun. I thought Aaron was overreacting and he and Gabi would kiss and make up. Maybe not right away if he came back smelling like cigarettes or anything else inhalable. But their fight wasn't my affair.

Thinking of siblings, I hadn't heard from my own adolescent brother in a while. I decided to text Danny to see if he wanted to talk. He almost never did, but I had to try. I missed him, but mostly I felt guilty leaving him behind. He wasn't as tough as me.

In retrospect, I suspect I was part of his problem. Our parents had delegated his care to me—my mom too depressed and my dad too busy with his deals—and I was all too eager to prove I could do anything grown up. It couldn't have been good for baby Danny to be brought up by his eight-, nine-, ten-year-old sister. Plus I got yelled at when he or I screwed up, and Danny paid for it indirectly. I took it out on him, and he lapped up my domination because I was all he had. Made me cringe to remember.

By the time I was fifteen, as old as Danny is now, I had figured out the scene was rotten and skipped out. I got an after-school job in a strip mall I could walk to and hung out with friends on the weekends. Nothing could keep me in that house. But Danny still lived there. He said it was okay because they left him alone. I pictured him turning into a mole with no friends and no future. I wanted him to break out, but I couldn't shake him long distance. I sent him a little money once in a while. Hard to do when you're living paycheck-to-paycheck.

I texted Danny. No reply. Brother trouble was another thing Gabi and I shared.

~ ~

At around two, José left, and Gabi went to the sink to wash dishes. Aaron wasn't back. I closed the blinds against the afternoon sun, and the apartment turned dusky. I checked the living room for leftover junk, and when I reentered the now cool kitchen, Gabi was seated at the table poking her phone. I took the other chair and waited for her to acknowledge me. She put down the phone and sighed. "Brunch was a disaster."

"It was delicious. Thank you."

She shook her head.

"Can I ask you something?" I said, daring to intervene. "Aaron thinks you've abandoned him. He thinks it's a big deal that you took José's side when they argued. I told him it wasn't."

Gabi threw up her hands. "They're all the same! José thinks I've abandoned *him* because I didn't kick Aaron out. I am so tired of the male ego!"

First time she'd said anything negative about José. I must have looked surprised because she leaned forward and grabbed my arm. "Don't worry. Aaron's family and I love him." She let go. "I love José, too." She sighed again. "He's my perfect guy."

I was all ears. "What makes him perfect?"

"He's strong and kind and he wants the same things I do. Almost."

I realized Gabi wanted to confide in me. "What's the problem?"

Gabi looked off into the nonexistent distance. "José has a child he never sees. The mother moved to California after the baby was born. José says *she* left him, and he's not responsible for the child because she got married. He says the husband should pay. I say he is responsible, no matter what. We argue about it." Her eyes teared up.

I gave her a hug. "I'm sorry you hurt."

She pushed me away. "I don't hurt. I'm frustrated! Men are so stupid. They turn everything into a contest they have to win." She freed a tissue from her back pocket and blew her nose. "Don't say anything to Aaron. I'm going to make peace between the two of them."

"Is that possible?"

"It has to be. I will teach them how to be brothers, however long it takes." She pushed her chair away from the table and stood. "You always talk about Continuity like you have a higher purpose. This one's mine." Her phone buzzed. She answered in Spanish and walked away.

I stayed at the kitchen table, a chill in my chest. This was the first time Gabi had put down my passion for Continuity. I knew my work didn't really turn her on, although she listened politely when I talked. She saw the world differently than I did; she liked the concrete, sensual stuff versus my abstraction, my ideals. She was happy in her skin and with her people, whereas I wanted to burst out of mine and climb the nearest mountain. In this world with so many gigantic problems, I thought Gabi's focus on family was too narrow. A shiver passed through me; what if mine were too grand?

The front door banged open and in a moment Aaron appeared in the kitchen. He poured himself a glass of water and sat in the chair his sister had vacated. He didn't smell like tobacco or weed, which was a good thing.

"Where's Gabi?" His color was better than when he'd walked out.

"On the phone. José left a while ago. You're safe."

He ran his fingers through his sweaty hair. "I scanned the neighborhood for 'rooms for rent' signs. There weren't any."

"You of all people should know everything's online."

"Not in my rental bracket." He stood up and placed the empty glass in the sink. "She say anything to you about me?"

I stood, too. "Your sister is a loving person. Talk to her. I'm not getting between you two."

"Thanks." He started to leave the room, but I stopped him with one hand.

"I suggest you wash that glass and put it away. Your sister left the sink spotless." I knew I was exploiting Aaron's momentary vulnerability.

He turned back to the sink, and I glided to my room feeling a little smug.

I had intended to spend the afternoon reading the book on "conscious construction" that Nate had lent me, but I didn't feel like it now. I turned on my music and took out an old college notebook from the box beneath the window. I opened it to a blank page at the back. Maybe I could write down what I expected from a higher purpose. The pen I dug out from the bottom of my bag didn't write. Just as well. I closed the notebook and texted my little brother again. I thought he was in better shape than Aaron, but I had to make sure. He texted back a flower emoji. Better than nothing.

17

Per his mother's request, Thomas Hammer drove me around the ranch for half an hour. He took an interior unpaved road I had only seen from the periphery. We drove through acres and acres of dried-brown, mostly empty fields pockmarked with rocks and prickly pear. He didn't respond to my request to see the mine. He said in the old days, they would never let a woman near a mine out of superstition, and that was still good policy. Actually, although he answered my questions, he didn't seem interested in much of what I said. Hard to figure the guy out, or maybe he just didn't care. But afterwards, he followed up promptly, sending me the pdfs of a couple of old maps as promised, along with a note saying he couldn't attest to their accuracy.

No kidding.

When the topo maps I'd ordered came, I did my best to match them up with Hammer's pdfs. I found both where the old mine was located and how to get there, at least so I thought. Despite the potential for "inaccuracy," I was prepared to take an icepick and baggies with me on a collecting expedition. Nate had said he might need soil samples, so I'd get him some. Bagging a little dirt couldn't be that complicated, and I wanted to show him I could take the initiative. But I also had a bigger goal. I was determined to discover what it was about the place that made my boss anxious. Something made Sy nervous, too. It was clear she didn't want me poking around it. Time to find out what the story was for myself.

Gabi fretted about my plan. She told her brother to go with me to keep me safe. The two of them seemed to have gotten over their spat, although I hadn't seen signs of different behavior on his part. Gabi couldn't stay hostile. Aaron probably knew he could get away with anything if he held out long enough. If he were my brother, that tactic wouldn't work. I'd kick his ass. Maybe that's why Danny didn't take my calls.

I told Aaron he didn't need to go prospecting with me. He said my assignment was ridiculous, but he owed me one for the trip to Mexico. He packed a flashlight, a hunting knife, and a couple of bandanas in case we ran into foul smells. I couldn't imagine that odor would be a problem, but okay. I told him I'd take him along just to make Gabi happy. Secretly, I wanted the company. I was slightly spooked by the idea of sneaking around uninvited, but I wouldn't show it.

We set off in the morning cool. We took a gravel service road off Cave Creek and came to a cattle fence at the edge of the Ranch. Aaron held the gate open for me to drive through. Then he re-looped the wire around the post and hopped back in the car, saying it was okay to go onto ranch property as long as you didn't let the cattle out. I saw no signs of cattle. Maybe they were in Texas, chomping greener grass. The rocky ground was the color of dust, with splotches of gray and black lichen. Leafless bushes here and there twisted their brown fingers skyward. If there were a good rain, green shoots would blanket the earth between the rocks, and tiny leaves would emerge between the thorns on ocotillo branches. I loved how this desert could green up overnight. And how creatures that lay hidden in the soil would suddenly emerge to do their thing for a wet moment. Evolution blew my mind. Desert creatures had developed so many tricks to stay alive. Some plants poisoned the soil around their roots to eliminate the competition, even if it was their own offspring. Some people poison the ground for their offspring and their offspring's offspring. You had to be careful with Mother Nature. Which was why I loved Continuity: compared to the other developers, we tiptoed around her.

The road twisted alongside a dry arroyo, turning into washboard on the rises and descents. My car shook like crazy as I powered over ruts and swerved away from holes. The car jarred so badly my teeth literally chattered. A trail of dust formed behind us. Wondering if my struts would survive the round trip, I slowed to a crawl. Aaron sighed in what I guessed was approval. He held the marked-up topo map in one hand and hung onto the door handle with the other. I was tempted to speed up just to jolt him, but reason and economy prevailed.

The road paralleled a sometime stream, as indicated by a line of cottonwood trees along its invisible bank. We crept along for a mile or so until the road reached one of the foothills and turned west. We followed an imaginary topo line around the base of the hill until we got pretty close to the spot I had marked on the map. Aaron pointed to a fragment of chain-link fence just below the road, and I pulled over. I had expected a mine site to look dramatic, but to my amateur eye, this place looked no different from the rest of the rocky landscape.

We clambered downhill a bit and saw that the fence blocked access to a double door-sized hole in the earth boarded up with railroad ties and weathered two-by-fours. Aaron said the Hammers were better than most mine owners who didn't bother to block abandoned entrances. I tested the fence, wishing I had brought a crowbar. It was solidly cemented into rock. Aaron said to leave it alone and follow him to find another way in. Since the miners had probably tunneled around underground, there would be other entrances. I shifted my pack on my back and followed him around an outcropping of boulders and along the hillside below the road. I kept scanning for the signs of prior activity that Nate wanted me to scout. Nothing but rock, dust, and clumps of brush that managed to make it through the drought.

Pretty soon Aaron pointed again to what appeared to be a little cave in the slope. We got closer, and I was about to look in, when he blocked me with his arm.

"Wait," he said. "If you want to poke your nose in there, we need supplies."

He filled one of his pockets with little stones. "Markers," he said in response to the question on my face.

Did he think we were some version of Hansel and Gretel? "Instead of breadcrumbs?" I stepped forward, but he pulled me back.

"What will you do if you see a snake?"

"Ignore it."

"No. You'll stop and tell me, and we'll both go the other way."

"Okay." I crossed mental fingers that there wouldn't be a snake and stepped into the cave's mouth.

"Wait. Let me lead." He held my arm.

"It's *my* job to look around." I pulled my arm out of his grip. I adjusted my headlamp and tiptoed ahead, pride intact. Aaron followed in single file. The cave became a low tunnel—we both had to crouch—angled downwards about thirty-forty degrees, obviously manmade, musty-smelling and cooler than outside. My boots slipped a little on some loose rocks, and I could hear my pulse in my ears. This little tunnel could be the only way for me to look inside. Too small and steep, but it might have to do.

About ten yards in, I told Aaron to hold up and swung my pack off my back to dig out my tools. As I bent down, the ground gave way.

I slid downwards in the dark.

My hands scraped rocks.

Knees smacked ground.

I landed on my back.

Aaron called my name. The beam from his flashlight played on the rocks above me. "Are you okay?"

I couldn't answer.

Couldn't breathe. Couldn't breathe. Chest would not inflate.

"Bee, answer me!"

I moved my parts, no sharp pain. The right side of my rib-cage hurt. I could breathe!

"I'm okay," I tried to yell but I couldn't push out enough air.

"How far down are you?" He sounded far away.

"I can't tell. My headlamp fell off." I groped the ground around me. I felt the lamp's elastic and pulled it toward me. The little beam showed me I was in a sizable room cut into rock, shored up by rough wooden pillars. There was some rusty equipment lying on the ground not far away. Would've been awful landing on that. I sat up gingerly, no stabbing pain, but I could tell my right side would bruise. I looked directly overhead into a chute of some kind. I could see flashes of Aaron's light maybe twenty, thirty feet up.

"I'm in a room. Maybe it's a staging area. Hey, lower my pack so I can take samples."

"Forget it! I'm going to the surface to call for help. Listen to me, don't move. And don't breathe deep."

I heard him scramble up the tunnel. I thought about looking for another way out of the room—there had to be an entrance the miners had used—but I couldn't see far and moving might get me into more trouble. You could break a leg and die down here. I started feeling nauseous, like maybe I'd vomit, but I pushed it down. I felt for my phone in my right back pocket. It came on. I panned the room, snapping photos just in case, for what I didn't know. I wanted Aaron to come back. What if he tripped or got lost going for help?

I heard Aaron in the tunnel and waved my headlamp over-head so he'd know I was alive. I yelled and my ribs screamed, too. I heard him muttering under his breath about fresh air. Then he called to me.

"The sheriff's men will be here in fifteen minutes. Are you bleeding?"

I scanned my body with the lamp. "I don't think so." A wave of relief washed over me because rescue was near. Then a wave of shame because I needed rescuing. Then I remembered my purpose in poking around. I scratched up some dirt from the floor and stuffed my pants pockets.

Two bandanas landed on me. One was wet.

"You can clean up with the wet one. Cover your nose and mouth with the dry one."

"Do you think there are creatures in here?"

"Do you smell urine? Is there water?"

"No. It's stuffy but dry."

"You're probably alone." He was quiet for a beat. "You should have let me lead."

"So you could've landed here instead of me?"

"I wouldn't have fallen into a hole. I would've tested the ground first."

"How?" He didn't sound mad or anything. Making conversation to keep my spirits up?

"The stones. I was gonna throw them on the ground in front of me, listen to the sound."

"That's clever. Where'd you learn that?"

"You know how Mark Twain got his name? Sailors used to stand at the front of the riverboat and test the depth with a pole. Mark twain is twelve feet."

So Aaron paid attention in school. "I guess you learned something in Ajo after all."

"This assignment you got from your boss? It's bullshit. No one should send a girl into an abandoned mine. He's working a con."

"He didn't send me in. He only said look around for evidence. *I* decided to go prospecting. I didn't think it was a big deal."

"Your boss should have gone legit, paid for a mine inspector."

"I wanted to see the mine for myself."

"So now you have. Satisfied?"

Maybe, just maybe Aaron was onto something. But this was not the time to discuss Nate's behavior and my dumb-ass initiative. I began to feel cold.

Aaron said, "I hear sirens. I'm going to the surface to meet the posse. Don't move. Don't breathe any harder than you have to. The air down there could be bad."

I heard him scramble away. What should I tell the sheriff? If I said we went into the tunnel for my job, Nate would pay the rescue fee, but then the world would guess Hargrove-Spence wanted the land. I could say Aaron and I were exploring, with permission from the owner. I'd charge the fee to my card and get reimbursed before payment came due. Surely Aaron would keep his mouth shut with the sheriff and let me take responsibility.

I heard men's voices and commotion. Then the room lit up, and I took a deep, awfully painful breath.

~ ~

Gabi fussed over me, changing the ice pack on my ribcage every half hour. She had set me up in bed with the TV on my dresser and chicken soup packed with cilantro, her mother's recipe, on a tray. She insisted on Tylenol every few hours because "you should not let the pain get ahead of you." I'd resisted the first time she offered the drug on principle, but I was too sore to tough it out, and too embarrassed to keep pretending to be cool. The second time she approached me bottle in hand, I opened my mouth like a baby bird.

She sat on the bed, placed two pills on my tongue, and handed me a glass of water. "You should rest now." She watched me swallow. She began to rise, then sat back down. "Aaron told me how worried he was. He thought you might pass out any second."

"Yeah, he kept talking to keep me awake."

"He said to tell you he's sorry he upset you. What's that about?"

"He saved me. I'd be eating dirt right now if he wasn't there. I can't believe I came so close." I shivered.

"How did he upset you?" Her voice was gentle, but I could see she wouldn't stop until she knew the score.

"He said my boss was a con man and I was an idiot for trying to inspect the mine."

"He called you an idiot?"

"He implied I'm too dumb to know I'm being exploited by a developer. 'Developer' is a dirty word in his book."

Gabi smiled. "Yeah, but he's a smart guy and cares about you. He's right some of the time."

It dawned on me that Gabi agreed with her brother.

She reached for my hand. "You could listen to me, too. I have your best interests at heart."

"I do listen to you. All the time."

She shook her head. "You listen when I talk about dinner or going out. You don't listen when it's about work." She squeezed my fingers. "I could help."

Wow. Did I really ignore my best friend?

I burrowed under the quilt, setting my right side on fire. I felt stupid and thick, disloyal to Gabi and pissed at Aaron. I felt hollow and a little scared. I closed my eyes.

Gabi rose. "Sleep is good for healing. I'll check on you in a while." I heard the door close behind her as I tried to relax.

I couldn't sleep. When I closed my eyes, I saw it again: the five minutes of terror while I waited alone for Aaron to call the sheriff. My heart sank, not because I might have died, but because I'd been stupid. So stupid about everything. My dad's prophesy—that I'd screw up—coming true. I wished I could cry, but I couldn't. It was all too much for my strung-out brain.

18

Iasked Sy if I could have a hard-backed chair because it hurt to sit on the couch. It still felt like a fire burned below my right breast. Her face scrunched in surprise, yet she gestured toward the dining room. I stepped slowly into the dining room and grasped a side chair with both hands. My ribs ached as I carried the chair into the living room. The doctor had said all I needed was time and to take it easy. I had kept our Friday date because both Sy and I looked forward to it, and except for carrying a chair, I considered it "easy."

"Tea?" Sy pointed to the service Leticia had left on the coffee table after I'd seated myself across from her.

"No, thanks." I didn't want to move more than necessary, not even to raise a teacup.

"What's wrong?" She arched her brow, commanding an answer.

What to tell her? I'd had permission to visit the Ranch but certainly not to poke around the mine. I felt flushed and hoped Sy wouldn't notice.

"Why are you getting red? Fess up, girl." She wagged a finger at me.

My brain whirred. She might hate me for spying, if not for stupidity. But I couldn't lie to her. She of all people deserved the truth. "After the Ranch tour, your son sent me some old maps, and I wanted to see if I could figure out where the landmarks were. I found the gold mine."

She shook her head. "Silver. My grandfather never found a grain of gold."

"I was hiking with a friend and fell into a hole that landed me inside the mine. I cracked a few ribs." My hand went to my right side automatically.

"Anything else?"

It seemed to me an extra worry wrinkle had appeared between her eyebrows. Did she suspect there was more to confess? I hesitated.

"Did you hurt anything else?" She lowered her teacup to the table.

I shook my head. "There was a bunch of machinery down there, but I didn't crash into it."

"I must telephone Thomas immediately." She rang the little bell for Leticia.

Uh, oh. He'd be pissed off, too. I couldn't look at her.

Sy said, "How did you get out of the mine?"

"My friend called the sheriff. The firemen brought me out in a sling."

"A mountain rescue?"

I got the point. "My boss is going to pay for it."

"That's very generous. Did he have something to do with your adventure?"

She's so damn smart. "Indirectly. I got interested in the mine in the first place because he thinks it will mean something to the people who will live in Continuity. History and all."

She nodded, as if to say *I thought so.*

"But it was my idea to go hiking Saturday, not his." I hoped she wouldn't press me because I didn't know if I could keep dodging.

Leticia appeared in the doorway. Sy asked her to dial her son and bring the phone. The woman disappeared and reappeared, handing over the phone.

"Thomas, can you come over right away? It's rather urgent." She paused. "I'm fine, I'm fine, but do come over before anyone else gets hurt." She passed the phone back to Leticia. "That will bring him."

I didn't know what to do, so I did nothing. Sy offered me a cup of tea again, but I couldn't stomach it, not with Thomas Hammer about to descend on me. I wanted to skip the confrontation and stood to leave. Sy told me to sit back down and wait for her son. She'd caught him in his car, and he'd be by in five minutes. I obeyed, hoping my flush would fade by then.

I cast around for something to talk about that wasn't the mine, and my eye landed on the painting on the opposite wall. I told Sy I'd been meaning to ask her about it for weeks. Her face lit up.

"My husband met the artist, Fred Darge, in New Mexico. He was living and painting in a van at the time, going from ranch to ranch. My husband invited him here. I liked him, a modest man making an honest living. We commissioned a painting of our son and the dog he loved. After Thomas was born, I wanted to bring Darge back to paint him, as well, but it didn't happen." She folded her hands in her lap, and suddenly looked old and tired.

"I'm sorry about your son."

She shook her head. "He died too young. I miss the life he never lived." Her voice quivered.

I wasn't about to press her, so I pointed to the painting. "Is the artist famous?"

"The painting might be valuable in cowboy art circles. It's more valuable to me."

We sat quietly for a minute, she in the past, me in my guilt for being too self-absorbed to be a true friend to her, or to Gabi. I heard commotion in the hallway. Thomas Hammer strode into the room, straight to his mother.

"Are you alright?"

"Yes, yes, I told you I'm fine."

"What's the problem?"

"You made good time. Sit for a minute. Tea?"

He shook his head.

Sy cleared her throat. "Bee was traipsing around the old mine and fell into a hole, as she put it. I want her to show you the spot so you can seal it up as soon as possible. We don't want any more injuries."

He shook his head. "You are a wicked woman. You had me worried."

Sy said, "Did you tempt her somehow when you toured her?"

"Of course not." He addressed me. "Tomorrow at two o'clock? Meet me at the main gate."

I nodded.

He bent and pecked Sy's cheek. "I can't stay. Don't get in any trouble this evening, Ma. I can't come to your rescue." He disappeared down the hall.

Sy turned to me with a sly look on her face. "Now, pour us a fresh cup of tea."

I was dumbfounded. Instead of scolding me, she had tried to blame her son for my wrong-headed expedition. I felt equal parts relief and confusion. I used my left hand to pour.

"Your son had nothing to do with my accident," I said when I handed over her cup.

"Oh, I know that. I poked him to make him react. Thomas has the best of intentions but he's lazy. As you see, my ploy worked."

"I thought you'd be angry with me."

She lowered her cup. "Bee, what do you see when you look in the mirror?"

What was she getting at? "Messy hair most always, and crooked teeth."

"I'll tell you what I see when *I* look at you. A brave young woman doing everything she can possibly do in order to learn. You should be encouraged, not disciplined."

I looked down in case I started to cry. No one had ever treated me with such compassion before. I didn't know how I'd earned Sy's support, but I relished it. I leaned over, ribs be damned, and took her cool, dry hand in my two. We sat like that for a minute, neither one of us wanting to let go.

~ ~

At a quarter to two on Saturday, I parked next to the Ranch's main gate and got out of my car gingerly. I was not looking forward to jolting over ruts, but I owed it to Sy to tough it out. The frame of my dollar store sunglasses had come apart at the hinge, and I shaded my eyes with my left hand. It felt like a hundred degrees already, which it could be in mid-May. In another couple of years of climate change, we'll hit a-hundred-ten in May and who knows what in July.

At two precisely, Thomas Hammer drove up in a Land Rover followed by a pickup with two people inside. He waved. I opened the Rover's passenger door and eased onto the seat, a little wary. Just because Sy had forgiven my misadventure didn't mean he had. We took off slowly, Mr. Hammer watching me from behind his aviators. The ride was a hundred times smoother than my car's, as if the Rover had balloons for tires. I gave him the high sign and he sped up a little. The pickup followed a couple of car lengths behind to avoid our dust. Neither of us said anything as he navigated around the gullies in the roadbed.

We reached the spot where Aaron and I had parked. I led Mr. Hammer along the imaginary topo line we had followed that day until I could point out the place of my accident. You could see that the sheriff's rescue crew had disturbed the ground all around the opening. Mr. Hammer whistled, and the two workmen stopped unloading tools and lumber from the pickup and strolled over to us. They were wearing the wide-brimmed, straw hats I'd seen on yard workers around town, and I wished I had as much shade. Mr. Hammer spoke to them in Spanish. The men shook hands, and then he told me we could leave. We got into the Land Rover; the two laborers trundled stuff toward the mine as we drove away.

"Thank you," I said as he downshifted. "I didn't mean to cause so much trouble."

"It's okay. We needed to check out the site anyway."

Without his cowboy hat, his thinning white hair made him look less intimidating. I tried asking a question to be polite. "Do you think anyone will ever mine here again?"

"Not on my watch." He eyed me behind his glasses. "Mining isn't profitable compared to housing."

My eyes widened. "Are you going to develop the Ranch?"

"No, but someone else will eventually. Your boss might."

"He wants to get Continuity up and running. I haven't heard him talk about anything else." I waited for Mr. Hammer to say more. He didn't.

"Is there a developer you prefer?" I tried again.

"Not really. Development is bad business. Too easy to go over to the dark side. Too many opportunities to lie to stakeholders." He faced me. "Russians park their dirty money in bogus real estate deals around here. Ask your boss about it."

"Your mother told me she doesn't like my boss, but she didn't say why. Did he do something on the dark side?" I couldn't help myself.

He sighed. "Did my mother tell you about the campaign?"

"No. What campaign?"

"She ran a campaign for a friend of hers for county commissioner, another woman. Your boss supported her opponent. He was just a pup at the time, and he followed the old boys' lead. They fought dirty. I don't think he'd do so now."

A whole new page in the book of Sy turned over in my head. "Could a woman win an election back then?"

"Sure. This is the town that produced Sandra Day O'Connor. She and my mother knew each other. Ma was kind of a conservationist ahead of her time, and the home builders association came out against her candidate."

Wow. I was going to have to find out more, preferably from the former campaigner herself.

"There have been plenty of women in government, even in Territorial days. Ranch women made good legislators. Ma liked pulling strings, but she always stayed in the background." He turned to me. "Please don't go prying into the business. Ma is a lot more fragile than she makes out."

She seemed fine to me, but what did I really know? Apparently, I'd already overlooked a couple of layers of the onion. I would have to find a good way to probe. Whenever I asked her about the past, she pooh-poohed and turned the subject of the conversation to me. When I shut up and listened, though, she said plenty.

It occurred to me that Thomas Hammer might say more now that we were in a chatting relationship. I decided to approach indirectly. "Did you know your great-grandfather, the miner?"

He adjusted his aviators. "Now there's a story from the dark side. He had a partner and a couple of East Coast investors. The partner disappeared one day. Rumor in the family was he tried to cheat the Easterners. The locals at the time blamed the Mexican workers. Nobody ever found a body, and the mine closed."

Wow. A murder in the Hammers' past? I made a note-to-self to investigate. I had a hunch the info might be useful in this "war" I'd been dragged into.

We reached the main gate. I apologized again and thanked him for the ride. As I stepped out of the Rover, he said "Thank you for being my mother's friend." He paused. "Be careful."

All the way home, I tried to figure out what he meant. Be careful with Sy's feelings, or watch out for the dark side of development? Or simply stay off his property?

I needed to be careful of all of it. Period.

19

First day back at the office, I picked up my phone to see if I could post any of the photos I took inside the mine. They were fuzzy—too little light—but I could identify stuff I was glad I hadn't landed on. A barrel-shaped thing wrapped in rope, maybe a winch of some kind, and a man-sized rusty metal cage lying on its side. A wooden board bearing some lettering lay against the cage. It looked weathered by time, but I made out the words "Johnson & Sons," and I remembered Thomas Hammer's story about the partner who disappeared.

Could Johnson be the guy? I decided to find out.

Online, I located a couple of academic books about the Arizona mining industry in the late 1800s, but there was nothing about individual miners. Bob, the most technical guy on staff, told me to ask the people at the State Archive for help. I made an appointment for the next day. It seemed to me some facts were missing from the conversations I'd had about the mine, and I wanted to get to the bottom of it. I cared about the truth more than my superiors recognized.

The Archive building didn't look like Hogwarts. Instead of piles of moldering papers and leather-bound tomes, a row of screens waited vacantly in a bland, chilly room. The librarian was pretty warm, though. She helped me find a link to a bunch of deeds that named a Johnson in the time period 1871-1900. We couldn't be sure, but it appeared that one of them was for land around where I'd fallen into that hole. It was hard for me to read the loopy cursive writing—I'd never learned it in school—but the librarian helped. Then she searched mining claims, court records, tax assessments, and census and voter rolls, but there was no trace of Mr. Johnson after 1882. Poof, gone! She said if the land had reverted back to the State, someone could have paid off the back taxes and gotten hold of it. But we might never know who did so. Powerful people were known to steal court records back then, and some even bragged about it. I thanked the librarian and hustled home.

I couldn't wait to tell Sy what I'd found.

~ ~

That Friday afternoon, as soon as we settled in the living room, even before I laid out the caramel cookies, I burst out with it. "I think I know why your grandfather's partner disappeared."

Sy's brows furrowed. "What on earth are you talking about?"

"I took photos in the mine. There was a signboard." I made air quotes, "'Johnson & Sons.' I went to the State Archive, and a librarian helped me find a deed that showed a Mr. J. Johnson owned a piece of land near the mine. Maybe he got killed for it."

Sy looked down her nose. "What else did you find?"

"Nothing definitive. But there's more to search."

"Don't you dare." Sy pushed the scooter's joystick and revolved away from the coffee table.

My gut contracted. Clearly, I hadn't been careful enough. "I thought you'd want to know more about the Ranch's past." I got up to face her.

"I want you to leave the whole sordid affair alone. It doesn't matter in the end."

"But this is your family and your legacy!"

"My family is the same as everyone else's. My family has its fools and liars as well as its heroes. At the time, they did they best they could for the Ranch."

"Did that include cheating Mr. Johnson?" Not to mention murder.

"I don't know the whole story, and you certainly don't. Drink your tea."

"Wouldn't your son want to know? He's the one who told me about the mystery. He cares about your reputation."

Her tone changed. "You don't know what you're talking about." She looked away from me. "There was some nasty business that my grandfather and his father fought over after he came back from the Great War. Their feud lasted into my childhood."

"What harm can it do to know the truth? It might even do some good."

"Good for whom? Your developer?"

She whirred over to her desk and put on her reading glasses. She riffled through some papers while I sat, holding my tongue. I hated getting shut down like that, and I began to think that my talking about the Johnson business might have frightened her somehow. I picked up my teacup. Then I put it down. "At least tell me why you want me to stop investigating."

Her head dipped ever so slightly. "If you trot over to Nate Hargrove and tell him your story, he will use it against me. Is that your goal?"

"Of course not! Nate doesn't want to hurt you. He sent me to help you in the first place."

"Such a child. You'd best go. My blood pressure is rising."

I got up and gathered my bag, leaving the untouched cookies on the table. My reception had been so different from what I'd expected. I thought she would compliment me, not blame me. I thought she'd welcome the facts, not squelch them. The steering wheel in my car was hot, but I held it in both hands. I decided to find Nate and prove Sy wrong for once. I called the office and heard he was on site. So, I headed north, driving extra carefully because being upset made me rash.

Nate's car was parked near the trailer. I went inside to wait in the AC. I thought I could feel *my* blood pressure rising, but maybe it was just another dumb blush. I pulled out my phone to distract myself and opened TikTok, which I didn't use much to promote Continuity because Nate disliked video. Unable to focus, I put the phone back in my bag. Then Nate and another man walked in the door. Nate saw me and asked the other guy to wait a minute. I wanted more than a minute. He came over, and I told him I'd discovered that someone other than the Hammers might have a claim to the White Bear Ranch. His stared at me. He told the other guy to meet him in ten at the lounge and took me into the nook inside the trailer he used for privacy. I sat in the VIP chair across from my boss and told him about Johnson & Sons. I blabbed that Sy didn't want me to investigate, which meant something dark might have happened.

Nate said, "I'll get my lawyer on it, but there are statutes of limitations. Send me the details." He leaned back in his chair. "I vaguely remember reading something about a scandal at the Ranch when I was in college, I think. If I were a Hammer, I'd want to shove it under the rug, too." He grinned.

"Sy said you'd use it against her."

"I don't blackmail old ladies." He leaned forward. "Listen, I doubt there's anything there. You just keep doing what you're doing. Stay friends with Sydelle Hammer, and keep me informed." He stood. "Thanks for coming to tell me."

I watched him chat with the construction manager on his way out the door, all smooth and smiles. I wasn't satisfied with his response. Both he and Sy were copping out, typical of their generations. I decided to keep looking for the truth on my own. I've always been good with challenges.

I drove home, turning over the fight with Sy in my brain, still more upset than I wanted to be. Gabi was in the kitchen, peeling cucumbers at the sink. I stood next to her and asked for her opinion. "If your grandfather had committed a serious crime, and you knew about it, what would you do?"

Gabi's eyes narrowed. "Are you talking about your grandfather?"

"No. I never knew either of my grandfathers. I'm asking about *your* grandfather because you care about your family."

She sucked in her cheeks, a sign of thinking. "How serious? Do the police know?"

"Murder. They don't."

Her eyes flicked from side to side. "I don't think we would tell the police because they usually don't take our side. But we wouldn't let him get away with it in the family. We wouldn't want the sin to be passed along." She finished peeling and reached for a cutting board. "No one in my family has done anything really terrible, as far as I know. And I'm pretty sure I would know. We all talk about each other all the time." She moved the cutting board closer and picked up a knife. "Why do you ask?"

"I'm trying to figure out a piece of Arizona history I came across at work. I really appreciate your thoughts."

Gabi seemed pleased. "Wanna eat with us?"

"Not hungry."

I headed for my room to change my clothes. I should have guessed Gabi's family would react differently than Sy's. Gabi's folks were close despite their differences. I wasn't sure that the Hammers cared about closeness, or about sin. Clearly, they cared about the business. I would need a lot more intel before bringing this up again with Sy. I went to the bathroom to wash the day's residue off my face. Then I went back to the kitchen, hungry after all.

JUNE

average daytime high = 106° F

days of rain = 0

20

It was eight o'clock in the morning, first Saturday of the month, and the dim office trailer smelled stale. My brain zoomed back ten years to the stuffy cabin my family rented once on the Jersey shore. No one had been there for months, and we had to open all the windows and turn on the fans before we could breathe. The air we let in smelled like seaweed, and I loved it. We had to cut the vacation short because my mom got sick, I don't remember with what. Danny cried when I packed his plastic bucket and shovel in the car for the drive home. My dad couldn't hide his contempt.

We never went on vacation again.

In the trailer, none of the weekend workers had yet arrived, leaving Nate and me alone. He flipped the light switch and entered "72" on the thermostat. When the AC unit on the roof shuddered into gear, a stream of warm air brushed the back of my head. The air would cool shortly, and the trailer would become habitable. I sat in the shaggy armchair next to the door while Nate unlocked the flat file. We were waiting for Mannheim to arrive for the first of the two meetings Nate was taking me to this morning. He'd called last night, and I'd agreed to come in on a Saturday because the second meeting was with Sy.

Nate opened the top drawer of the flat file and riffled through layers of blueprints. I pulled out my phone to check messages, not really expecting any. Nate had said Mannheim wanted to show us his latest discovery. The architect was your classic divergent thinker, Nate said. You never knew if his idea might be worthwhile. I nodded, wanting him to think I understood. Mannheim would be late as usual, but we'd make it to Sy's by eleven. I didn't want Sy to face Nate alone. I had to be careful of her.

Apparently, the blueprint Nate wanted wasn't in the top drawer. He opened the next one down. He was into the third drawer when Manheim showed up, a roll of papers in his hand and a shit-eating grin on his face.

"You are going to be happy," he said flourishing the roll. He sat at the conference table and unrolled the papers, smoothing them flat with a loving gesture. Nate and I each leaned over one of his shoulders to look.

"I calculate if we use super-reflective paint on every inch of the exterior surfaces, including the roof, we can eliminate at least seventy percent of the air-handling units." Manheim stared at Nate. "You don't look overjoyed. You should be."

"You're a designer, not an engineer."

Manheim pointed to a matrix on the top sheet of paper. "See the numbers? This stuff is straight out of the laboratory." He turned to me. "The paint prevents the walls from heating up and transmitting heat to the interior. With smaller windows and this paint, we can go completely off the grid. It's a brand-new product. We could be one of the first to use it at scale." He looked Nate in the eye. "This is the beauty shot. It'll make us the self-sufficient, emergency-proof community we have envisioned. The paint is expensive, but we'll save big on HVAC equipment. Think of the energy savings going forward!" Manheim slapped the table. "Fantastic! Do you see?"

Nate hesitated. "I see good thinking on your part, but it won't work."

"Why not? I can get the drawings re-done in just a few weeks."

"Because it won't meet code."

"But the code is obsolete with the new paint. The engineers can prove it."

"It's too hard to sell at this point."

"Ask your politician friends for help. You have important friends."

"Yes, and I need to keep them. I can't ask for little favors."

"This is not little! This is innovation! This is what you are known for." Manheim's brow furrowed.

"You mean that award? My peers don't know what to make of me, so they call me an innovator and turn their backs. It won't work. I'm sorry."

I remembered that last year Nate had been named innovator of the year by the homebuilders' association for converting an old hotel into affordable housing with a daycare center built around the ground-floor swimming pool. He'd installed store-front windows so passers-by could see toddlers splashing, and some downtown boosters had been charmed. Nate thought the award had been ginned up to coax him into buying multiple tables at the association's fund-raising gala. Even so, I enjoyed the fancy dinner, sitting next to Dana Hargrove who provided running commentary on who was who. I had bought a sec-ondhand slinky dress and almost felt glamorous. I remember giggling a lot—my first experience with unlimited champagne— and making Mrs. Hargrove laugh.

Nate straightened, stepped to the flat file, and pushed the drawers closed. "I *am* sorry, Victor. Please excuse me. Bee and I have work to do off site."

We left a flustered Manheim poring over his papers, as if he could make another calculation to break through to my boss, and got into Nate's car. All the way to Scottsdale Road, Nate had that preoccupied look on his face. I figured he was rolling Manheim's suggestion over in his mind. I decided to argue the case. "That paint sounded amazing. Why is it too late? We don't even have walls yet."

"Jesus, you, too!" Nate leaned into the steering wheel. "It's complicated. To do what Manheim wants would require new engineering, new permitting, going back to the investors, going back to the bank. Things have to be done in the right order, and the opportunity for that big a change has passed."

"Wouldn't the life-cycle savings be huge? In energy and money and climate-wise, like you always say?"

"We'll use it in phase two."

"This is something that would turn on younger buyers."

"Let it go. We've already done a helluva lot climate-wise. We're way out ahead of everyone else."

"Right." I sat lower in my seat. Case closed. Sy's words about Nate's "opportunism" came rushing back. I got chilled wondering if Sy was right—that Nate might be too willing to compromise. What would happen to Continuity then?

We reached Lincoln Drive, and Nate turned west toward the central Phoenix neighborhood where what was left of the old guard still lived. In a minute, Leticia opened Sy's door and gave me a quick hug. She said she was glad I had come too. Nate and I followed her into the living room, where Sy was sitting on the couch behind a silver tea service, her lips in a tight smile. The scooter was parked in a corner. Nate shook her hand and sat opposite her. I thought it best to sit next to him rather than in my customary spot since I wasn't sure she'd want me closer.

She spoke as soon as we'd seated ourselves.

"I'm glad you were able to come today." She gestured to the pot. "Tea, or would you like something stronger?"

"Too early for me, but thanks for the offer." Nate nodded. "It's nice to see you again, and to see you looking well."

"Indeed. How is your wife? We volunteered together years ago. I liked her."

Nate said, "She's fine, thanks. I'll tell her you said hello."

"My son takes me to lunch on Saturdays. I will discuss your proposal with him afterwards. Very convenient, wouldn't you say?"

"I'm happy to make things convenient for you," Nate said. "In fact, that's why I asked for a meeting."

"Bee, would you like tea? Help yourself, dear."

I poured a cup and sat back in my chair. It felt wonderful to be called "dear" after our fight about Johnson & Sons. Maybe our relationship could return to normal?

Nate said, "No doubt you know there's a drainage issue between us. Your Ranch is uphill from the foot of my parcel. I propose to build whatever it takes to keep your water on your property in return for an early investment. I'm sure you're aware that containing your additional run-off is required by law in Maricopa County."

"Yes, yes." She waved her hand.

"We're in the field right now, so it'll be cheap to build whatever containment features are necessary. Even if it's contaminated. It won't cost you a dime."

She pursed her lips and leaned deeper into the pillow behind her. "Why do you say our water could be contaminated?"

"Might not be, but generally old mines cause problems. I'm willing to take the risk of needing to do remediation in exchange for the timing of your investment. I believe you have the paperwork?"

"Yes, I looked at it."

"I propose to use your five hundred thousand for marketing right now, when it counts. Your endorsement will also mean a great deal in this town, and to me personally."

I looked down so I wouldn't have to meet Nate's eyes, remembering what the Hargrove-Spence comptroller had said about a loan coming due. Nate was pressuring Sy to invest. I hoped he wouldn't ask me to lean on her, too.

Sy folded her hands in front of her chest, jewels glittering on several fingers. "You won't be selling homes for a year or two. Why are you here now?"

"Because I'm building infrastructure, and this is the time to address drainage. If you ever want to sell the place, you'll have to clean it up. It could be expensive."

Shit, I thought, Nate's trying to scare her. Or blackmail her. Then I remembered Aaron's saying something was fishy about Nate's interest in the mine. The bottom dropped out of my stomach.

Sy unfolded her hands and fussed with the collar of her blouse. "I see. I have no intention of selling the Ranch, but I will inform my son of your offer. I don't want to constrain him from beyond the grave."

My hand flew to my mouth.

Sy leaned toward me. "At my age, one is realistic." She addressed Nate. "Thomas calls your development Starbucks. They say you can have your coffee any way you like if you have it our way. He doesn't believe your 'clusters,' as you call them, can be individualized."

"Starbucks?" He chuckled thinly. "I'd love to see Continuity on every corner."

"Thomas says there's no benefit to clustering, but he seems to be interested in hearing you out."

"I would appreciate the opportunity to show him these figures. There are huge economic advantages, as well as environmental ones." His face contracted.

"Bee, dear, what do you think about the proposal?" Sy asked me directly.

"I haven't read it." Dammit. I hated looking stupid.

"Then why are you here?" She turned to Nate. "I will talk to Thomas. If he sees any advantages, he will contact you." She nodded. "It was nice to see you again. Goodbye."

Nate rose. "Please tell your son I'm at his service."

I rose, too, shocked by Sy's slap in the face. Was she still angry at me or was she warning me not to get caught up in whatever Nate had going? I followed my boss out to the car. He held the door open for me, while I tried to get a grip. I could hear my heart in my ears. Nate drove east, and I took a breath.

"Is the water contaminated?"

"Don't know. We'll need to hire a hydraulic engineer ASAP if it is."

He glanced at me with a flicker of something in his eyes. "I guess I should have hired a specialist to examine the mine. Thanks for the samples."

Was this an apology in Nate-speech? I was pissed. I didn't trust myself to reply.

"Do you think Sydelle will listen to her son, or will she make up her own mind?"

"She'll listen to him and then make up her own mind."

I couldn't keep my mouth shut. "Does he have a point about Continuity being like Starbucks? I mean, not offering a meaningful choice?"

"There's no pure choice in this world; everything has a context. We're offering an extremely attractive context. Our subscribers want to live in a community where people feel responsible for the collective good."

So what about individual good? Blackmailing is okay? Or making me look dumb? "Why is Thomas Hammer against Continuity?"

"He's probably an ideologue."

"What does that mean?"

"He doesn't get it."

"Do you think he'll invest?"

"Hammer doesn't have to like Continuity to make money from it."

We drove the rest of the way back to the site in silence. He pulled up beside my car. As I opened the passenger door, he said, "Wait a minute. Do you have any advice for me on how to handle your friend Sydelle?"

"She handles herself."

~ ~

I tromped into my bedroom and stripped as fast as I could. Too hot to hike, but the public swimming pool had just opened for the summer. I put my bathing suit on under my clothes and drove my hot car down Dunlap. I had to do something with my fury.

The outdoor pool wasn't crowded because it was lunch time, only a couple of white folks swimming laps. In a few hours the place would be packed with brown kids cavorting while their abuelas watched from under the awnings. I paid my three bucks and went to change. The City of Phoenix did not provide booths or lockers, and patrons usually left their belongings poolside. But a little voice told me not to, and I handed my purse to the attendant for safekeeping. I'd learned the hard way that you should always listen to that inner voice. Now, I wanted swimming to make it easier to hear.

I ran across the so-called cool deck, burning my feet, and jumped into a lap lane.

I rolled onto my back, began swinging my arms past my head and kicking. I had my own style since I never had swimming lessons. I found my rhythm: smash the water right and breathe, smash the water left and breathe, kick double-time all the time. Smashing water instead of beating on Nate for taking advantage of me and threatening Sy. I propelled myself to the end of the lane, turned and headed back, heart pumping hard, head getting clearer. Two more laps. One of the teenaged lifeguards kneeled at the edge of the pool and waved a wristband at me. I paddled over. She explained I should have taken a swimming test, but she was giving me a pass because I looked safe. As I wrapped my wrist, I realized I could do *my* job *my* way, like she was doing hers. I could separate my anger at Nate from my feelings about Continuity. I could introduce the world's best housing to a young market even if I had to cancel my boss. And I'd be damned if I backed away from the woman who was teaching me so much, whether I liked the way she was doing it or not.

Swimming had freed me up, all right. I knew I could stay strong

21

On Monday, in the office, a mass email from Katie Morrison popped up on my screen. She wrote cancelling the Friends' June meeting and urging everyone to go to a county budget hearing on Thursday night instead. Hargrove-Spence had an item on the agenda relating to water supply for the area abutting White Bear Ranch, and the Friends should show up in force. She attached a bunch of stuff, including instructions on how to protest.

I forwarded the email to Nate. He wrote right back asking me to join him at the hearing in case media showed up. I said yes. I wanted to know whatever there was to know.

I searched "water supply in Arizona." I followed a couple of threads and learned that the key idea was managing the different sources: river water, ground water, and recycled water, although there wasn't much of the latter. I read that the State had designated six "Active Management Areas," mostly urban locations, where the water supply was regulated. Outside the AMAs, the rest of the state was a free-for-all, although some people wanted that to change. A Saudi company had bought thousands of acres in southwestern Arizona and drained the aquifer beneath the ground to grow alfalfa for the Middle Eastern beef industry. Arizonans held conflicting views: the free-market types thought since the Saudis paid for the land, the water beneath it belonged to them. The social-welfare types thought the aquifer belonged to the local people and the water rights should be controlled.

The governor used a legal loophole to kick the Saudis out, but the issue hadn't been resolved. Typical for a purple state.

Continuity was in an AMA. Turns out a developer must prove that any subdivision in an AMA has a "100-year Assured Water Supply of sufficient quality and quantity." The State doesn't seem to care how you *get* the water, as long as it meets the goals of its AMA.

A tiny shoot of doubt bloomed in my chest.

I called Bob, who was the only practicing engineer on the staff of Hargrove-Spence. He said yeah, we had an assured hundred-year supply, or we couldn't have proceeded. Ours was a combination of well water and city-treated water, same as in the nearby towns. I asked about the hearing coming up; he said no big deal. Some bureaucratic thing had changed, and we needed an amendment to one of the contracts. I didn't tell him that it was a big deal for Mrs. M. I ended the call, sorry to have doubted Hargrove-Spence's legitimacy.

Then it occurred to me the Gen Z market would care about water supply if I could find gripping images to show them. Nate had promised special financing for the younger market who were priced out of the best locations because investors wanted property for Airbnb or VRBO rentals. I searched "wells in Arizona" and hit an info gusher. How deep should a well be? How long will it last? What happens when it rains? What happens when it doesn't rain? There was too much information to process at the moment. I powered down and went to the conference room to see if anyone had left something decent to eat in the fridge.

~ ~

On Thursday, it was still hot when I walked across the county parking lot at six-thirty-five, feeling prepared for whatever might come up. Luis was standing under a tree near the entrance to the auditorium wearing a green T-shirt with a stylized white bear on the front. He was giving out T-shirts to Friends and offered me one. I thought it best not to cover the yellow dress I'd worn for Continuity's sake, but I asked him to save me a size small. Indoors in the blessed cool, I spotted Nate on one side of the hearing room, and Mrs. M in a sea of green-and-white on the other. I could sense the tension in the air. I sat next to Nate and studied the agenda he'd handed me. He was quiet, looking around the room and back at his phone.

After about five minutes of people shuffling in and out of the council chamber to adjust mics, et cetera, the council members took their places on the dais and the hearing began. The politicians argued about minutia at length: the number of dog catchers, the routes of garbage trucks, and on and on. Our water deal was number twenty-six on the agenda, probably an hour away. When the council adjourned for a ten-minute break, Nate and I followed the rest of the audience into the courtyard and the hot night. Nate went to talk to someone, and, as I meandered away from my boss, Luis appeared. He signaled I should follow him.

"Feels odd to see you on the other side," he said. "You look nice in that dress, by the way."

"It's weird. I'm not sure what I'm supposed to be doing." I caught my breath. "Wait!" I grabbed his arm. "Look over by the door. Is that Thomas Hammer talking to Mrs. M?"

Luis glanced behind him. "Yes. You know him?" He pushed his glasses up his nose.

"I've met him."

"Katie found out the chairman of the council is an old buddy of his. I think she wants to show off the new logo. What do you think?" He pointed to the bear on his chest.

"Why did he come?" I was channeling my friend Sy.

He pushed his glasses up his nose. "Maybe he's interested in Katie. Maybe the fix is in."

"What fix?" The skin on my neck started to crawl.

He looked around to check for eavesdroppers. "I suspect Hammer can get the council to do whatever he wants."

"What does he want?"

He shrugged his shoulders. "Beats me."

"I have to tell my boss." I took a step towards the knot of people around Nate.

He caught hold of my arm. "Stay. I'm sure he knows. Power brokers think alike." He let go. "Listen, how about getting a beer afterwards? Make something of the night."

"Text where to meet." I turned away to hide the blush. If he hadn't asked, I might have. I wasn't usually forward with guys, but Luis was different: nobody where I grew up looked like him or studied science for real.

The crowd began to edge back into the council chamber. I took my seat next to Nate, who looked at me with raised brows. None of his business where I went. I shrugged.

Later, when the green T-shirts got up one after the other to comment on item twenty-six, I kept my eyes focused straight ahead. Evidently, Mrs. M wanted the council to re-examine the deal Nate had cut with one of the local water suppliers. When it was her turn to speak, she went on and on about needing to keep water reserves in the ground because the climate was changing. She kept looking at the council chairman, as if confirming she'd taken the right tack. When all protesters had spoken, the chairman tabled our item until next month.

Nate got up to leave, and I followed.

"Should we be worried?" I asked as soon as we stepped outside.

"No. My lawyer says it's for show. The council had to respond to the Friends' objection, but if they'd wanted to kill our amendment, they'd have done it. We'll get our due next month."

"You don't sound relieved."

"I don't count chickens. We've worked with the water department for over two years. I trust Hanson. He's the sharpest real estate lawyer around."

"So Continuity is okay?"

"Think so. Thomas Hammer showed up. What can you tell me about that?"

"Sy hasn't said anything." My conscience pricked. "Luis said the council president is a buddy of Thomas's."

"Luis is the guy you talked to tonight?"

"He's Katie Morrison's intern. We met at the first Friends meeting, remember? He's a climate scientist."

"Then he should be on our side." Nate turned toward his Lexus, talking to me over his shoulder. "I don't think we need any follow up. Thanks for coming. Good night."

His car peeled out of the lot. I was glad he hadn't asked me about Luis. I didn't need another spy assignment.

Thinking of Luis, I checked my phone. He'd texted the address of a bar in North Scottsdale. I pasted it into Waze and got into my car. The AC wasn't pumping cold like it ought to. I should take the car to the mechanic on 12th Street, but it was hard to find the time, not to mention the money if the AC system needed replacement. I pulled out carefully, changing my focus from Nate to Luis. I drove slowly, growing nervous—the good kind of nervous—as Scottsdale appeared ahead.

22

When I entered the trendy bar Luis had selected—doesn't every bar in north Scottsdale try to be trendy? —he was sitting in a booth looking at his phone. He didn't notice me until I slid in across from him. I said hi, he tapped a bit and then tucked his phone into a pocket.

"I was checking to see if my collaborator sent the data he promised. He's in China. It's daytime there."

"I thought China was off limits."

"Not in science. My advisor and I use satellite imagery to measure climate artifacts. We get data from Europe, China, everywhere. We have to, to get the full picture."

"The government lets you?"

"They want us to. I mean, the agencies that fund research."

A waiter appeared. I realized I was hungry as well as nervous and ordered nachos and a Negra Modelo. He ordered wings and a Medalla Light. The waiter said they didn't carry "East Coast beer," so Luis followed my lead.

"I can't eat early," I said when the waiter had gone. "I used to study in the cafeteria at school after it quieted down. I ate at home, later, to save money."

"With your roommate?"

"Sometimes, not usually. How about you?"

"My housemates and I don't share. I doubt they'd like what I cook."

A scientist who cooks! "Are you a good cook?"

"My mother's parents came from Puerto Rico. I learned to cook a few dishes from my grandmother. Someday I'll show off my *pastelon*, if you like. It's lasagna made with bananas."

I laughed, still ridiculously nervous. "I grew up on hot dogs and chicken nuggets. I'd love to try your bananas."

The waiter brought our order on a tray and placed the food in the center of the table. He laid a stack of paper napkins and an empty plate in front of each of us. I forked a glob of nachos onto my plate. Luis helped himself to a couple of wings. He offered me one. I bit into it, and it was so hot I had to swig my beer. Luis swigged his, too, as if to keep me company. A few more swigs and I'd calm down some, I hoped. I didn't want to say anything stupid.

"Tell me more about how you grew up." He ate a wing without blinking and reached for another.

"I'm from a small town in Pennsylvania. I got out of there right after high school. This is home now."

"Do you stay in touch with your folks?"

I shook my head. "Do you stay in touch with yours?"

"Not really. But they're good people. Except they named me Luis Mordecai, one name for each grandfather. They met in pharmacy school. I was an accident they didn't repeat."

The beer was doing its thing in my bloodstream. I wiped wing sauce from my fingers and forked another blob of nachos.

Luis held a wing in his left hand—left-handed? —while he talked. "My parents bought a fixer-upper in an iffy neighborhood in Queens in 1990. I watched the neighborhood gentrify while I was growing up. Made me ask a lot of questions about who gets to live where."

"Did you get answers?"

"Not from my folks. They were too busy pursuing their American dream." He paused, took another swig. "I stopped focusing on social class when I found out there was a bigger problem. If we don't fix the climate, there's no sense worrying about anything else."

"I know. That's why I love my job." The nachos had hit the bottom of my belly, yay. He laughed. "Tell me more."

"We're building the most climate-forward housing any-where. Every business sector has to do its part, and we're modeling what real estate can do." I dabbed at my greasy lips with a napkin. He pointed to his cheek, and I understood he wanted me to wipe my own cheek in the same spot. "I'm chan-neling my boss again. Sorry."

He reached across the table with a napkin in his hand and brushed my cheek softly. "Are you sure your boss is a good one to channel?"

"What do you mean?"

"You got upset when you saw Thomas Hammer and I said the fix was in. I should have said the second fix. The water deal your boss cut was the first." The right side of his mouth turned up.

My brain went on high alert. "Is this your idea of how to impress a date?"

"Touché." He raised his bottle to me.

"Seriously, if you have evidence, tell me. I'm tired of being left out of the conversation."

"What conversation? At Hargrove-Spence?"

"Uh huh." Too soon to say anything more.

"Sorry, no evidence, just conjecture. This internship has cor-rupted me." He fingered a cheesy tortilla chip that hung over the edge of the plate.

"It sounded like Mrs. M was channeling you tonight. But I can tell you hate the Friends." The beer had loosened my tongue. "You flinch every time Katie Morrison asks you to do something."

"She's an upper-class NIMBY. You know, Not-In-My-Back-Yard? She'd do anything to advance her own interests." He took a long swig.

"Isn't the preserve a good idea?"

"Depends on what she does with it. She doesn't care about the Ranch or the ranchers. She wants to turn them into a meme." He took another swig. "She doesn't care about climate. I'm window-dressing." The right corner of his mouth turned up again.

I knew what it felt like to be window-dressing. "Then why do you stick with her?"

"No choice. My prof is launching a new algorithm, and I've got a big piece of it. I need the internship to stay in the program." He pointed to the nachos. "You mind?"

"Help yourself. So, what do you do? I won't get all the science, but I'll get enough."

He smiled and pushed his glasses up his nose. "I'll bet you get more than enough. I think you're a closet scientist."

"Why do you say that?"

"You want evidence." He hunched over his plate toward me. "What did you major in?"

"I got an associate's in communications. It was the shortest route to a job."

"Yeah, but what did you really like? Chemistry? Biology?"

I threw my cheesy napkin at him. "Biology. How did you know?"

"My secret." He leaned back. "I'll tell you since you're nice. Most girls I met in college liked biology or chemistry but were afraid to major in it. So they took art history instead."

"Duh, maybe those girls liked art."

"That's charitable of you." His face narrowed. "Can you meet me on campus at five o'clock tomorrow? My prof made a video to explain the project to donors. We'll hit the demo theater before it closes."

"I'd like that."

We finished up the last of the food, me talking about my hiking habit, him talking about working in his folks' pharmacy during the pandemic. He went to New York to help them out of a pickle: too many sick, confused customers, too few staff. He told me about some of the weird stuff he saw there. Plus, he laughed at my jokes. When I came back from the bathroom, he'd already paid the check.

Outside, the warm night air smelled like sautéed garlic from the Italian restaurant across the street. He walked me through the parking lot to my car. I asked what he did when he went out with his PhD friends. He said they argued. He steadied my shoulder with one hand and ran his other thumb between my eyebrows along the frown line that had recently shown up in my mirror. He said not to take him literally because graduate students were caustic sons of bitches. Then he kissed me on the lips, a polite, introductory kiss. I kissed back. If I hadn't had my own car, I would have gone home with him in a heartbeat.

The next day, I arrived a few minutes early at the campus address he'd texted. At five on the dot, he led me into a small auditorium with screens on three walls and cushy seats. He fiddled with the controls at a podium at the side of the stage. The lights dimmed, and views of the earth from observation satellites flowed across the screens. A male voice-over explained how researchers used them to understand climate variables, like retreating glaciers and rising sea levels. Then the screen filled with a rotating globe that looked 3-D, and I caught my breath. Our beautiful blue and green planet spun slowly against the blackness as little golden sparkles indicated places where conditions matched the narration. Then a bunch of graphs of trend lines appeared showing the conclusions Luis's prof was drawing about urban sprawl. I was so impressed I tingled from head to toe. I had no idea Luis's work was so important.

When we stepped outside, Luis suggested we get a bite. I suggested we get take-out and go to his place. We did, and made love before the meal. We were both so eager it didn't last very long. We sort of fell into each other's bodies and flowed to a gentle orgasm—I hadn't known an orgasm could be gentle—and I clung to him until he got out of bed to reheat the food. While we ate, he said I had a tight little body for a tall girl. I was too happy to wonder what that meant, still feeling him on my skin and savoring his smell. I told him I would find something wonderful for us to do on our next date. He said he was looking forward to it. I was too.

23

Dana Hargrove had sent me a hand-written invitation to have dinner with her family. I wondered if she had gotten tired of waiting for Nate to move on her idea. The note read "business casual" and included a printed map of where to park. I was a little nervous about invading my boss's private space and a little worried that I might not fit in, but curiosity won out. I put on my yellow dress, which Mrs. Hargrove had never seen, and Nate would not remember, and drove up a hill at the edge of Sunnyslope.

Theirs was a two-story house stuck onto the rocky hillside close to the peak, all concrete and glass nestled into the rock-face. I parked on the street below where the map indicated, and followed a stone path to a one-person elevator that raised me a flight. Opening the elevator door, I turned a corner into the living room and was stunned by the view. Sunnyslope spread out beyond the picture window looking pretty and peaceful in the setting sun. I walked past the window onto a travertine deck and stood at the rail, picking out Central and Dunlap and Seventh Street and Seventh Avenue, looking like the arteries I once saw in biology class with cars flowing like red blood cells. You didn't hear their noise up here or smell any diesel, and it felt ten degrees cooler than on my block.

Mrs. Hargrove appeared and gave me a hug, insisting I call her Dana and asking if I wanted to tour the house. You bet I did: for intel on my boss.

She led me past the living room into a gleaming stainless steel eat-in kitchen, and beyond into the master suite with that same fantastic view and his-and-her bathrooms with closets as big as my bedroom. We took a spiral staircase down to where the kids lived. In the family room, a worn lounger facing the big TV contrasted with the rest of the sleek, Italian furniture. Dana saw me eyeing the old chair that stood out from the rest of the décor and said with a laugh that Nate refused to give up his throne. She called out to Madsion, who emerged from behind her bedroom door. She was blonde and big-boned, like Nate, and seemed not particularly interested in my company. Dana suggested we chat about the transition from school to work since Madison was about to take a gap year. Madison said okay and retreated to her room.

Dana knocked on another door. She said fourteen-year-old Matthew was into video games and probably had headphones on. When he didn't answer, Dana walked in, motioning for me to follow, which I thought might be totally embarrassing. You shouldn't walk in unannounced on a teenage boy. But Dana knew her kid. He was seated at a computer, talking to someone via a headset. When his mother touched his shoulder, he startled. He twisted to face her and said he needed another fifteen minutes to finish the round. He was small-bodied and dark-haired, like his mother. Dana introduced me and told him no more than fifteen. We left him gaming away.

We walked past another two doors and out onto another deck. As lights began to twinkle on across the city, Dana explained that they had bought the lot from an estate and torn down the existing house to build this one. Nate wanted a view, she said, because it inspired him. She wanted the school district because she was committed to public schooling, and Sunnyslope High School had an excellent reputation. Madison was a swimmer there and a good enough student. It was too soon to predict

Matthew's trajectory. She said Nate was impatient with his son, but Matthew would find his niche in time because he was smart as well as sweet.

I didn't know what to do with the confidences Dana was sharing, but I felt I should reciprocate. I told her I was concerned about my little brother because he didn't seem to have initiative, although it was hard to judge long distance. As we climbed the steps to the living room, Dana invited me to say more. I didn't want to get into the subject of my family, so I told her Danny was obsessed with paintball. Dana laughed and asked why is it that boys need targets? All Matthew wanted to do was rack up virtual fatalities. She advised patience. I could feel my cheeks begin to burn. Danny didn't play paintball, as far as I knew, and my convenient little white lie sat badly on my conscience. When Dana and I arrived in the living room, Nate offered me a drink. I asked for wine. He made her a cocktail and didn't ask about our conversation.

Dana excused herself to "tend to the kitchen," and Nate and I took our drinks onto the upper deck. A sudden breeze swirled down the hillside, kicking dust into the air. We shielded our drinks with our hands. The Soleri bell hanging from an eave began to chime. Nate said only a strong wind from an advancing weather system could make the metal clapper hit the metal dome. He liked the sound because it presaged change. "Look around," Nate said with a sweep of his arm. "If I had a magic wand, I'd wave away all the palms. They're cheap, non-native, unimaginative. We can do better. We are doing better." He sipped his drink.

That was the Nate I used to admire, committed to change and a better future. The wine went down easily.

Nate said, "You met the kids? Maddy's going to do great things. She has tremendous self-confidence, more than me at seventeen." He took another sip. "Not Matt, he's tender like his mother. I grew up fighting with my brothers and it toughened me. I want Matt to face up to bullies at school. Won't happen at Sunnyslope, too many students, too easy to hide. I'm going to enroll him in private school as soon as Dana lets me." He took a sip.

I thought the bigger the high school, the better. My school had been too small for me to find my people. But I wasn't going to share my opinion with my boss. "I noticed your wife calls the kids Madison and Matthew. What should I call them?"

"Anything they'll answer to." He grinned. "Dana has a thing about names. When she starts a book, she flips through the pages to find the characters' names and charts them. Then she reads the end. She says the journey's better if she knows where she's going."

I wonder what Dana would think if she saw my driver's license.

"By the way, we don't talk business at the dinner table. Anything you need to tell me now?"

"No. But I'd like to know about the water deal. Is Continuity in the clear?"

"No sign-off yet, but I'm sure we're okay. Hanson's on it." His face lightened. "Let's go in. Dana's calling."

I followed him into the dining room that contained a rectangular glass table surrounded by upholstered chairs and took the seat Dana pointed me to. I watched Maddy flounce onto her chair—looking much younger than I had at her age—and pout at her dad. She could use a gap year, all right, to get out of her protected cocoon. Matt sent a shy smile my way. I decided I liked the kid, despite his supposed lack of self-confidence. It might be hard for a boy to bloom in Nate's shadow.

Dana told me to serve myself salad and pass the bowl. I did, and dinner began. Dana's chicken was lemony and delicious, and I helped myself to seconds. Nate ate quickly, Dana cut her chicken into tiny pieces before eating, and the kids picked at their food. Dana asked them what was happening in school. Then she asked me to talk about my coming west and how I found my job. At her urging, Maddy asked me a few polite questions. I told her about the job counseling service at my community college and offered to help her find help for resume writing, not that her parents couldn't help. She rolled her eyes and asked me to text the link. Then she asked if I thought I was doing enough to fight climate change because that's our generation's mandate since the adults had abdicated. Dana leaned back in her chair with a silent sigh. I said working for Continuity meant I was doing my part. Maddy shook her head. "Continuity doesn't count."

"Why do you say that?"

"Because the concept is too narrow. The world is more messed up. Besides, Dad follows the seventy-five percent rule."

Nate interrupted. "That's family shorthand for the art of compromise."

Maddy said, "Some art."

Nate shifted to address me: "My grandfather used to say that at least three-quarters of his water company's customers were content with their service, but the rest made his life miserable with their impossible demands. He realized he'd never be able to placate those folks, so he decided pleasing seventy-five percent of his customers was good enough. It's a great rule to follow in a business like mine where so much is beyond my control."

Maddy said, "You have to deliver water to one hundred percent of your customers, or else they could die."

"Continuity will deliver the *essentials* to one hundred percent of our residents. We may not make our stretch goals for the rest, but I'd be more than happy to reach seventy-five percent. Getting to eighty-five would be a smashing success."

Matt piped up. "My friends and I are more practical than Maddy and her friends. We like math."

Dana asked if everyone was ready for dessert, and Maddy sulked. I traded glances with Matt across the table. He shrugged his shoulders. I wanted to ask my boss to define exactly which twenty-five percent of the vision he was ready to sacrifice, as if you could cut off an arm or a leg and not notice it.

I worried: if Nate was prepared to downgrade his vision, could I get downgraded, too? I remembered him brushing off Mannheim's proposal to use the super-reflective paint. Maybe Sy was right, and I'd been a fool to trust that Continuity would make a meaningful difference. I could not touch the berry cake Dana passed around.

"Dad?" Matt asked. "Can I show you my game after dinner? I leveled up again."

"We have company, Matt."

I jumped in. "Oh, that's fine. I should leave. I have to get up before dawn to go hiking." Not true. "It's been a pleasure getting to know you all. Thanks for everything."

I pushed my chair from the table and retrieved my bag from where I'd left it on a couch. Nate thanked me for coming over and turned to his son. Dana ushered me to the door, thanking me for encouraging Madison. She said feel free to call her if I wanted to discuss anything. I told her I thought she was a great cook and walked out. I followed a flagstone path that wound down the side of the house to the street below and got in my still warm car. Then I stopped to breathe.

It was only eight thirty, maybe early enough to call Sy? We'd never talked by phone before, but I felt an urgent need to apologize. Leticia was in my contacts. I waited for an interminable three rings, and, thank goodness, she picked up. I apologized for the hour, saying I really needed to talk to Sy. She came on the line in a minute, and the story of the evening spilled out of me, word for word.

Sy said, "Why have you called me?"

"I think you were right about Nate." My chest squeezed tight, and it was getting hard to think.

"In business, achieving seventy-five percent of your ambitions is altogether respectable. I'm glad to hear that Hargrove is capable of realistic analysis."

I was shocked. "But he's ready to abandon his principles."

"In the long run. He seems able to run his business in the short run."

I didn't get it. "If he lops off a quarter of Continuity, it could fail."

Sy said, "It could fail anyway. Most likely it will."

I didn't understand where she was coming from, and I felt small and stupid. "I am so disappointed in him."

"Did you expect me to comfort you?"

I wasn't sure what I'd expected.

Sy said, "I'm sorry but it's my bedtime. We can resume this conversation on Friday. I prefer seeing you in person."

In other words, don't phone again.

"Goodnight. Rest well." She, or Leticia, ended the call.

I put on my seatbelt and cranked the engine, utterly confused and embarrassed by Sy's reaction. Then an idea dawned: I *thought* I'd called to apologize for doubting her warning about Nate, but maybe I really did want her to comfort me for losing faith in my work. What a baby thing to do! I must have disappointed her. I would be glad to wait for Friday to try to make up for it because I needed time for my feelings to get back to normal, whatever normal meant now that I'd eaten at Nate's table. I turned on my headlights and drove downhill toward home.

24

For a couple of months, I'd been noticing a string of snarky comments on the Hargrove-Spence Instagram account I monitored from someone called @nobs8819. No threats or conspiracy theories, just mockery. Today, @nobs8819 claimed Hargrove-Spence didn't care about the big picture, otherwise they wouldn't be creating a barn (picture of Continuity) for animals who ate too many other animals producing too much methane pollution, i.e. cow farts. I didn't normally respond to such low-level trolling, but something made me pause.

I realized I had seen the number "8819" recently ... on the invitation to Dana's dinner party. Jesus, Mary, and Joseph, as they said in Pennsylvania. Could @nobs8819 be Nate's daughter, Maddy? I sat back in my chair, trying to digest this realization. Then, an idea bloomed in my brain: maybe I could get Maddy to work the internet for me.

I had spent hours at the Archives, looking at newspapers from the 1880s to the 1920s, scanning for a headline about a Johnson murder. The old stuff wasn't searchable, being just photos, not a database, and there were dozens of newspapers back then, the social media of the day, according to the librarian. She told me to concentrate on the biggest paper, *The Arizona Republic*, and I'd finally found one article that mentioned White Bear. Evidently Sy's grandfather had come home from WWI a hero, and they held a welcome celebration for him. The reporter wrote that after the loss of the mine and his partner in "dubious circumstances," Sy's grandfather had volunteered to fight with the British in France and earned a Purple Heart. The article said, "all thoughts of the silver mine scandal were forgiven and forgotten" in light of his heroism. Not according to Sy, who'd said her great-grandfather protested against his son for decades. I guessed that the older man knew something about the way his son had engineered "the loss of his partner" and hated it. But I hadn't been able to find any details.

Now, Maddy might offer me a new angle on the matter.

I trotted over to talk to one of the mothers in our apartment complex whose kids got on the school bus I saw every morning. She told me Sunnyslope High School got out at 2:45 unless your kid did extracurricular stuff. It was 2:15. I hopped in my car and drove over to the school. I figured I would stand in a conspicuous spot when the doors opened, and Maddy would find *me*. If she was in school that day. Most likely she was. I have to admit, it thrilled me to set a trap for living prey.

Kids started to flow out the door closest to the parking lot right on time. Maddy said goodbye to another girl and approached slowly, as if she sensed danger. Good for her.

I waved. "Hi, nobs8819. Can we sit in my car where it's not cool but not hot either?"

She followed me to my ancient vehicle and sat in the passenger seat without a word. I began to feel sorry for her. To break the ice, I asked, "What's 'nobs8819' mean?"

"It's not 'knobs,' it's 'no B S.' I'm the only one at 8819 who doesn't bullshit."

"Clever. Don't worry, I won't tell your dad. I just want your help."

Her body slumped an inch. She adjusted the backpack on the floor at her feet. I could read skepticism in the tightness of her lips and decided to lay it all out.

"I've discovered that a man in 1882 owned some of the land your dad has his eye on for future expansion. Only the guy disappeared from official State records. I have reason to believe he may have been murdered sometime before 1914. I'm asking you to put the word out to your followers and their followers. Use your influence. See if anyone can find anything about his story. Sound good?"

Her head whipped around to face me. "Why do you want to know?"

"Background. I'm a very thorough person." No leaks from me. "I won't tell your dad what you're doing if you don't tell him what I'm doing."

"Why do you want my help?"

"Because you have a network of people interested in social justice. May I text you the details?"

She took her time thinking it over. "Okay. Give me a lift home? My ride already left."

"My pleasure." A long shot, but it launched.

I drove to the physical 8819; Maddy sat silently all the way, despite my attempts to chat. I deposited her at the foot of the driveway. I waved, and she waved back as she climbed uphill.

I turned my car around to head for Scottsdale where Luis was waiting at Mrs. M's. His car was in the shop, and I'd offered to drive him wherever he wanted to go. I couldn't wait to see him, and touch him. He'd been hovering in the back of my brain, distracting me, ever since our date. I was looking forward to seeing him front and center.

It took twenty minutes to get to Scottsdale. I eased Mrs. M's front door open and tiptoed in. The dining room table was covered with pamphlets, and Luis sat behind his computer, tapping away. I snuck up behind him and whispered, "Is Mrs. M home?"

He startled, then reached for my hand. "No, but I expect her back any minute. Don't get me fired."

I pecked his cheek and sat in the chair next to his. "How long will you be?"

"Dunno. Katie asked me to wait. My time is her time."

I wanted to cheer him up. "I know something Mrs. M would probably kill for." Just like a kid, I wanted to share my treasure. "The White Bear Ranch has a deep shadow in its past." I told him the details, but not about coercing Maddy Hargrove to help me search, which he might think was over the top.

"Are you going to look for the names of others who could claim the land? Mexican names, or Spanish names before them? Or Native American names before *them*?" He placed his hand on my thigh. "Your search is not going to produce anything actionable."

"That's okay. I just want my friend Sydelle to have the whole story."

"To do what with?"

He had me there. To tell the deep-down truth, I wanted to find out stuff too important for Sy to ignore. I wanted to help protect the Ranch, and I wanted her to respect me for it. My cheeks tingled as I realized how childish this might sound to Luis's sophisticated ears. "I guess that depends on the story."

We heard noise in the vestibule. Mrs. M walked in followed by a woman I recognized from the Friends' meeting. They complained about the heat as they pulled out chairs. Mrs. M said she was surprised but delighted to see me. She flashed her thousand-watt smile. She asked Luis to review the statement she and the other woman had prepared from a scientific point of view and handed him a tablet. Turning to me, "You're welcome to stay, but this may take a while."

Luis shook his head, mouthed "Uber" at me.

I pushed away from the table and said I had to go. Mrs. M rose, too, and walked me to the door. Maybe because she'd ruined my plan for a lovely evening, I decided to needle her. I stopped at the threshold for my parting shot.

"By the way, did Thomas Hammer tell you about the tragedy at the Ranch in the last century?"

Her smile looked frozen in place. "I'm not sure what you mean."

I was enjoying her effort not to show surprise at hearing the name. "He told me that a partner in the silver mine may have been murdered. The Friends should know about it." I stepped beneath the transom. "See you at the next meeting."

I hustled to my car, gloating a little about turning the tables on Mrs. M. I'd reverted to my teenage troublemaking habit, only this time I was on the side of the righteous. As I cranked the ignition, a touch of remorse set in. What sort of person did this sudden bout of scheming make me? A trickster? Or a full-fledged combatant in the land war into which I'd been plunged? Or maybe just a girl pissed off that some woman had stolen her boyfriend for the night.

~ ~

On the following Friday, before leaving for Sy's, I checked out @ nobs8819 one more time. Maddy had activated her following as promised, but nothing useful had emerged. But today, one of the comments said Ancestry.com might be a good place to look. The helpful librarian at the Archives had showed me that Arizonans can look things up on Ancestry without paying, so I searched. I found two J. Johnsons living in Maricopa County at the time, one from Wisconsin and the other born in the Territory, who could have been in the mining business. But I couldn't figure out how to pin either to the deed. I had nothing to report to Sy, which was probably a good thing since she didn't want to know anyway. I decided to let Maddy off the hook, but there was no way I'd let go of Johnson & Sons. Not yet.

I wrote to @nobs8819, saying we were quits and wishing her a happy gap year. I was sure she would keep my secret as long as I kept hers. Then I wrote to Luis, my only other confidant, telling him that he was right about my search hitting a wall. I suspected he was a person who liked being right, and I wanted to please him. Our second date was coming up this weekend, and my anticipation had no bounds. I wanted to know him better, not just screw him, which I totally wanted, but I also wanted him to get to know the real me. I was so tired of lurking around Nate and Mrs. M, collecting bits of intel and pretending to be cool. I wanted to feel free to blow my cool with Luis and be liked for it. Maybe even loved?

I packed up my bag and headed out to the car to pick up a snack for tea at Sy's. As I backed out of the too-tight space, a wave of pleasure hit me. I realized that I had stopped lurking around Sy a long time ago. She and I were real together, although I had to be careful of her fragility. Like she said, we could agree to disagree. So far, so good.

25

That first night Luis and I had gone out, I'd sat across the table thinking I had never dated a guy who wore glasses before. Most guys wore contacts, like girls. Luis was different in so many ways. First of all, he was half Puerto Rican, from New York, and getting a PhD. I'd thought that with all his big city experience, he wouldn't be interested in me. But he was. He seemed to understand my interest in Continuity, and I totally got his commitment to climate. I hadn't been so attracted to anyone in a while. I hadn't had sex in a while, either.

In high school, I had been crazy about a boy named Jeff whose his father had acted in commercials in New York before the family moved to Pennsylvania. Jeff read books no one else did and taught me to think about what I read. I was thrilled when he'd picked me over the pretty girls. We hung out, and he popped my cherry. But when I left home, I said good-bye to Jeff and didn't look back. We stopped texting one another after a few months.

My first year in Phoenix, I hung out with other students at the community college and played around, but nothing serious. Then one of my teachers asked me out after the course ended, and we went on a couple of heavy dates. But we didn't talk about anything besides campus stuff, and we never went anywhere, so I finally told him I wasn't interested anymore, which hurt his feelings, and for which I was very sorry. When I got the job at Hargrove-Spence, I was so involved in my work that I didn't miss dating. When Luis entered my orbit, I went back on the pill.

This evening, Luis showed up at my door right on time for the adventure I had planned for our official second date. It had occurred to me while dressing that he could give me technical advice, so I asked him to come in for a minute. He followed me into the living room, looking around at the furniture and the *Fin de* Año decorations still strung overhead. Aaron peered at us from the hallway.

"Hey, Aaron," I said. "This is Luis, my friend from work. I want to show him something. Would you play host while I go get it?"

"*Quieres una cerveza?*" Aaron asked.

"No, thanks. I should tell you my Spanish isn't very good." Luis sat on the couch and crossed his legs.

I went to my room and dug out the map to the mine. When I got back to the living room, Aaron was seated on a chair opposite Luis, legs wide, a sneer on his face.

"So, what do you do as intern?" Aaron asked Luis.

"Some clerical work, some historical research. I try to make the group include climate science in their decision-making."

"Do you get paid?" His right leg began to jiggle.

"The internship is part of my program at ASU. I'm a grad student." Luis pushed his glasses up his nose. "Nice place. Feels homey."

I sat beside Luis and unrolled the map. He helped hold down the corners as I traced the boundary between Continuity and the White Bear Ranch with one finger and ticked off contour lines to the west. Our thighs pressed against each other.

Aaron cleared his throat. "What are you two up to?"

I glared at Aaron and faced Luis. "I want to know if there could be drainage issues between these two properties. My boss mentioned there might be contamination."

Gabi pushed through the back door carrying glasses and a half-empty pitcher of iced tea, José on her heels. "Getting buggy out there," Gabi said. She noticed Luis and wagged the pitcher. "Hi. I'm Gabi, Bee's roommate. Want some iced tea?"

"This is Luis, the climate scientist I told you about. Hi, José."

"No, thanks," Luis said. He pointed at a spot on the map where circles of contour lines indicated a hilltop. "What's over here?"

"There's an old silver mine somewhere around there." My heart quickened.

"Could be acid mine drainage. Old mines are a known environmental hazard. Mineral deposits lying around can leach. But it's outside my expertise."

Gabi said, "I'm about to order pizza. Would you like to eat with us?"

Luis stood. "No, thanks. We should head out."

I rolled up the map and dumped it in my room. Tomorrow I would Google acid mine drainage. I said goodnight to Gabi and company and followed Luis out to his car.

The sky was still bright at seven o'clock when we parked at TopGolf, and mountains in the distance glowed pink in the lowering sunlight. Luis looked at the sign on the three-story building as if to ask, what is this place? As I had suspected, he didn't get out much just for fun. I told him here's where ordinary folks play golf without belonging to a country club. The building had three walls; the fourth side was open to face a driving range bounded by a giant net. You could stand at the edge of the floor on the open side and hit balls into the range. Luis cleaned his glasses.

We entered the lobby along with two other couples and a family with a grandma in tow. A group of men with "Cox Communications" embroidered on their shirts swarmed past.

Since we were a little late, I grasped Luis's hand and pulled him toward the reservations counter. I flashed the reservation QR code to a girl wearing a black TopGolf T-shirt and a nose ring. The girl checked my phone and looked us up and down and told us to take bay number two-oh-one before anyone else got there. I led Luis up the stairs and down the corridor to the alcove numbered two-oh-one, where two banquettes formed an L around a coffee table. I sat on one of the banquettes and spread my arms to claim the space. He followed suit on the other banquette. A knot of people showed up half a minute later. They called over one of the black-clothed teenaged hosts and conferred. After the host radioed someone, he ushered those folks away. I grinned at Luis and said let the games begin.

Luis looked around; I could sense him analyzing the place. Our alcove, one of about twenty on this floor, contained furnishings on three sides and overlooked the driving range on the fourth. Close to the open edge, a machine dribbled golf balls onto a fake grass mat from which a rubber "tee" protruded. I pointed to several net-covered holes built into the driving range at various distances from the building, maybe thirty-feet wide. The object of the game was to sink your ball into one of the targets and accumulate points. We could hear balls being whacked by chattering people in the bordering bays.

Luis said, "Must cost plenty to keep this set-up cool." He squinted at the targets.

I stepped over to the rack of golf clubs behind us and pulled out two. Then I used the touchscreen mounted on a column to select a simple game for starters. I also pulled up the dinner screen. "What do you want to drink with the burger I'm ordering for you? Best thing on the menu," I said.

"Beer?"

I punched the screen, then handed him a club.

"The only time I ever held one of these was at a miniature golf course in an amusement park in the Bronx." He swung it like a pendulum. "Geez, it's heavy."

I showed him how to grip the club. He hit five balls into the net that served as a gutter along the edge of the bay, cursing under his breath. Then I hit five balls, scoring thirteen points. He hit another five balls, managing to dribble one into the closest target. We both cheered when three points showed up in his column on the screen.

A chubby teenager wearing TopGolf black appeared with the food. He placed the tray on the coffee table, and Luis sat next to me to eat. He said he hadn't realized how hungry he was, and the burger *was* good.

In between bites, I told him about the first time I came here with Gabi and four girls from her call center. "I tried to pay attention to the game while the others gossiped and flirted with the guys the next bay over. We all laughed a lot, and I realized why Gabi had brought me here." I looked him in the eye, challenging him to figure it out. "To stop taking myself too seriously."

Luis shook his head. "I don't need to stop being serious. Climate doesn't wait."

I felt the heat rise up my neck and seep into my cheeks. "I hope you don't think this is a waste of time. I thought it would help us get to know each other."

"This is fine. Better than a golf course. They use technology rather than wasting water."

"Oh?" I stopped eating.

"There could be fifty balls flying through the air at any given moment, and the software figures out who hit what, where. The balls must be tagged."

I put down my burger. "You're the only one I know who thinks about algorithms at TopGolf."

"Yeah, I always stand out from the crowd."

"Where's the evidence?"

He paused, as if he were weighing how much to reveal. "I dated a girl named Melissa in New York. She brought me home to meet her parents on Park Avenue. They ignored me the whole time. She said they'd never liked anyone she dated. But then I found out she had a birthday party, and I wasn't invited." He reached for a fry. "Melissa went to all the right schools but didn't learn anything." He chomped the fry.

I told him I didn't fit into the crowd where I grew up either. He offered me a fry, and I ate it. I was about to offer him one when the chubby host appeared asking if we needed another round of drinks. We said no simultaneously. As soon as the host retreated, I said, "That's how TopGolf makes money. Three-fifty for a Coke that costs them ten cents."

"No one ever *needs* a Coke. No one needs plastic grass, either. It's an environmental disaster."

"You'd have a hard time explaining that to the management." I pointed a finger at him, like Sy would.

"People have to give up a lot of stuff if the species is going to pull through." His voice had taken a dark tone.

"When do you think we'll realize that?"

"Not soon enough. When I think about the odds against the majority accepting science, I want to drop out. But I can't stop being my parents' son. I inherited their work ethic."

"So you're not quitting school?" I hoped he'd laugh.

"I'm leaving as soon as I get my degree. Do you know that Pluto is a planet according to the state legislature, although astronomers all over the world disagree? This is Arizona. We do what we want."

"Don't go. We need you. I mean, Continuity needs good science."

"Your boss thinks he has that covered." He shook his head.

I stood, picked up my club. "So, how about we don't think about the climate for the next half hour?" I wanted to have fun, and I hoped he would, too.

I set a ball on the rubber tee and handed him a club, saying it was his turn. I had forty-five points, and he had thirteen. He adjusted his glasses and stepped up to the tee. I told him to keep his wrists and hands still and stood behind him to guide his swing, steering him by the shoulders. He followed directions. The swing landed him ten points. He gave me a hug and mumbled in my ear, "I'm doing this for you, you know." I hugged back. He said he couldn't help wanting to feel competent even in a trivial endeavor. We each took another turn, and then the game timed out. I asked how about another? He shook his head.

We returned the clubs to the rack and made our way past alcoves of loudly carousing golfers. We headed down the stairs, and out to his car in the crowded parking lot now illuminated by streetlight. The mountains in the distance had merged into the dark.

Luis cranked the engine. "I should really go back to the lab. We take turns on the supercomputers, and there are more slots at night."

"Luis, it's the weekend."

"I'm kidding. Shall we go to your place or mine?"

"Mine, please." I wanted to feel his arms around me and mine around him, but a little voice was saying something wasn't right. I tried to swallow the message as Luis drove toward Sunnyslope, but it wouldn't go down. He remembered the way without prompting from me—the guy knew his urban geography—and pulled into a spot opposite the complex's gate.

"I hope you enjoyed TopGolf," I said as he cut the engine.

"I enjoyed the company." He reached for my hand. "Shall I come in?"

"Not tonight."

"I thought you liked me." He tilted his head in mock surprise.

"I like you a lot. I'm not sure you like me."

"Of course I do." He pushed his glasses up his nose. He did not appear surprised by what he'd heard.

I leaned over and gave him a kiss. "I'll text. See you soon." I escaped before he could press me for an explanation.

I had had such high hopes for our date, but everything at TopGolf had annoyed him: the cost of air conditioning, the kid bringing Coke, the plastic grass, the triviality of it all. I couldn't make him lighten up, and it made me sad. Worse, I couldn't tell if his problem was with TopGolf or with me. Compared to him and the well-schooled Melissa, I was a TopGolf kind of girl.

26

It was past ten o'clock when I opened the apartment door after seeing Luis drive away. Gabi was sitting in the living room watching TV. She never watched TV alone, so I figured she was waiting for me. I did not want to talk about Luis, but I knew she wouldn't let me escape. I kicked off my sandals and sprawled on the chair across from her.

Gabi asked, "Did you have fun?"

"Yup." True, if not the whole truth.

"Did Luis have fun?"

"Yes. Otherwise I wouldn't have."

"Do you think you're fancy enough for him?"

"We got along fine." How did she know exactly where I hurt?

"You're missing the big red flag waving in front of your face." She'd taken on that maternal tone I didn't appreciate. She was only a couple of years older than me.

I rolled my eyes. "What?"

"You know what we call someone like him in my family? *Arribista.* Someone who thinks he's better than the people he comes from and imitates the people above him."

"Why do you say that?"

"When he picked you up, he wouldn't talk to Aaron or me."

"He's a quiet guy."

"He pretended he doesn't speak Spanish."

"His mother was born in New York City. His father isn't even Puerto Rican."

"Okay, but that's no excuse to be rude. Aaron thinks he's a prick."

"Aaron's jealous. Your brother should follow Luis's example and go to work instead of minding other people's business."

Gabi's voice rose. "Aaron's making progress. He got an internship at Chicanos Por la Causa."

"Good for him."

"Why don't you give him credit? It would mean so much to him."

I sat straighter. "You want me to date your brother? Is that it?"

"I want you to be good to him. He thinks the world of you." She glared, "He's not a snob."

"Your brother is not datable."

"Why not?" She crossed her arms across her bosom.

"Because he sucks at relationships. He once told me you do too. He said you pick losers who push you around." I felt mean telling on Aaron, but she was wrong about him.

Gabi paled. "I've made mistakes," she said. "But I've learned from them. I guess you're going to have to learn from yours."

"What mistake? Dating a guy you don't like?"

"You are turning into a snob. With your high-and-mighty cause, and your puffed-up friends. Me and my family aren't good enough for you anymore." Lips tight, she got up and stomped to her bedroom door. She slammed it hard behind her.

I hated fighting with Gabi. When we'd both gotten the coronavirus from the Memorial Day party we'd gone to, both sick as dogs at the same time, I'd watch her trudge into the kitchen to make Jell-O for the two of us and told myself if she can move, so can I. She was my inspiration—and my competition—and I got my shit together. Later she confessed she had had the same reaction to me. We buoyed each other up those three weeks and had been super tight ever since.

I remembered Aaron's face when I glared at him, but I wasn't putting him down, just telling him to butt out. Luis hadn't done anything snobby. I didn't envy the rich people I met at work. I wanted Continuity to succeed because it would protect human beings from harm. People needed shelter of some kind, and shelter at Continuity was good for the planet. It was an honor to work for something … revolutionary. I'd never imagined I could make a difference. My motives were solid. Gabi didn't get that some ideas were more important than some people.

I got up and gathered my sandals and purse. I went into my room and closed the door carefully. I wasn't a bad person, but I'd hurt my best friend, and that was bad. I went to the bathroom to brush my teeth, wondering how to make it up to her. Gabi had done so much for me. She was kind and generous, and I'd slammed her for criticizing a guy I hardly knew. I would apologize in the morning. I went back to my room, took off my clothes, and lay down on the bed to wait for sleep. My eyes popped open.

It was Luis!

Luis was the problem, and I had taken it out on Gabi!

I felt crummy, Pennsylvania crummy. I didn't love family the way Gabi did, and I certainly did not want to date Aaron, but so what? It was wrong to disrespect your friend. I got up and went to the kitchen for a glass of water. It might be a long night.

~ ~

Leticia had asked me to come early on Friday, but not stay long, because Sy had a lunch date with her son, and it took a while to prepare. I found Sy in the kitchen in a fluffy, white bathrobe, a glass of water and an array of plastic pill boxes labeled with the days of the week on the table in front of her. Leticia poured us some water and left us alone.

Sy pointed to the pill boxes. "Now you see how my day proceeds. Twelve drugs to keep me going." She paused. "I'm sorry to disrupt our routine, but my son needs my counsel. We can chat for a little while before I dress."

"I'd like your counsel, too." I hadn't meant to lay it on her like that, but ... "I had a date over the weekend that's got me worried."

"Continue."

I told her Luis's basic biodata and that he'd gone along with me to TopGolf but grumbled about everything. I said I didn't know whether he hadn't liked the place or if he was unhappy with me because I wasn't classy. Plus, my roommate and I had fought about it. She accused him of being a snob, and me by association. I didn't know what to do.

"Why does she call him a snob?"

"Because he didn't chat with her and her brother when he came to the apartment to pick me up. We were in a rush, though."

"Have you slept with him?"

"Once."

"Is he a considerate lover?"

"It was quick but good. Totally good."

Sy tapped the table with one bent finger. "My dear, there are men who are open to women. They have soft edges. Then there are men who are not and never will be. They are impermeable."

"What do you mean?"

She sighed. "My husband was one of the latter. Of course, I didn't know that in the beginning. After he died, I met an Australian who had come here for business. He was in agriculture, too. We had a fling, and I found out what I had been missing. Martin was so attentive. He thought every word I said was inspired. He would have married me and moved here if I'd let him."

"Why didn't you marry?"

She waved her hand. "Oh, too complicated financially. He had a family. I had a family. My point is, he was attuned to me and supportive. Nothing else matters." She leaned toward me, as if sharing a secret. "Years later, when I fussed about the birth of my first great-grandchild, he sent a koala bear."

She still cared about the guy! I pictured Sy making geriatric love to a sun-wizened Australian with a bald head and white goatee. Lots of affection, not much performance. She made me smile.

"There's another thing. He's a fanatic about climate change and his work. I get the feeling that nothing else really counts for him. That would include me."

"My dear, I don't worry about the climate. I am done with all that."

I wasn't done—how could I be, when the future was a stake? —but I wanted to come first in my guy's priorities. I guess hanging around with Gabi and Sy had rubbed off on me.

A bustle in the hallway. I could hear the low murmur of Thomas Hammer's voice and Leticia's high-pitched response.

"I'd better go. What should I do about Luis?"

"Date him, and you will discover what sort of man he is. You are a smart cookie."

"I'll take your word for it."

I got up and pecked her cheek. On my way out, I bumped into her son in the hallway carrying a giant bouquet. "Is it your mom's birthday?"

"We celebrate her birthday every month. My mother claims she's not sentimental. Don't let her fool you."

For a nanosecond, I considered asking him about Johnson & Sons, but that might get back to Sy, and I didn't want to provoke her without evidence. Thinking about evidence made me think Nate's lawyer might be able to help me. If I talked to him and Nate found out, he'd forget about it as soon as something new popped up on his screen.

I hustled out of the house and got into my warm car. The AC came on after a minute in its feeble way—gotta get that fixed—and headed for Sunnyslope. Sy had given me a course of action to follow with Luis, and I always felt better with a plan. Her praise had me glowing inside, too. My brain drifted to Thomas Hammer's flowers. He must be one of those soft-edged men to treat his mother like that. Which would make him super vulnerable to Katie Morrison. I realized I should report this tidbit of intel to my handler, but I didn't care to talk to him in my current mood.

I drove to the office and sidled up to Maria. When she squinted at me, I asked for Nate's lawyer's coordinates, saying I had to deliver a package. Such blatant lying curdled in my stomach, but I had a mission. Back in my corner, I called Mr. Hanson's office, and in a few minutes he came on the line, such was the power of the Hargrove-Spence name. I said I was following up on the Johnson deed case, and he told me straight out it was dead for all practical purposes. No heirs, no complaints, not even worth drafting a memo. He hung up and I drove straight home.

Sitting on my bed, I opened my phone to try to find if Johnson had heirs, but I had no idea where to look other than the State Archives. I realized I had to admit defeat on this front. But I wasn't out of the game. Instead I searched "acid mine drainage Arizona." Then a text from my little brother arrived. A miracle. He wrote he had an opportunity to transfer to a different high school for senior year to take a course our school didn't offer, and he wanted my advice. And money for the fee. I typed my reply—go for it! —and Venmo-ed two hundred bucks in case there'd be extras, totally emptying my account. I closed my eyes and visualized the cafeteria where I'd snuck in every day after the bell to avoid talking to the other students. I never felt comfortable in that school outside of class. Danny could make better friends somewhere else, as I had here.

27

My phone woke me at ten in the morning on Sunday. Nate. Oh, crap. I swiped into the call.

"Hey," Nate said. "I want to give you a heads up for tomorrow."

"What's going on?" It would have been nice to get an apology for disturbing my Sunday. I bet he apologized to VIPs.

"You go see Sydelle Hammer every Monday, right?"

"I go on Fridays." I could feel myself getting pissed.

"Oh? Sorry, I got the day wrong. You don't need to anymore."

"Why don't you want me to see her?" I tried to keep the edge out of my voice.

"Something turned up. I'm going to concentrate on her son instead."

"What turned up?" I started to worry.

"If I told you, I'd have to kill you."

"Seriously, what's going on?"

"Look, you don't have to waste time with the old lady anymore. Come to the office tomorrow for a new assignment."

He ended the call before I could protest. I had no intention of staying away from Sy. I got out of bed and pulled on shorts and a tank top—over a hundred degrees outside—and drifted to the kitchen.

Aaron was setting the table, and Gabi was at the sink cleaning vegetables. She said, "Want brunch with us?"

She had been careful since our fight about Aaron. I had, too. "Sure. Can I help?"

"Take the tamales out of the pot and watch out for the steam," she said, nodding in the direction of the stove. As I obeyed, I wondered what if Nate had learned something that could hurt Sy. I wanted to protect her. I felt a wedge insert itself between Nate's interests and mine.

"After brunch, I need to go to the construction site. There's something I have to see."

Gabi said, "It's already over a hundred out. And it's Sunday."

I shook my head. I wanted to check out the landscape where Continuity met the Ranch to see if there really could be a drainage issue. My boss was known to exaggerate in order to land a deal.

Aaron said, "I'm going with you."

"No, thanks."

Gabi said, "Yes, thanks. Aaron will keep you out of trouble."

I did *not* want company, but here was a chance to make it up to Gabi. "Okay." I turned to Aaron. "I'll pack water for both of us." On second thought, Aaron might be a big help; he knew about mines, and he could read a map.

We settled down to one of my favorite Arizona meals: two pork tamales topped with a fried egg. Gabi let me put salsa on top of my tamales, a concession to my gringa taste. I ate every bite because it was good, and to fortify myself for the road.

~ ~

I parked next to the Continuity construction fence closest to the Ranch. There were only a few hard-hats on site, and none of them had tried to stop me driving across the property. We stepped out of my barely cool car into the blazing Arizona summer. I put on my dollar-store hat and slipped the pack onto my back. Aaron, who had been quiet in the car, donned a baseball cap. He grumbled, "Jesus, it must be a hundred and ten and climbing."

"You volunteered."

"I did. Which way?"

"I want to walk toward the White Bear mine. To see the path water would take from there to here."

"You mean after a rain?"

"Or after human activity."

"Crazy girl. Water travels mostly underground."

"Over ground, too, when it's too dry to soak in. I read up on this. There might be signs left on the surface." I checked the map and got my bearings. "See that saguaro that looks like it's growing out of a boulder up there?" I pointed. "The mine is behind that ridge, I'm pretty sure. We need to go there."

Aaron held the chain link fence steady so I could climb over. The toes of my sneakers barely fit into the links, not like when I was a kid. Then I steadied the fence for Aaron. He hauled himself up over the top with strong arms and landed hard. Fifty yards farther we came to the Ranch's barbed wire cattle fence. Aaron stepped on the bottom wire and pulled the next wire up to make a hole for me to climb through. I did the same for him. Poor cows were too dumb to escape.

We headed uphill, scrambling around bushes, slipping on loose rock all the way to the top of the ridge. The surface was a dry beige, the bushes brown and crinkled. I did not see evidence of past rain, which didn't worry me, not yet. From the crest of the ridge, the ground dipped down, then up to a higher ridge. We had to bushwhack slowly in the broiling sun, Aaron frowning the whole time. I stopped for water and to cheer him on. To cheer myself on, too, because I was beginning to feel a little foolish chasing after water in the desert. I took the pack off my back and fished out the water bottles. We each drank a few swallows. Then he put the bottles into the pack, zipped it shut and swung it onto his back. I said nothing, glad to have my load lightened. My *physical* load.

At the top of the next ridge, the ground dipped again, and then rose again. But on the distant hillside ahead of us, something metallic glinted in the late morning sun. It had to be the mine—there was nothing else manmade on this side of the Ranch—and I yelled *Yahoo!* in relief. I hadn't screwed up: the mine *was* directly uphill from Continuity. Even if we hadn't seen dried-up washes on the route we'd taken. I stopped climbing.

"We can turn around now. I've got my answer."

"What was the question?" He lowered the pack and took out our bottles.

"I had to know if water from the mine could reach the construction site."

Aaron poured some of his water on the ground. It disappeared. "Not too likely."

"Let's head back." I didn't want to argue about likelihoods.

"Is this connected to that scouting trip we took?"

Oh, shit, I thought, he's onto me. I tried to keep my voice neutral. "I wanted to see the land for myself. I care about people on both sides of those fences." I waved my arm downhill.

"You really buy into your boss's propaganda? It's called greenwashing, you know. I don't get why you're loyal to that asshole."

"Aaron, cut it out. It's too hot to argue."

"I'm not arguing, I'm asking why you stick with that guy. What do you really want?"

"A million dollars and world peace." I crossed my eyes.

"I'll ask you again in the shade." He hefted the pack.

We retraced our steps, the torturous sun almost directly overhead. I pretended to concentrate on my footing, circling around cacti and patches of dessert crust. Aaron's question had zinged me to the core. I didn't stick with Nate; I stuck with Continuity. Could I find something equally important to do, or maybe better, if I looked? Until this very moment, it hadn't occurred to me to try. I shook off the thought. But there was a small creature inside my chest trying to scratch its way out.

JULY

average daytime high = 110° F

days of rain = 4

28

The third meeting of the Friends of White Bear Ranch started on time. Most of the usual suspects sat around Mrs. M's dining room table. On an open laptop at the far end, a Zoom grid displayed the faces of a few others, presumably dialing in from cooler places. The Arizona upper class reminded me of the British Raj I once saw in a movie. The sahibs sent their wives and children up into the mountains in Simla while they sweated for profit and glory down below. Mrs. M's Friends were modern-day sahibs.

The AC kicked on, but it was well-oiled, and we could hear Mrs. M clear her throat. People hushed and she called the meeting to order. The Friends seemed eager to report on their accomplishments: one after the other, they brandished their assignment sheets and told the group about the potential supporters they'd contacted. I sat quietly in the background stealing glances at Luis. He had a good poker face. When the last person finished speaking, Mrs. M complemented the Friends on their progress. She thanked those who went to the budget hearing for demonstrating their commitment so effectively. Applause broke out around the table. Luis flicked his eyes at me. Various people commented about the experience of protesting. Some talked about the Hargrove-Spence water deal, as if they'd forgotten I was present.

Then Mrs. M cleared her throat again.

"I have one more item to discuss. You remember I wrote you that I'd had a conversation with Sydelle Hammer. With her on board, no one could turn us down, and I think I've found a way to motivate her to join us."

She had everyone's attention, including mine.

"If we name the future preserve after her late son, John, I think she'd be appreciative. I haven't approached her, of course, not without your approval. What do you think?"

Hubbub ensued. Someone said it was a bad idea because it would make the public think the preserve was private and therefore turn off donations. Another man replied nobody boycotts Scottsdale, and it's named after Winfield Scott, for goodness' sake. One of the quieter Friends said she was concerned about valuing the name; how would we know how much to ask for? People murmured in agreement. Someone offered to poke around town and catalog naming donations. Someone else warned of ways it could get complicated and offered to consult a trust attorney. Mrs. M asked each Friend to email his or her questions or concerns to Luis, who would collate them. Then a study team would be formed to find answers. Heads nodded. The naysayer leaned back in his seat, looking mollified. His opponent blew his nose. Mrs. M said they'd completed the agenda and invited everyone into the living room for snacks.

I waited for the others to clear and headed over to Luis, who was sorting the assignment sheets into stacks. I checked that Mrs. M was nowhere near before taking hold of his arm. "Is she really asking for approval, or is this a done deal?" I remembered the conversation in Sy's living room and worried she might be hurt by talk about her dead son coming from perfect strangers.

"First I heard of it. I'm off the case now that she's friends with Thomas Hammer."

"What do you mean?"

"I came over here to go over my findings a couple of days ago, and he was in the living room looking comfortable. I suspect she's got him in her tentacles." He tucked his stuff into his carrier bag.

Wow. I wondered if Sy knew. "How close do you think they are?"

He shook his head. "I wouldn't put anything past her. She wants John Hammer's name on the preserve, and she'll get it any way she can." He zipped his bag and faced me. "I'm going to a conference this weekend. How about I cook you pastelon when I get back? You said you'd like to try it."

I nodded. I would take every opportunity to follow Sy's advice. My heart twisted with anticipation.

"I'll call." He bent and brushed my forehead with his lips.

Despite everything buzzing in my brain, I wanted to kiss him back. All of me warmed, and it wasn't a blush. I told him to have a safe trip and told myself to focus on the problem at hand. I considered warning Sy about what might be coming. I certainly wouldn't tell Nate, not without knowing what he had going with Sy's son. This war over the Ranch was pulling me in three directions at the same time.

I meandered into the living room, but couldn't bear the chit-chat. I bent over to pat the dog, thanking him for his silence the other day. I looked for Mrs. M to say goodnight, planning to spend the next few hours on Netflix emptying my brain. Mrs. M took my arm and reminded me about my promise not to share with Sy. I smiled, not sure I would keep it. As Gabi always said, family came first, and Sy was becoming part of my Arizona family.

At home I scanned the Netflix new arrivals but couldn't shake the image Luis had planted in my head of Mrs. M and a "comfortable" Thomas Hammer lounging together. I tried not to leap to conclusions, but if Mrs. M *had* seduced Thomas Hammer, she'd trumped Nate. My boss could be ruthless, but he didn't screw around for profit, as far as I could tell. Dana Hargrove wouldn't put up with such conduct. She struck me as a total straight arrow. But what did I really know?

When I went to the kitchen for a glass of water, Aaron was sitting on the floor poking the back of the fridge that he had pulled away from the wall. A bucket and towels stood nearby. He looked up. "Do me a favor?" he said. "I need more tubing." He held up four inches of skinny rubber tube.

"Did we have a leak?"

"The ice maker is busted in this piece of shit José brought over. Can you go to Home Depot and get me three meters of this?"

"I thought you couldn't fix things." I took the tubing from his hand.

"This is no big deal. Or lend me your car? Gabi's out with José with her phone turned off."

"I'll go." I picked up my bag. "Anything else you need? I'm not going twice."

"They're open until ten." He looked relieved.

I drove to the intersection of Cave Creek and Cactus, where Google said I could find the nearest Home Depot. I parked as close to the entrance as I could—it was still over a hundred degrees—and walked up to a double door. As it slid open, the smell of raw lumber hit me. Sweet and clean, a promise of better things to come. At Continuity, I was more comfortable with the hard-hats than with the paper people even though I never picked up a hammer. Home Depot felt like my turf. I made my way to the plumbing aisle and found the right size tubing. Then I went to pay. In front of me in line, a middle-aged couple pushed a handcart with an install-it-your-self shower unit looking like it would fall off at any moment. Behind me a youngish dad held his little daughter's hand in one of his and a portable drill in his other hand. It seemed like an awful lot of activity for a Thursday night in July. Suddenly, my brain opened, and an idea slid out: *all* people tried to build in their own way using whatever tools they had. We at Hargrove-Spence weren't so special.

I played with the idea as I paid for the tubing and walked out of the big bright building. Driving down the hill toward home, I felt linked to every person prowling the aisles at Home Depot, and Lowes, and all the hardware stores scattered in between, and it was oddly comforting. My world felt wider.

At home I found Aaron behind the fridge, drinking a beer. He put it down and reached for the tubing. He cut a length same as the old tube and examined the ends. Then he fitted the tube into place, working steadily as if he had a plan. Of course he had a plan! He was one of those millions of people trying to improve their homes in their own way. I should be grateful.

Aaron got up from the floor and shimmied the fridge back against the wall. He reached for one of our plastic drinking glasses and activated the water dispenser. Water trickled into the glass. Aaron knelt and felt under the fridge's door. He straightened up, smiling.

"No more leak. I've saved that creep's reputation."

"You've saved all of us. Thanks."

He said, "Want to have a beer with the hero?"

"Nice idea, but no." I wanted to show him I was sincere. "Gabi said you got an internship with Chicanos Por la Causa. What are you doing?"

He picked up his beer. "Research. I'm finding all the kids in Maricopa County who could have been Dreamers if they'd applied. CPLC is making new policy, and I'm helping."

"Look who's trying to save the world!"

He waved his beer. "*Basta.*"

"Seriously, sounds great."

"Yeah, it's a long shot, and I don't get paid, but so what."

"Tell me about it tomorrow. I'm going to bed." I left him putting away his plumbing tools.

Tomorrow, I would have tea with Sy. As I undressed and slipped on my nighttime T-shirt, I wondered what to tell her when she asked about the Friends meeting. She *would* ask, because she kept up with my calendar, although she pretended the Friends were her business, and I knew she didn't give a crap about them. She always preferred to hear about my life, the bad stuff as well as the good stuff. Her attitude toward the bad stuff seemed to be "shit happens, and you'll get over it." I didn't think she'd gotten over her son's death, though. Maybe I should ask Thomas Hammer about his brother?

I got into bed, grateful for the quiet in my room. As I waited for sleep, Home Depot came to mind, and then I visualized Aaron fixing the fridge. I realized he was like all the other plumbers everywhere doing the best they could with whatever they had, and I identified. Neither Aaron nor I would ever give up.

29

Mrs. M sent an email marked "high importance" asking me to meet her at the Lost Dog Wash Trailhead in the McDowells. I didn't usually hike in those mountains since the closest entrance was a forty-five-minute drive from my apartment while North Mountain was next door. I wrote back that I could meet her at eight-thirty. Any later, and it would be too hot. She sent a thumbs up and a GIF of a dancing cactus. Back East, I hadn't enjoyed the outdoors, but hiking the desert made me feel alive and strong enough for whatever Mrs. M had in mind.

The lot looked crowded for a weekday in July. I found a spot at the far end and trudged to the trail. At the entrance, a rust-colored building shaped like a trapezoid had a concrete slab roof that extended out from the building for twenty feet, making shade. Mrs. M was sitting on a concrete bench in that shade. The big dog lay on the ground next to her. She waved and patted the bench beside her. I sat. The dog heaved itself onto its feet and came over to sniff me.

"Spike won't bother you. When he was a pup, he would clamber over everyone, but not anymore. We're aging together." She pushed her sunglasses on top of her head. "I hope you don't mind dogs. We have a grooming appointment right after this."

"Isn't it a little hot for him? He'll hurt his paws." I'd seen plenty of dogs wearing trail booties.

"Oh, we're not hiking. Spike can't take the heat, nothing over eighty-five. He used to be a great companion. Once when he was young and frisky, he saved my ass on that trail," she pointed. "We were headed home, and he kept stopping every few yards and looking at me. I thought he was playing and kept shooing him ahead. Finally he blocked the trail in front of me and refused to budge. He stared behind me, and when I turned to follow his gaze, I saw the coyote that had been stalking us." She patted the dog's back. "You don't run into many coyotes here these days."

Spike sat down at her feet, panting, and peered through the legs of a Japanese tour group passing by. I reached over to feel his coat, which was soft and smooth, even before the grooming.

Mrs. M said, "Ten years ago I would have said good riddance to coyotes. But I've learned that disturbing the natural order of things produces unintended consequences. The ranchers around here imported buffelgrass to feed their cattle, and now buffelgrass has taken over and raised the fire risk for everyone."

I nodded, wondering if she planned to show me some buffelgrass.

"I wanted to meet here because I would like you to understand that the White Bear Ranch could be the gateway to an amenity like this. Take a look around. We'll wait right here."

I got up and strolled over to a signboard attached to the trailhead building. Plastic pockets on the board held trail maps and fliers for kids' activities, guided hikes, a nature photography contest, and some other stuff. A couple of people were filling bottles at the water fountain across from the johns. A skinny guy in a safari hat and bright blue T-shirt with a whistle around his neck was pointing toward the hills and talking to the Japanese tourists. Behind him, the trail led slightly uphill to a metal grating that formed a bridge across a dry stream bed—no rain this month—and then continued toward the mountains to the east. I crossed the bridge and came to a signpost. Ahead of me, two trails branched left and right, rising uphill toward the McDowell peaks. To the far right, a trail paved for wheelchairs had those metal signs you see in national parks about the local plants and animals. Everything looked lush by Sonoran Desert standards: brittlebush, grasses, cacti and agave, even some scraggly mesquite and acacia trees, fed by runoff from the mountains I would guess. Just then, the tour group trudged past to take the steepest uphill trail. I smelled sunscreen and sweat as well as the dust kicked up by their shoes. They were all wearing hats and had water bottles hanging on straps around their necks. Their outfitter had done a good job.

I turned around and went back to Mrs. M, who was on her phone. She put it in her purse when I approached.

"Seems like a lot's going on," I said, taking off my sunglasses as I sat down to wait for her next move.

"Magnificent, isn't it? Thirty thousand acres in all, pieced together over the years. Do you know how many people enjoy these mountains annually? Not to mention the school groups. It's also part of an important wildlife corridor." She sat straighter and wrapped the leash around her wrist. I thought she was going to get up, but she faced me instead.

"How old are you?"

"Almost twenty-three."

"You know, I was only a little older than you when I came to Arizona. I grew up in Chattanooga. I fell in love with the son of the president of the country club where I was working. We got married when I graduated from UT. I taught school for a few years until I got pregnant."

Why was she telling me this?

"I was an outsider in Chattanooga, but I learned how to make things happen watching my husband's family try to renovate the downtown." She paused. "It's always a long haul."

"That's why I love Continuity. We think about the future."

Spike yawned and rolled over on his side. Mrs. M said, "Look how patient he is. If you are ever interested in getting a dog to hike with, I can refer you to a terrific rescue operation. Their dogs are healthy."

I shook my head. I had no intention of following in her footsteps.

"Did you know this Preserve was started by one woman who didn't want the mountains eaten up by development? It took decades to get a whole lot of people behind her, and the City of Scottsdale as well."

"I heard."

"I don't claim to have her skill and courage, but I do see an opportunity for the Friends of White Bear Ranch to do something similar. I hope you will help."

"Me? I live in Sunnyslope."

She reached down and petted the dog. "I would like you to get more involved with the Friends. I can teach you what I've learned about real estate. You won't always be an outsider." She smiled her devilish-looking smile.

I should have been flattered, but something didn't feel right. Why would Mrs. M single me out? "I intend to keep going to your meetings."

"Wonderful. It will be mutually beneficial, you'll see."

She bent to get something out of the carry-all at her feet, a big leather thing too hot and heavy for summer, in my humble opinion, but classy. She took out a book. She handed it to me saying, "I remember you said you read for work. I think this may be instructive."

I turned the book over, glancing at the blurb: a book written in 1516, in Latin, about an ideal society. Huh?

She said, "Have you heard of Sir Thomas More? No? He's the original thinker about utopian community. I thought you might like to deepen your knowledge. It's a satire, but you might be pleasantly surprised to find how relevant it remains."

She stared at me, as if daring me to object.

"Thanks. I'll read it next." I meant it. My background in this stuff was pretty thin, and who knows, there might be a clue to Mrs. M's schemes.

"You don't really expect your boss to create a paradise, do you? No one in his industry tells the truth. Developers, contractors, they say what's convenient, even if it's impossible. Surely you know this by now?"

Nate had often said that his competitors and vendors were full of shit, but I hadn't been in the business long enough to accumulate evidence. As for Nate himself, to tell the truth, from time to time I did think about how hard it would be to keep Continuity going over the years. When the pipes broke or a neighbor threw a fit, who would actually fix things? Would Nate's commitment extend that far, or would other people lead, maybe one of the residents? I'd pushed down my doubts—I was not naïve—because I wanted to see the experiment through.

"Thanks for the book." I stood to leave.

"One more thing. I know you spend time with Sydelle Hammer. She doesn't leave the house these days, but I'm sure you would want her to be included in the project?"

Aha: the real reason for this meeting.

"She asks about the Friends, and I tell her what happens at meetings."

"Then I can count on you to keep her informed! What can you tell me about how she feels about us at this point?"

"She's neutral."

Mrs. M pursed her lips. "I know you joined the Friends because Nate Hargrove sent you, but I promise that you are going to get more and more enthusiastic as the plan develops and you begin to see all the good we can do. Permanently. Not on the scale of this Preserve, of course. We'll start small."

She stood; Spike got to his feet. "I'm so glad we had this chat. Thanks for meeting me."

A small dog trailing a leash came bounding by, and a woman approached flapping her arms and yelling, *Trixie, come! Trixie!* The dog stopped short beside Spike, then sniffed his rear. Spike didn't much care. Mrs. M stepped on Trixie's leash, and the woman caught up to us out of breath.

"Thank you, thank you!" She puffed. "I don't know what I would do if I lost her." She bent over, still puffing, and picked up the leash. "She's such a minx. Thank you."

Mrs. M said you're welcome and walked on. I followed her to the exit. She turned to me and said, "If you do get a dog, make sure you can manage it. Goodbye."

Mrs. M was a piece of work. I wondered how a teacher from Chattanooga had turned into a monster environmentalist in Phoenix. If she tried to use me in some sort of disinformation campaign against Nate, okay. But not okay against Sy. My best defense would be silence.

30

What luck! Thomas Hammer stepped out his mother's front door as I drove up. I'd been wondering how to get hold of him. I wanted to ask about his brother's death so I could help Sy handle whatever the Friends planned to spring on her. Google had told me nothing about John Hammer, and I didn't look forward to another trip to the State Archive. I also wanted to know what he was talking to Nate about and what he had going with Mrs. M but doubted I'd be able to uncover *those* pieces of intel on the fly.

"Do you have a minute?" I stood on the flagstones directly in his way. "There's something I'm worried about that affects your mom."

He looked piqued but stopped and crossed his arms in front of his chest. He was wearing his cowboy hat and steel-toe boots like a construction worker. "What's on your mind, Miss Wells?"

I screwed up my courage. "You're familiar with the Friends of White Bear Ranch. Do you know they're thinking bigger than the Ranch? They want to make a two-hundred acre preserve."

"So I've been told."

By whom, I wondered? "Do you know they want to name it after your brother?"

He blanched, which I didn't think possible for a man as tanned as he. Clearly, Mrs. M hadn't told him.

"Thanks for alerting me."

"Can you tell me about your brother? Mrs. Morrison made me promise not to say anything to your mom yet, but I want to be prepared."

"There's not much to tell. John was T-boned his senior year of college by a drunk driver who walked away. He had been driving home from a party. He didn't drink."

"Oh, how awful. I'm so sorry."

"Ma was mad with grief for a while. But my mother has always been resilient."

"What about you?"

"I was still in high school. Made me cautious. Probably made me a dentist. I like a small, controlled field of operations."

Manheim was right about him.

He uncrossed his arms, his color returning. "My brother loved the Ranch. He would be running it now."

"With you?"

He shook his head. "When we were kids, he was the cowboy. I was interested in school."

"And your brother wasn't?"

"My brother was good at everything. *I'm* the black sheep. I left ranching behind."

"But you're running the Ranch now?"

"My mother needs me, and she deserves it. I'll sell when she's gone."

Suspicion entered my brain. "Phase two of Continuity?"

He pulled aviators out of his pocket and put them on. "As I told your boss, that's a long shot. I've had other inquiries." He took a step. "If you'll excuse me."

I seized his arm. "Please don't tell your mom about this conversation."

He frowned. "Let me handle anything to do with my brother."

I let go, nodding. Nate had propositioned him, Mrs. M was communicating with him, and Sy had suffered an awful tragedy. So much intel!

When I headed toward the house, I saw Leticia peering out the foyer window. She opened the door before I rang. She asked if I was making friends with Mr. Thomas, and I said I'd like to. She held both my shoulders and said that he was a good man. So loyal, she said, and handsome. I had never considered his looks—he could be my grandfather! —but I stopped to think. He was lean with enough white hair and clear blue eyes. I bet Leticia had a crush on him.

Sy was sitting on the couch, the scooter parked beside it. I'd brought Swiss chocolates rather than cake. She peered into the box I held close to her nose and made a face. She pointed to a milk chocolate cup filled with cream and nuts, which I had been eyeing. I put it on her plate and sat down with a sigh, saying that was the one I wanted. She said she thought so, and that's why she took it. I selected a dark chocolate square with a pink blob on top. We both nibbled, told each other mine was better, like two kids sharing Halloween candy. Contentment was a feeling almost unknown to me in my previous life, before I came to Arizona and met Gabi and Sy.

I poured the tea, telling Sy I'd talked briefly with her son outside. "He said he was on his way to the Ranch. Everything okay?"

"Yes, yes. We need to drill another well. The water table continues to recede. You will tell me it's climate change and I will say it's too many housing developments sucking from the same aquifer, and we will both be right."

She knew everything, and I felt proud to be her friend. I didn't think *I* would wind up as wise and caring as she, but so what.

Sy said, "What were you and Thomas discussing?"

"We were talking about you." True enough.

"Oh, I hope you don't listen to him go on and on about my condition. He is overprotective. His experience with my daughter-in-law taught him to anticipate the worst. You know, she died of a wasting disease."

"Sounds tough."

"They had help, of course, but Thomas hovered over her for years. It was a love match." She paused, seeming to watch a scene play out in her mind. "Now he hovers over me. I don't want him to, but he's a good man. He never adopted his father's bad habits."

"Leticia admires him."

"As well she should. My husband could be demeaning to the female hands, and Thomas stood up to him. They fought constantly after my son, John, died. It was how they mourned him." She took a sip. "Tell me, what have you learned about the Friends group? They had a meeting, I believe."

I wanted to reveal all, but I had agreed to let Thomas Hammer handle the naming issue, so instead I described the Friends' enthusiasm as they discussed expanding their numbers. She asked me to name names. I said I would after Luis collated the info. Speaking of Luis, I told her, he invited me for pastelon after he returns from a trip. She nodded emphatically, and I waited for her to comment, but she went quiet. I was about to segue to Nate's latest doings when she rang the little bell on the scooter tray. She looked past me to the threshold where Leticia would appear. I swallowed my words. Sy asked Leticia to help her onto the scooter because she wanted to lie down. I watched them maneuver, knowing not to interfere. Sy wrapped her arms around Leticia's neck and Leticia encircled her back, like they were getting ready to dance. On the count of three, Sy lifted, and Leticia pulled, pivoting her onto the scooter. Turning to me, Sy said she was sorry to end our tea early, but Thomas must have tired her out. I was to bring something adventurous next Friday. Leticia thanked me for coming as she followed the scooter down the hall. The rubber wheels made no sound crossing the tiles.

I let myself out the front door, disappointed. When I was with Sy and enjoying her sparkle, it was easy to forget she was frail. Maybe it was a good thing her son hovered, as she called it. This was not the first time I'd seen her need help getting into her scooter. Obviously, she didn't like needing it.

31

No one I want to hear from calls at eight in the morning, so I didn't answer the phone. When it chimed again a minute later, I glanced at it and swiped in.

"My dear," Sy's voice. "I want you to visit me."

It took me a second to get into gear. "Don't we have a date for Friday?"

"I had a little fall, and they're keeping me in bed. It would be good to have your company."

Uh, oh. "Are you hurt?"

Sy laughed. "Only my pride. I have something to show you."

"I'm on my way."

I drove too fast on the 101, weaving in and out of lanes. Everyone else was driving above the speed limit, but not as fast as I wanted to go. I was frightened: I'd heard that when seniors fall and break their hips, they go downhill fast. I needed Sy to be okay.

Leticia opened the door. Thomas Hammer stood behind her, bareheaded, and asked me to follow him. I perched on the couch in the living room, scared of what he was going to say.

"Leticia found my mother on the bathroom floor this morning and called the doctor. My mother says she slipped. We think she had a TIA. You know what that is?"

I shook my head.

"Transient ischemic attack. A little stroke that's temporary because the blockage goes away. There's no damage, but it can lead to a full-blown stroke."

"How is she?" I felt awful.

"She's resting and in good spirits. Nothing broken. She insists on seeing you. Please don't stay long." He pointed to the hallway that led to Sy's bedroom.

I hustled down the hall and knocked on the door gently in case she was dozing. Sy said to come in. The room smelled like her floral perfume. She was propped up in bed, leaning on a quilted headboard and looking like a pink island in a sea of white. I had never been in her bedroom before. There were books and papers and at least a dozen figurines crowding the tops of the dresser, night table, and chaise longue. A bookcase held what looked like family photos—weddings, children at the beach, graduations—and a vase full of dried flowers. Next to one of the photos a miniature amaryllis sat in a mini pot, both made of cloth. Someone knew what grandma liked. I should bring a real one.

I moved over to the bed.

Sy looked pale but motioned for me to come closer.

"How are you feeling?" I asked.

"Good, good. Just a little sore from lying on the floor." She pointed to the bookcase. "Bring me the albums on the bottom shelf, the two on the left. I want to ask you something."

The scrapbook covers were faded, edges crumbling. I laid them on the bedspread beside her. She opened one gingerly. A few loose photos slid out. She pointed to the other scrapbook. "That's the one. Look inside."

I opened the album and saw a mess of photos, some stuck onto pages, many loose. Most were black and white, some had old-time, lacy edges with the corners tucked into bits of paper shaped in right angles, like the corners of frames. Some photos were really old, sepia tones on cardboard. I turned a few pages. "What am I looking for?"

"For me." She lay back into the pillows.

I turned pages and found a bunch of kids posing beside a Christmas tree. A little girl holding a teddy bear looked straight into the camera. I rotated the album towards Sy. "This you?"

"Yes, and that's the original white bear. My grandfather wanted the Ranch to remain in the family, so he renamed it after my favorite toy. He said that way I would always know it was mine no matter my last name. He wanted me to treasure it."

"What a nice story!"

"No one alive knows the story, except you."

Not even her son?

She raised her eyebrows. "I suppose you want to know why I told *you*?"

"I'm honored, but yeah."

She pushed on her hands to sit more upright. "Unlike my grandchildren and great-grandchildren, you are interested in the Ranch and its past." She folded her hands on her chest, like an otter. "I would like you to digitize these photographs. Now. I'm running out of time."

Did she know what she was asking?

Sy pointed a gnarled finger at me. "Of course I know what *digitize* means. I told you I might have a project for you months ago. The time has come. Will you help?"

"Absolutely."

"We'll start tomorrow. I'm tired and Thomas is hovering."

I pecked her cheek and returned to the living room where Thomas Hammer sat doing paperwork. He got up and walked me to the door. I felt I should clue him in. "I'll be back tomorrow morning to collect your mother's albums. She asked me to digitize the photos for her."

He shook his head. "Only my mother would start a new project at the end of her life."

As I stepped across the threshold, he called out, "Miss Wells, thank you."

~ ~

The apartment was empty, thankfully. I hustled to my room to research digitizing. I discovered I could send Sy's photos to a service, which might take time, or scan them myself with an expensive piece of equipment or with cheap software on my phone, depending on what kind of end product Sy wanted. I had a lot of questions. How many photos did she want scanned? How would she store them? Did she want them in the cloud? Did she know what that meant? I should have checked my work email, but I didn't care about Nate's demands.

Too antsy to keep sitting, I put on my big hat and went outside. I walked half a mile east to the edge of the Phoenix Mountains Preserve under a heat-whitened sky. It was way too hot to climb the hill, but I knew a shady spot, a cave of sorts, actually a fold in the rockface halfway up. I picked my way around the brittlebush and found the shortcut to the cave. I climbed into it. Someone had scribbled graffiti on the rock at the back. I was disgusted. On my block, no one respected anything. People left garbage in the gutters and dog shit along the walkways. They got into arguments and shot each other. I sat on a flat rock in the mouth of the cave and looked out over streets and rooftops. Both the White Bear Ranch and Continuity seemed impossibly far away. I'd come West to make a better life. I wasn't sure I'd succeeded.

~ ~

Sy looked okay the next morning, in bed but wearing lipstick. I had brought my backpack to carry the albums. She told me to put down my pack and pull up a chair. She sounded like herself, and I relaxed a little. My conscience nagged at me, though. I had gone to bed wanting to tell Gabi how the White Bear Ranch got its name. Then my thoughts had segued to who else would like to know the story, and I thought of Nate, which made me feel guilty. I had not been one hundred percent truthful with Sy, either. I had not explained Nate's drainage scheme or Mrs. M's maneuvers. Sy had placed her memories in my hands, but I wasn't completely trustworthy. I tried to think of a way to confide in her that wouldn't hurt her.

I had printed out screen shots of various scan resolutions. I fished them out of my pack and placed them in front of her on the duvet. I hesitated, and she picked up on it.

"Cat got your tongue?"

I took a deep breath. I could feel my heartbeat quicken out of fear of blowing the friendship. "The first time I came to see you it was because my boss sent me. But I didn't come back for him, I came back for you."

"Yes, I assumed as much."

"And then you sent me to the Friends group. My boss wanted me to spy on them, too, so it was convenient. But the Friends told a different story about the land than he did."

A little smile played across her lips. "Now you see what I have to deal with. Go on."

"You know my boss wants to build more housing, and he doesn't care about the Ranch. Katie Morrison wants to use the Ranch as the anchor for a giant preserve, and she doesn't really care much about it either. I can't tell which of them would be better stewards of this land. I need to ask: what do you want to happen to it?"

She waved her hand. "It'll be up to Thomas. I imagine he'll sell it off as soon as he can. He never liked ranching, and my grandchildren don't want to be involved. He knows my cousins are gold diggers."

"But what do *you* want?"

She paused, and a faraway look came into her eyes. "I want the Ranch to go to whomever will take the best care of it. My family has worked so hard for generations to improve the land, to keep it good for grazing despite the pressure of numbers."

"Who should take over for you?"

"That's a difficult question."

I wanted to help her answer the question.

She shook her head. "Thomas will decide, and that's as it should be."

I didn't believe her. She was a fighter. Why give up now? "But what do *you* think should happen?"

She patted my hand. "My dear Deborah, there's more than one way to skin a cat. I will let Thomas handle this one. I've had my turn."

But I haven't had mine.

She reached for the pink reading glasses on the night table beside her and picked up two of the screenshot print-outs. "What am I looking at?"

I left Sy's house with instructions to buy a high-end scanner and supplies. We planned to set the machine up in one of the spare bedrooms; I would come on the weekends and consult her about duplicates and partial images. If she wanted to, we would have tea. The plan was good, but my chest hurt. She seemed so fragile.

I drove north to take another look at the Ranch buildings that might appear in the old photos. It was too hot to explore on foot, and I hadn't fixed my car's AC, but I wanted to think about Sy's legacy. What did it mean to "care for the land" if no one was raising cattle on it? Nate wanted to build houses on it; Mrs. M wanted tourists to admire the view. They were both crummy as people, but their ideas were good. Maybe Luis could help me sort out my thoughts. Science might have the answer. I stopped at a light on Cave Creek Road and called him. He said he was about to give a presentation and was pressed for time. I blurted my question: in the long run, would the land be better cared for if my boss or the Friends owned it? He said probably the Friends because they would mostly leave it alone. But if Hargrove-Spence succeeded in actually developing high-density, sustainable housing as advertised, *and* it was affordable, it might be more beneficial for the community in the long run. "You should ask a city planner or an engineer how to calculate that," he said.

"Right." At least he'd given me a lead.

"If the climate collapses, it won't matter anyway. It might even be too late for the desert already."

What did *that* mean?

True, I had noticed changes in the plants from when I first hiked here four years ago. Some things were bushier now while others, especially scraggly desert trees, had withered. I had thought little of it. But perhaps the desert was actually signaling something. A scientist might be able to interpret. Not Luis, evidently. I mumbled my thanks.

The White Bear buildings lay ahead. I pulled to the side of the road and idled the engine. One of the Friends was a city planner. I would get an appointment ASAP. I got out of the car and snapped a few shots for reference. The White Bear photo archive would be my gift to Sy. I got back in the car and drove south, organizing the project in my mind. But my brain kept twisting. I'm not good at indulging my feelings—I'd rather just do something—but I couldn't avoid my fear. I couldn't pretend that Sy and I would have an unbroken string of Fridays together. It didn't seem fair that when I'd finally found a mentor, a woman I could admire and emulate, she'd disappear. I was already starting to miss her even though she was still there. I told myself to stop worrying about an event that could be months, even years away.

But there remained the question of who should wind up with her land. She pretended she didn't care, but I was sure she did and was too tired to fight about it. So I would figure it out for her.

32

Driving to the Best Buy on Tatum and Cactus, which had the scanner I wanted in stock, I pushed Nate's latest antic out of my brain.

I'd gone to the office to pick up my new assignment, as requested, and found Nate seated at his desk, spreadsheets glowing on both his monitors. When I knocked on the open door, he didn't respond. I told his white-shirted back I'd spent an unplanned morning with Sy because she'd had a TIA. He whirled his chair around. He said he was sorry to hear that, although he'd known she was on the way out—I wanted to smack him! —and I didn't need to cultivate her anymore. Thomas Hammer had asked for a proposal after all, and Nate would deal directly with him. I said I had an errand to do for Sy, could my new assignment wait? He said "sure" in a way that made me think he'd forgotten all about it. I scooted before he could dream something up.

Best Buy smelled like cardboard, plastic, and carpet glue. The tattooed, pierced clerk led me down an aisle to the printer section and pointed to the model I'd asked about. When I nodded, he disappeared for a few minutes, brought back a box in a shopping cart, and turned away without a word. I could have saved the gas and ordered online. I put ink and photo paper in the cart in case Sy wanted to print anything and checked out, using the credit card Leticia had handed me. Being efficient stopped my brain from looping. I focused on the next steps to take to document Sy's past, not on the sadness ahead. It was too late to go back to her place, so I went home.

I couldn't leave anything in the car. It could get hot enough to melt the plastic bits, and I didn't want to invite anyone to break in. I unloaded the stuff in two trips, piling the printing supplies on top of the scanner box inside the living room door. Gabi came out of the kitchen to see what I was up to. I'd told her Sy had a TIA, and, much as I didn't want to talk about it, I had to explain the boxes. I told her Sy had commissioned me to digitize her photo collection. My throat closed up. "She said she's out of time to do it herself." I choked on the words.

Gabi enveloped me in a silent hug. I leaned into her softness. Gratitude washed through me. I headed to my room, not wanting to face José on the couch with the remote in his hand. My friend Gabi could love whoever she pleased as long as she kept on loving me.

~ ~

The next morning, Leticia helped me unload my car. We carried the stuff into a spare room, and I placed the machine on top of a dresser near an electrical outlet. I followed the set-up instructions and tested the scanner. Leticia brought in the folding table and wastebasket I had asked for, and I told her to expect me to spend Saturdays in this room for the next little while. She gathered up the discarded packaging and took back the credit card. I packed up my bag to go to work.

As I walked past the living room, I did a double-take. Dana Hargrove was seated on the chintz coach and the table was set for tea. She caught my eye and beckoned. I closed my open mouth and approached.

"Sy is getting dressed. Come sit with me." She patted the couch.

How come she was sitting in Sy's living room? I sat in the upholstered chair opposite her and bit my lower lip to keep from saying something inappropriate.

"I'm glad to see you," Dana said with a big smile. "I'd been meaning to connect with you again. I'm sorry to meet under these circumstances." She was wearing a navy-blue sleeveless dress that wouldn't be out of place at a funeral.

"Has Sy had another TIA?"

"No. She says she's feeling better. But she's ninety-two, and—"

"Excuse me," I interrupted. "Did your husband send you?" Instead of paying respects himself, the jerk?

She shook her head. "Hell, no. Sy and I worked together for a charity years ago. When I heard about her TIA, I offered to help with her volunteer activities. I count her as a friend."

"So do I," I blurted. I realized I was gripping my bag and placed it on the rug at my feet.

"Nate mentioned your meetings. Sy is a fabulous mentor. You're lucky she's taken you on."

"I thought she was supposed to rest."

Dana leaned toward me. "I imagine you know her by now. If she feels up to a cup of tea, she'll have one."

I heard the scooter behind me and turned around. Sy rolled toward us wearing lipstick and a turquoise sweater over black pants, white bob freshly combed. Dana rose and pecked Sy's cheek. I stood, too, almost tripping on my own bag. "I came to drop off the scanner. It's ready. I'll see you Saturday."

Sy motioned for me to sit. "Stay for a cup. Leticia was impressed by your technological skills." She positioned her scooter next to the couch. "Dana, will you pour? I take cream, no sugar. Bee as well."

Dana poured the tea gracefully, as if she did so every day at four o'clock. Compared to the two of them, I felt awkward and shabby in my Target shorts and T-shirt. I didn't want to horn in on their conversation, but I couldn't refuse Sy. I sat back and sipped while they chatted about a school where they had both volunteered. Evidently a new director they both liked had gotten into trouble with some of the trustees neither of them liked. The tone of the conversation changed: in lowered voices they discussed who might agree with them and how to line those people up against the others. Dana made notes on her phone. I didn't follow the plot, but I watched Sy with increasing concern. She had not touched her tea or eaten her customary two cashews; the cup and saucer trembled in her hands more than usual. I snaked my long arm forward and took the saucer from her, placing it on the table.

Sy addressed me. "Yes, I *am* tired. I'll go rest." To Dana. "Thank you. I'm confident you'll make it right. Excuse me." She pushed the little joystick and whirled away.

When the scooter had disappeared down the hallway, Dana said, "You are the only person I've ever seen Sydelle Hammer take direction from." She put down her saucer and faced me square on. "That's a compliment."

I swallowed. Not used to compliments from a Hargrove.

"Madison said you contacted her. Thank you for reaching out. She needs role models closer to her age."

"Did she say what we talked about?"

"Something about a project you are working on about Sydelle's ranch. She didn't go into detail. She doesn't confide in me the way she used to." Dana gave a little smile. "I'm grateful for whatever you can do for her."

Clearly, Maddy had not blabbed about Johnson & Sons. I couldn't imagine why she'd mentioned me at all.

Dana sat up straighter and clasped her hands in her lap. "Tell me, Bee. Do you enjoy your work with my husband?"

Oh, boy, what to say? "I love Continuity. I think the compassionate people of the world should have a safe, sustainable place to live."

She laughed, "You sound like Nathaniel." She paused. "I'm not talking about Continuity. My question is about *you*. What do you make of your job?"

"I like learning new things. I'm glad I have a lot to do besides posting every day." What was going on?

"I understand you are waiting for a promotion. Have you wondered why it's taking so long?"

"I don't think about it." A white lie.

"Perhaps you should. I've kept track of you. I think you have a lot of talent, but you won't go far with my husband. He's an inspired developer, but he's not good at cultivating staff. It's his blind spot."

Why was she telling me what I already knew?

She went on. "I'm not making excuses for him, but he's been under a strain these last few months. He really doesn't like to stick his neck out, and I sometimes wonder if he's in the right line of work."

"He has seemed a little off lately."

She sighed. "Sometimes I worry about what could happen to him, to us." She sighed again. "In any event, I don't want the staff to bear the brunt of it."

I was tempted to tell her to pay attention to her own family first, her devious daughter in particular, but only for a nanosecond. I didn't know what to make of the fear she expressed. Why share with me?

Her posture changed, as if she shook it off. She began to smile. "I know Nate appreciates your work, but you can't count on him to advance you."

"I don't think about advancing." Another lie. I really needed the promised raise. "I think about opening Continuity."

"And what will your job be then?" She sat back, took a sip of cold tea.

"Maybe running events for the younger residents? We'll still need a social presence."

"Does that sound interesting?"

"Sort of." Ever since the conversation with Mrs. M, I had been thinking differently about the future. The book she gave me showed that, no matter the century, people screwed up even when they thought they were doing good. The book made me question my motives for loving Continuity, which was probably Mrs. M's intention. I still believed in the promise of a cleaner life, but some of the glow had gone off. Plus, now I had something more important on my mind, Sy in danger of dying.

Dana put down her cup and saucer. "Let me ask that differently. What do you want to be doing five years from now?"

I hadn't thought that far, and I felt itchy. "Nate hasn't said anything definite. I always have to figure things out in real time."

She nodded. "He *can* be elusive. His older brothers were merciless, and he learned to keep his cards close to his chest."

Was that supposed to be an explanation? Poor Nate, in trouble with his wife, his daughter, his brothers, and whoever he borrowed from. I shrugged.

"Bee, I think you could have a career in business. But Nathaniel may not be the best the person to guide you."

My skin started to crawl. "Is Nate going to fire me?"

"Oh, no!" Her face opened in surprise. "He thinks you're a great Girl Friday. I'm not speaking for him. I'm speaking for myself, as an observer."

"Are you telling me to quit?"

"I'm asking you to think about your future. You can do more than be a Girl Friday."

I still had a job. My heart slowed and I tried to smile.

She leaned forward. "I suppose you're wondering why I bring this up?"

I nodded.

"I don't work *in* the office, but I feel responsible for the people side of the business, especially for the staff. I benefit from your hard work."

I nodded, still confused about her motives.

"The most important thing is respect."

Had Nate said I didn't respect him? Or that he didn't respect me?

Dana leaned back. "My husband acts bold, but underneath he's fighting for recognition. I don't want you to suffer collateral damage." She paused. "Perhaps you have a fight of your own?"

"I spy on the competition, that's all."

She picked up the purse lying beside her on the couch and stood. She dipped into it, producing a card. "I'm sorry if you feel I've intruded. Here's my cell. If you want to talk about anything, please call." She closed the purse. "And I won't be offended if you don't."

~ ~

The apartment was quiet and stuffy. The blinds were closed against the summer heat, and it felt like eighty-five degrees inside. Gabi had rules for saving money: the last person to leave the apartment was supposed to set the thermostat to eighty-five, the first person back could lower it to eighty. At night, Gabi lowered it to seventy-seven. She was the only one allowed to go lower than eighty. I surmised that Aaron, leaving last, had obeyed the rules for the sake of sibling harmony. I went to the thermostat to lower the temperature. Then I went to my room and unloaded my laptop. I *should* post the latest construction vids with bits of tantalizing copy about the units priced for Gen Z, but I didn't want to. Because then I would have to monitor the conversations, and I didn't feel like writing smart, sassy replies. I didn't feel smart or sassy. Dana Hargrove's conversation was occupying my brain.

I went out to the patio to sit under the neighbor's tree because I always think better outdoors. But pretty quickly it got too hot even in the mesquite's spotty shade. I opened the back door to go inside, and there was Aaron, sprawled on the couch, beer in hand. He waved the bottle at me.

"I figured you had to be home. I *know* I set the damn thing to eighty-five."

He sat up. "Have a beer with me. No more work today."

I shook my head but sat down anyway.

"What's the matter?" His face grew serious.

I had to spill it. "My boss's wife just told me to quit, I think."

"Maybe you'll listen."

I got up to leave, but he held my arm, and I plopped back onto the couch.

He let go of my arm. "I'm sorry, that was crude. What happened?"

I repeated the conversation I'd had in Sy's living room as accurately as I could, leaving out the parting question. Dana Hargrove's words about a career in business felt foreign on my tongue. I doubted Aaron understood them any better than I did, but he kept nodding. I said, "I just don't get it."

"I get it," Aaron said. "She knows your boss is up to something, and she's warning you. You ought to quit. Like I said."

I stood up and glared. "I don't know why I told you. Forget about it. I'll figure it out on my own." I turned my back and stomped to my room. I should have known Aaron would automatically crap on my job. I locked the door, although I knew he wouldn't follow, and threw myself on my bed face down. It felt like my heart was knocking on the mattress. I rolled over onto my back.

If I didn't work for Continuity, what would I do? Nate was a jerk, but I had proven to myself I could take it. It was the vision that mattered, not him and not me. A vision in which, to tell the truth, it was getting harder to believe.

If his own wife didn't trust Nate to treat people right, how could I trust him to treat Sy right, and the land? The small creature that had been scratching in my chest for the last little while had grown longer claws.

AUGUST

partial monsoon

average daily high = 106° F

days of rain = 5

33

The door to Sy's bedroom was open, but I knocked softly in case she didn't feel up to talking. She called me in. I slipped to her bedside with another file of photos in my hands—we'd worked out a good editing system these last two weeks—and pulled over a chair. She was propped on pillows, wearing her fluffy pink bed jacket and lipstick, Leticia's handiwork.

She waved me closer. "I'm glad you're here. Recovery is boring."

I pecked her cheek and spread the photos on the duvet. "I can't tell what's going on in this batch." The black-and-white snapshots showed Sy with several other youngish women wearing cowboy hats raising wine glasses in a toast.

Sy squinted at the photos. "Oh, dear. I'd forgotten we posed for the camera." She petted one of the pics. "My husband called me foolish. He never really understood what he had in me."

"It looks like you were having fun."

"We were on strike at the Maricopa Cattle Growers annual meeting. The men wanted to form a women's auxiliary with a silly name. Cow-belles. It was a play on cowboys, of course, but I imagined a cow with a bell around her neck. My friends and I felt equal in every respect to our husbands except for the Y chromosome and what comes with that. You can't run a ranch by yourself. We were partners with our husbands, not auxiliaries."

"Wow. You were a troublemaker." I couldn't help grinning. "Good for you!"

"Sometimes trouble is appropriate." She tapped my hand. "You don't need to digitize these. The next generation will fight its own battles."

"But this is history. Don't you want your grandchildren to know that you were a fighter?"

"I want them to respect the land." She paused. "I've been disappointed so often by people who promise everything and do only what serves themselves. Politics are a distraction." She flicked her wrist: end of subject.

I pulled out another set of snapshots: a middle-aged Sy standing to the side while a bunch of adults and kids mugged for the camera in front of the old ranch house. "I can't place these."

Sy picked up one of the photos and looked closely. "Oh, that's my husband's family. I never cared for his sister. A social climber. I managed to tolerate her."

"Why did you?" I felt my button zinging. "You don't have to love your family if they don't deserve it."

Sy raised those imperial eyebrows. "'Love' is the wrong word. 'Embrace' would be better. I discovered my sister-in-law had her reasons for doing as she did." She dropped the photo.

In my family of origin, no one embraced the way Sy meant it. "Should I make a folder for these?"

Sy shook her head. "Those people have no connection to the land."

I wasn't going to challenge her. I stuffed the snapshots back into the file. "If you change your mind about anything, all I need is the approximate year."

I stood to leave but Sy reached a hand toward me.

"Speaking of family, I have something to discuss with you."

I sat back down and leaned close.

"When my husband died, he left no instructions beyond his will. It became my duty to distribute mementos. I don't want

Thomas or my lawyer trying to read my mind after I'm gone, so I'm making provision for you now. Hand me my purse, please."

I spotted her purse on the crowded bookcase and brought it to her. Did she feel bad enough to die? My throat tightened.

She opened the purse and took out a bulging combo wallet-checkbook. Gnarled hands trembling, she struggled with the checkbook, managing to rip out the top sheet. She handed it to me and returned the wallet to her purse. I heard it snap shut while I read, "Pay to the order of Deborah Wells, the sum of five thousand dollars." My heart thudded.

Sy said, "Now, fix your teeth. When you look in the mirror, I want you to see who you are: a confident, smiling Deborah, not a worried Bee. Then you can get a move on."

"Sy, I don't know what to say." No one had ever given me such a generous gift before. Tears welled.

"Go find yourself an orthodontist, and don't ask my son for a reference. His peers are too old. You need someone with the latest technology. And let me know if it costs more. I complete what I start." She frowned. "I would do more for you, but I have grandchildren and great-grandchildren to think of."

I froze as my brain whirled. I had been sent to spy on this woman and to sneak around behind her back, which I did. When I broke into her mine, she forgave me without a word. I could feel my cheeks redden. "I can't take this. I don't deserve it."

"Yes, you do. Now, hurry up about it. I want to see some progress before I die."

I leaned over and kissed her cool cheek, feeling overwhelmed by the money and her vote of confidence. When she did die, there'd be a hole in my life. Not just because I'd miss my once-a-week shot of attitude. Sy made me feel okay about being opinionated, like her. She made me feel good about being me.

Voices sounded in the hall. Leticia emerged in the bedroom doorway, asking if Sy could take company. Her son had brought someone to see her. I started to leave, but Sy motioned for me to stay. I pulled my chair away from the bedside and sat in a corner, busying myself with the photos so I wouldn't look out of place.

Next minute, Thomas Hammer escorted Katie Morrison into the bedroom. My mouth nearly flew open. He held her by the elbow and paused for a second when he saw me. Then, placing his arm across her shoulders, he guided her close to Sy. Mrs. M was dressed up in a white blouse, black skirt, and heels. She and Sy's son seemed a lot friendlier than the last time I saw them talking together at the budget hearing. My skin started to crawl. I started imagining her plotting against Sy the way she plotted against her own son, and I fought to stay quiet.

"Ma, you know Katie. She came to me with an idea about the Ranch. I told her you were the decision maker. She has a time constraint and asked to speak to you. I thought you would want to hear her out."

Mrs. M said, "May I?" and sat on the edge of the bed without waiting for permission. "I won't stay long. I know you need your rest."

Sy looked her in the eye. Her lips puckered, which meant she was holding her tongue. If I were Mrs. M, I'd fear a tongue-lashing.

"I'm speaking for the Friends of White Bear Ranch, not just myself. We would like to offer you the opportunity to name the future preserve after your late son, John, in perpetuity. We haven't worked out the details since we didn't know if you'd welcome the idea. But if you do, and I hope you do, we'll work with Thomas to dot the 'i's and cross the 't's."

Sy looked at her son. "Was this your idea?"

"No. I thought you should hear it from the source."

Mrs. M said, "Your son's name would head the preserve's legal name on signs, maps, and a host of other things. I imagine hikers would tell each other 'Meet me at the John Hammer trailhead.' It's not complicated to add his name at this juncture, as we're still early in the project. It could be tough to do so later."

Sy's eyebrows knitted. "What's the price?"

At least Mrs. M had the good grace to cringe.

"It could be land, or financial support, or a combination of both. I'm sure Thomas and I could work it out to your satisfaction."

Thomas Hammer said, "Ma, she has more."

Mrs. M lowered her voice. "I think this would be a way for you to ensure the White Bear would be viewed positively going forward, to pre-empt anything unfortunate that might emerge from the past. The public relations campaign would be stellar."

Sy said, "Please go, I'm tired. Thomas will get back to you." She turned her cheek to the pillow.

Mrs. M looked at Thomas, who nodded. She rose, leaving the impression of her presumptuous ass on Sy's duvet. Thomas Hammer bent to give his mother a kiss. As he and Mrs. M left the bedroom, he nodded at me, whatever that meant. I was angry at him, at both of them, for bothering Sy in her delicate state. Ruthless, that was the word for Katie Morrison. She even dressed like a vulture. I stepped close to see if Sy was okay. She turned her face to me, and there was a tear in the corner of her left eye. My anger soared.

"Oh, Sy, I'm sorry." I stopped in my tracks. "Should I leave you alone?" The last thing I wanted was to make her feel worse.

"No. Give me a minute." She wiped the tear with one bent finger.

I'd give her an hour. Anything.

She sighed. "When I'm gone, John will truly be gone. That makes me sad. But it can't be helped. Certainly not by plastering his name on a trail."

That's my Sy!

"No more photos today. I *am* tired. Go home and deposit that check." She leaned back and closed her eyes.

I returned Sy's purse to its place on the bookcase and left quietly. The check was burning a hole in my backpack. My father had refused to pay for braces: would straight teeth have made a difference in my life up to now? I wasn't sure I needed to fix them at this point, but Sy usually knew better. I started my car and cranked the AC. My poor brain was in a jumble. Sy was dying, and Katie Morrison knew it. Nate knew it. Both were trying to take advantage of her frailty. Neither deserved her land. One of them might get it.

As I pulled out of the driveway, I decided to channel Sy and make appropriate trouble. I phoned Nate even though it was Saturday. "I've just seen something you should know about. Thomas Hammer brought Katie Morrison to meet with Sy this morning. The Friends want to name the preserve after Sy's dead son if she buys in. She didn't say yes or no."

"Well, I'll be damned."

"I got the impression Thomas Hammer's in on it. He seemed cozy with Mrs. Morrison."

"How much money is involved?"

"They didn't say. Do you want to tell me what's happening with him?"

"Uh, not now. Thanks for the tip." He ended the call.

I had expected more of a reaction, not that he'd spill his guts to me, but maybe he'd share *something*. I hoped he was squirming inside, although that's not what you should wish for your boss. Would he be equally indifferent, I wondered, if I said I was quitting? I was not about to test that out with my credit card maxed and my student loan payment and rent due. I pushed the gearshift into drive and headed home. It was nearly noon, time enough to get to the bank to deposit that red hot check rather than let it fly around the internet. A few cotton-candy clouds were spread thinly across the August sky. It might rain later in the day. August meant the paralyzing heat of summer was about to relent.

Not for me.

~ ~

Gabi was sitting at the kitchen table, on the phone, when I approached. She said *"momentito"* and lowered the phone to her chest. "My mother. This could take a while. I'll come find you."

Agitated, I stepped onto the patio. It was still less than a hundred, and mildly muggy because we'd had a monsoon the night before. Aaron was standing beneath the neighbor's mesquite, smoking weed by the smell of it. I asked for a toke. He grinned and passed me the joint. I disliked marijuana but took one deep drag to calm down.

Aaron said, "Problem?"

"Why do you say that?" I handed back the joint.

"Because I've never seen you smoke."

I leaned against the dilapidated block wall separating our building from the neighbor's and thought about taking another hit.

Aaron said, "*I've* got a problem. Gabi wants to give a party for my twenty-first birthday and the family is gonna drive up from Ajo. Parents, uncles, aunts, asking questions I don't want to answer." He offered the joint. "Can't you talk her out of it?"

I took another deep drag. "Doubt it. You know how she feels about family. Be grateful you have a closet to sleep in." I couldn't help jabbing him.

"Whoa. Give me that back before you get really mean."

I took another deep drag and felt like crying. "Sorry. It's not you. I'm totally disgusted."

"Wanna tell me about it?" He spoke gently.

The tears came with a feeling of release. "I want to help Sy figure out who should buy her land. Both my boss and his rival want it, and neither of them deserve it."

"Is this really part of your job?

"Not technically, and I don't know what to do."

"You need a new job." Aaron passed me the joint and I pulled so hard the entire business end glowed. Then he took it back, saying something I didn't catch. I stopped listening.

I leaned against the wall, the rough surface pressed into my skin. I ran my hand over the stucco, dislodging pieces in the worn places. Someone should fix the stucco before it crumbled in the Arizona sun. The landlord didn't care. Could you patch the surface, or would you have to tear the whole thing down, I wondered? I didn't know. I tried to hug the whole warm wall against my chest. I spread my arms and felt friendly roughness on my cheek.

Hands pulled me off the wall. Aaron said, "Let's go in. You need to come down."

Why was he telling me what to do? Everyone told me what to do. Sy. Dana Hargrove. "I like it here."

"You'll like it inside, too." He wrapped an arm around my waist and led me into the apartment. I could feel the muscles of his arm pressing against my back. They felt strong and I leaned into him. He whirled me around and pressed his lips against mine.

I pushed him away. "No, no."

He stepped back, mumbling sorry, sorry.

"You might be nice to kiss if I were some other girl."

"Be some other girl."

"Ha!"

I sailed past him through the living room and into my bedroom. I flopped onto the bed and hugged the pillow, remembering why I avoided marijuana. It turned me off people; I much preferred the company of my own super-sensitized brain. I wiped Aaron's kiss off my lips with the back of my hand and reached both arms up to the ceiling, weaving my fingers together. I looked through the finger web at the popcorn up there: those little bumps covering every last inch of ceiling, the last century's fashion. I wanted to run my fingers over them, pull off loose flakes of paint. How had I wound up in Sunnyslope sleeping under a popcorn lid? I turned onto my side and closed my eyes. Aaron was right. I needed a new job. But the idea of leaving Continuity scared me. What would I do instead? Damn Aaron and his truth-serum weed. And what about Sy? I wanted to talk to her, but couldn't. I closed my eyes to rest my loopy brain.

3 4

Two Saturdays later, a couple hours before Aaron's birthday party, I went to the office to pick up some brochures. At seven that evening, a crowd would gather in our back yard. Gabi had invited the neighborhood as well as her extended family, and if strangers asked about my work, I wanted to be able to hand them a brochure. You never knew when someone would be interested. Speaking of interest, I had invited Luis—although I wasn't sure he'd come—so he could gain ground with my roomies. We hadn't seen each other in a couple of weeks, and I wanted to know when the invitation to eat his pastelon was going to materialize.

As I headed down the office corridor to the exit, box of brochures in hand, I spotted Nate out of the corner of my eye. He was seated at his desk talking to a young guy wearing a blue blazer despite the August heat. Nate spotted me, too, and called me over. Okay, I thought as I detoured toward his desk, Nate shouldn't be here at five on a Saturday. Something had happened.

Nate said, "I'm surprised to see you."

"I needed a resupply." I waved the box in front of me.

"Let me take advantage of your being here to introduce you. Bee, meet Chris, my new hire."

The guy offered his hand, and I shook it. He didn't smile. He wore one of those "I'm too busy to shave" shadow beards and short hair. I smelled prep school.

Nate said, "Chris, you should know that Bee used to visit with your great-grandaunt on our behalf."

One of Sy's relatives? The hairs on the back of my neck stood up.

Nate addressed me, "Chris recently graduated from the same real estate program at ASU as I did. He's going to take over Continuity. You can show him the ropes next week."

The words plowed into me like a bullet. "What do you mean 'take over'?'

"He'll handle the day-to-day communications. And White Bear Ranch. He knows the neighborhood." Nate winked at me.

"Is this what you've been cooking up with Thomas Hammer?" I thought: you idiot, she hates that side of the family.

"You did a great job with his mom, but as I told you, the situation has changed."

I pointed to the guy, "If he has communications, what am *I* supposed to do?"

Nate looked surprised. "Your job is as my assistant. I have a few things coming online we haven't discussed. Maddy told us you wanted to do something new."

My heart fell into my gut. "This is bullshit!" I plopped the box of brochures onto a chair and stalked out of Nate's office all the way to my car. A few drops fell on the windshield as I steered for Sunnyslope, trying to untangle my feelings, hoping for Gabi's sake it wouldn't rain.

Did I just quit?

No, I was rude. But Nate infuriated me. Not bothering to talk to me before changing my life. Using his brat kid as an excuse. Maybe he was afraid I'd revolt? More likely he assumed I'd trot along doing his bidding, business as usual. A horrible thought burst into my brain—that I'd snuck around for two years, muddying my morals, for what? To help him ambush my friend? My hopes came crashing to the ground. I had betrayed my better self for nothing.

I reached our block. A bunch of dusty vehicles had taken all the parking spaces in front of the apartment complex—probably Gabi's folks up from Ajo—so I parked around the corner. Gray clouds were bunched overhead. If it rained a little, drops would form pock marks in the dust on the vehicles. If it rained a lot, the cars would wash clean, but Gabi's party would fizzle. I went inside and found her loading bowls with homemade salsa.

"I'm going to leave the food inside in case of rain," Gabi said. "The drinks won't melt. Do me a favor, see if my uncles need anything?"

I stepped out the back door into the alley running the length of the apartment complex. Two chunky men with facial hair were tying down an inflated bounce house at one end. At the other end, I saw the barbeque they'd already set up. When the party was in full swing, the adults would stand around eating hot dogs and drinking beer, while Gabi's Latin playlist blared from a pair of speakers and the kids bounced themselves silly. I asked the uncles if they needed help. They waved me away with big smiles. I went back to the kitchen, dying to talk to my best friend about what had gone down at my office, but she was hunched over the stove, flushed with cooking and hurry. I swallowed myself and asked her what she needed done next.

~ ~

Two hours later, calmer, I stood on the kitchen threshold surveying our guests. The rain had held off, and at least fifty people crowded the yard, now and then coming into the kitchen to fill paper plates with Gabi's cooking. Some of the men shouted over the music as a few guests danced. Little kids shrieked in the bounce house. The teenagers flirted like crazy. Gabi's uncles tended the barbeque, sending the sweet mesquite smell into the night. Aaron, presiding over the beer supply, seemed happy, toasting with his uncles, singing along. I saw no outward sign of the embarrassment he had feared, and I was glad. Gabi hung onto José's arm and seemed a little tipsy. She deserved to have fun at her own party. Trying to get into party mode myself, I stepped over to the bounce house to chat with one of the aunts who was supervising. She was younger than Gabi's mom and spoke perfect English. We watched a little girl in a frilly dress stop the boys from getting in. I felt a touch on my shoulder: Luis, finally, carrying a six-pack.

"Where should I put this?"

I pulled him over to the deserted drink table. Aaron popped up a nanosecond later. Luis said, "*Feliz cumpleaños.*"

Aaron opened his mouth to answer but I interrupted. "I'll bring Luis back in a bit, okay? I need to talk to him."

I pulled Luis through the crowd out to the front steps where the sounds of the party dimmed. I couldn't wait another minute.

Luis said, "You know, I could use a beer. I've been wrangling data all day."

Suddenly I felt foolish, looking at myself through Luis's New York eyes.

He leaned against the railing. "What's up?"

"Nate hired a guy to take over Continuity. He's taking it away from me." The words burst out of me. I'd only been this angry once before.

"Male chauvinism?"

"No, nepotism. He's a relative of the owner of the White Bear. Nate is playing politics with my life, and I'm disgusted."

"Quit."

My chest squeezed shut. "Continuity is the best thing that ever happened to me."

"What do you mean, best thing? It's a real estate deal." He frowned.

I took a couple of deep breaths, searching for how to explain my confusion in a way that would make sense to him. Luis had to measure things before he believed them.

He put his hands on my shoulders. "Look, whatever it is that you like about Continuity, you'll find it somewhere else. The one thing I've learned in science is that good ideas persist."

This isn't science, I thought. Listen better!

"Besides, utopias never work out." He dropped his arms. "How about that beer?"

I looked away so he wouldn't see the disappointment in my eyes and led him back around the building to the party. Sy would call him impermeable.

We made our way to the drinks. As Luis opened a can, Aaron hustled over. I braced for bad behavior, but they talked civilly about their internships, and I stopped paying attention. I turned my back, realizing that I didn't want Luis as a boyfriend just like I didn't want Aaron. While the two of them joshed with each other, I slipped away to nurse my urgent, painful anger. It would be hours before the party would end and I could go to my room and lick my wounds.

~ ~

At eleven the next morning, Gabi, José, and I sat down to brunch in the kitchen. We'd spent the last couple of hours cleaning up while the birthday boy slept in. Our guests had left three garbage bags full of mess, even after we'd collapsed the cans and boxes. José had worked fast, muttering under his breath, emptying the barbeque and deflating the bounce house. I'd been watching him these last few weeks but hadn't seen any signs of his mistreating or devaluing my Gabi. Maybe Aaron just didn't like José's style. But Gabi liked it, and that was that. Her family had praised Gabi to the skies before driving away last night, and she'd floated on air in the kitchen while cooking our scrambled eggs and bacon.

I was hungry and dug in. I'd come to a decision in the wee hours after the party ended. When I'd laid down, Luis's comments had echoed in my brain. I talked with Sy about it in my mind. She seemed to say, "Look for the portion of truth and discard the rest." She also said, "I trust you to think it through." So, I would trust myself.

I examined everything honestly, and an image of the future came to me, an image disconnected from Nate and the Ranch war. After a little while, I fell asleep and woke up energized. The eggs tasted like salsa even though I'd washed the pan before Gabi used it. It reminded me of something else Sy once said: traces of the past sometimes persist, but you shouldn't let them stop you from enjoying the present.

Gabi poured a second coffee for José and came over to me. "Guerita, I need a favor. Wait for the vendor to pick up the rentals? We're going to see José's mom. She couldn't come last night. We're taking her to church." Gabi's face was shining. Who could resist?

"Sure. Do I pay them?"

"No, no. It's covered. Oh, and I put a plate in the fridge for Aaron when he wakes up. We'll be back in a couple of hours." She kissed my cheek. "Thank you!"

José carried his coffee cup out the front door behind Gabi, and I was alone, savoring my newfound peace. I placed the brunch dishes in the sink and was about to go check my phone when Aaron loomed in the doorway, yawning and rubbing his eyes. He had to be totally hungover.

"Where is everyone?" he said with gravel in his throat.

"Your sister went to church with her boyfriend's mother. She left food in the fridge for you. Want me to warm it up?"

Aaron shook his head and eased himself onto a chair. "I need coffee."

"You need water first. You're dehydrated. I'll make you coffee after." I handed him a glass of water and stood over him while he drank it.

He squinted at me. "Why are you pretending to be Gabi?"

I laughed and smelled the coffee left in the pot. "What's going to be different now that you're twenty-one?" I dumped the stale dregs and started fresh.

He muttered, "Nothing, except I can buy liquor and cigarettes and marijuana and guns."

"Aaron, I'm serious." The coffee maker began to spit and steam. I nudged the pot so it lined up with the spigot.

"Why are you dancing around? Something happen last night? Hot date?"

"None of your business." My mood was so good I could let that go. I cranked the water faucet, planning to soak the dishes. "Leave your plate in the sink after you eat. I'll wash everything later."

I went to my room and unplugged my phone from its charger. I thought about texting Sy to thank her for the advice "she" had given me last night, but it would be better to pop in tomorrow in person.

Then Aaron appeared in my doorway. "Hey, I'm sorry about that crack. I keep screwing up around you."

"Yeah, you do." Poor, hungover guy. I wanted to give him a birthday present. "Something did happen last night. I decided to quit my job. I'm going to tell my boss tomorrow." It felt so good to say the words out loud.

Aaron straightened up. "Wow. Good news. Took you long enough."

"Don't be nasty." I wasn't annoyed, not in my current frame of mind.

"I mean, what are you going to do?"

"Look for work. Go to school. I might have to move. Then you could have my room."

"I'd rather have you." He looked dead serious.

"There you go again." I stood up and pocketed my phone. "I'm going outside for a while before it rains."

Puffs and streaks of white cloud populated blue sky. In a couple of hours, more clouds would appear and form a gray mass. If it rained, the air would cool, and plants would release wonderful smells. Back East, we always hoped it wouldn't rain so we could keep playing outdoors. Here, where everything was thirsty—the ground, the plants, my skin—I wished the rain would go on and on. In the last four and a half years, Arizona had changed my feelings about a lot of things.

~ ~

On my way out of the Hargrove-Spence office for the last time, I phoned Sy and told her I'd quit my job and had something important to tell her. She said, "Well, well, come over right away." I drove mechanically, turning things over in my busy brain. In my night-time mental ramblings, I'd realized the question was bigger than whether Nate or Mrs. M should take over White Bear Ranch. I loved the desert, not just for hiking, but as a place for life, however tough. It really came down to what was best for the land *and* for the creatures who had to, or, in the case of humans, chose to live there.

When I knocked on Sy's door, Leticia ushered me straight to the bedroom. I hurried to Sy, my heart beating hard with ... what? Excitement, yes, and also fear. What if she scolded me about quitting without having another job? But I knew it wouldn't take me long to find work, and I had to make the change. She was waiting in the wingchair.

"Sit on the ottoman over there," Sy pointed. "Now, tell me what happened."

"I quit my job this morning. Now I can speak freely." The words came out in a rush. "I don't think you should let your son chop up the Ranch. It's *your* legacy. I don't trust my former boss to live up to his promises, and Katie Morrison is a manipulator, but I think you should give the Ranch to the Friends before ... it's too late. I've spoken with a city planner. They'll probably take better care of the desert."

I held my breath.

 Sy nodded. "Thank you for telling me your truth."

"What will you do?"

She folded her hands. "I need to tell you my truth." She sat straighter. "I disappointed you when you came to talk about the Johnson affair. I should have explained how painful it was to hear my grandfather and my father fight all those years. My grandfather enlisted to atone for his misdeeds, but he returned from that awful war even more damaged. I was just a girl, but I understood that he had shamed our family. I have protected my family's standing ever since." She paused. "I could have trusted you to understand."

I shrugged. "It doesn't matter now." I had let all that go in the night.

"Yes, it does." She nodded again and took a breath. "While I appreciate your advice, I will not take it. The White Bear belongs to Thomas. He is better suited to grapple with it than I am. I belong to another time."

My turn to nod.

She unfolded her hands. "What will you do now that you are free?"

"I'm going to go to ASU to finish my education. I want to understand, *myself*, how people can live well in the desert." My heart boom, boomed.

"Does this have anything to do with your young man, the scientist?"

"Luis? No, we're barely speaking." Uh, oh. She thinks I'm not up to it.

"Good. You don't need his permission."

Relief flooded through me, and I could feel the excitement rising hot in my cheeks. "If you don't mind, I'm going to use the teeth money for tuition and start as soon as possible. I'll get a part-time job and a student loan and a deferment on my old loan. I'd like to pay you back eventually."

"Nonsense. I support education. But promise me you will fix your teeth ... *eventually*." She gave one of those coy smiles that had charmed ranchers and politicians and everyone else for nearly a century.

"Thank you."

I got up to give her a hug. I could feel every bone of her ribcage through her bed jacket and tried not to squeeze. I wanted to protect her, one of Arizona's living treasures, and one of mine.

"You're welcome. Go home now. But don't be a stranger."

"I won't. I promise," I said, and I meant it.

MAY, FOUR YEARS LATER

Gabi stood with legs spread and baby on hip in my tiny living room—I'd moved out of Sunnyslope to be closer to campus—and beamed with mama pride. She'd come to see me graduate and, of course, to show off her daughter and the ring on her finger. Such a cute kid, with José's coloring and Gabi's soft, round face. Little diamonds sparkled in the toddler's ears. She'd been making eyes at my brother, then burying her face in her mother's shoulder, then peeking out at him again. Two years old, and already a flirt. My brother flirted right back. He'd come to my graduation with an ulterior motive, as I'd discovered when I picked him up at Sky Harbor the other night lugging his guitar case. Nineteen now, past the worst of his acne, Danny had learned to charm, and he was shining it on all three females in the room.

It had taken me almost four years to finish my BA as I didn't have the precursor science and economics courses required for my major, and I worked part time. But working had never troubled me, and I loved studying sustainability, not in the blind way I had glommed onto Continuity, but with eyes open to the problems ahead. To fulfill a course requirement, I'd done a research project on urban parks, and it had produced a couple of job leads. I planned to interview later this summer after a much-needed break. I'd finally learned not to put work ahead of everything else.

I loved having Gabi and Danny watch me get my diploma. I wished Sy could have seen it, with the words "Deborah Wells" written in old-fashioned ink. She lived almost a year after that first TIA and totally supported my goals, although she continued to pester me to fix my teeth. The day she left the planet was the saddest I'd known, and I called an orthodontist right after the funeral. At least Sy had known that I followed her advice and took back my name. I'm Deborah, called Dee by my college friends. Just thinking about Sy makes me smile.

Gabi put the baby down and sighed. "She's getting too heavy to carry anymore." She fished around in her gargantuan bag and handed her daughter a toy keychain with a bunch of neon-bright, plastic keys. The little girl toddled over to Danny and banged the keys on his knee. He swung her up on his shoulders and stepped outside to play piggyback—not enough room inside my place—and the toddler squealed happily. Gabi followed them with her eyes, then she turned to me. "I almost forgot. This came for you." She reached into her bag and handed me a glossy brochure. "Those people need to update their mailing list."

It was a sales piece for a ballot initiative to fund the future White Bear Ranch Preserve. In Arizona, citizens who gather enough signatures can ask the electorate to vote on a proposition to become law. I skimmed and then I reread carefully. I had dropped out of the Friends group and stopped following their progress after the Preserve became a reality thanks to a fifty-acre gift of land from the Ranch. If I had to bet, I'd say Katie Morrison offered to take the mine off Thomas Hammer's hands so she could use "the gift" for political reasons. Now the Friends wanted public money to complete their two-hundred-acre plan.

I looked at my friend. "Would you vote for it, I mean if you could vote?"

"Probably, now that I have a kid. Would you?"

I had spent the last few years learning how environmental science crosses economic development and cultural values, and I'd learned there are legions of interlocking considerations, no clear-cut rules, and individuals still made a difference. I hoped Thomas Hammer would hand over the rest of the Ranch to the Friends, either gift or sale. I hoped they would prove to be good stewards.

I smiled at Gabi. "Yeah, for your kid's sake."

I laid the brochure on top of my laptop on the desk in the corner of the living room. Gabi stepped to the door and stuck her head out. Then she perched on my Goodwill couch.

"They're sitting on the curb. He's good with kids."

"He's trying to ingratiate himself. He wants to stay with me for a while." I made air quotes: "To check out the scene."

Gabi's head pulled back. "Where will he sleep? On this couch?"

I laughed, remembering Aaron on her couch and in our closet, and the hard time I had given her about it. Aaron and I still texted now and then, and he brought me some of the tamales his mother sent up every Christmas.

Gabi said, "You know why Aaron finally moved out? He said it was because he fell in love. I think it was because he couldn't stand hearing an infant cry. It's hard to shake a little brother." She rose. "I should go feed my baby."

We hugged tight. I texted Danny to bring back the kid. He met us at the door. The baby toddled over to the potted amaryllis standing on the floor inside the doorway and grabbed at a red blossom that had just opened. Gabi sprang forward to rescue the plant. She gathered her little girl in her arms, and we four exchanged kisses. Danny and I waved as Gabi drove away. I felt warmed head-to-toe by her friendship. We were the best kind of family.

That night, while Danny streamed music into his headphones, I opened my laptop and Googled the White Bear Ranch Preserve. I couldn't find a map of the fifty-acre donation, only of the grand scheme, which looked acceptable.

Then I Googled Continuity.

It seemed Nate had run into obstacles, but the first phase was now mostly subscribed. I was glad to see the experiment continuing, and I wished Nate luck.

My brain segued to the project I'd been planning in my head ever since I finished my coursework. I wanted to make a dryland pocket park where the end users decide the design—I borrowed the best of Nate's ideas—alongside a landscape architect, a climate scientist, and a lead partner from the community association. I hoped to start in Sunnyslope, where the locals would be willing to speak up, on a patch of empty desert near the main drag. It might take years to complete, and it might fall through anyway for who knows what reason. But I would keep going because it was the right thing to do, for me and for Arizona. Sy would approve.

~

Photo credit: Scott Foust

ABOUT THE AUTHOR

SHEILA GRINELL earned a B.A. in English literature at Harvard University and a Certificate in creative writing at Phoenix College. Her debut novel, *Appetite*, was published in 2016 and a second novel, *The Contract*, in 2019. After a 40-year career in science museums, Grinell now gives talks at libraries and bookstores and engages with readers on social media about "writing as a second act." A resident of metro Phoenix since 1993, she has served as Writer-in-Residence for the Mesa, AZ, Public Library system and was inducted into the Arizona Women's Hall of Fame. For more or to contact her, go to sheilagrinell.com, or FB: Sheila-Grinell-author, or IG: @sheilagrinell.

ACKNOWLEDGMENTS

The character of Sydelle Hammer was inspired by four nonagenarians and two centenarians I had the pleasure of knowing: Bettie Crawford, Lucille Kinter, Ada Korf, Maxine Lakin, Betty Van Denburgh, and Dot Webb. Many friends, neighbors, and colleagues told me about their experiences in community-building in Arizona: Brian Baehr, Stacie Beute, Jim Burke, Marc Cavness, Nikal Conti, Keri Garcia-Wright, Wendi Goen, Eric Gorsegner, Dennis Knight, Christine Kovach, Sally Lakin, Raina Maier, PhD, Kim Moody, Spalding Olmsted, Mac Perlich, Mary Jane Perrone, Suzanne Rothwell, Kori Tueller, Patricia Watts, and Doug Young. Maureen Donovan kindly escorted me around Tamaqua, PA, the model for Bee's hometown.

Trish Cox and Linda Valdez read early versions, and Pam Hait stuck with me through multiple iterations. My late friends Lois Zachary and Lynn Multari read partial drafts, and Laird Hunt and the other finalists in his section at the 2022 Tucson Festival of Books Master's Workshop provided encouragement. Agent Najla Mamou gave useful advice (although she didn't represent me). My brilliant developmental editor, Carol Test, helped me complete the work. I am grateful to all these people for their support and guidance.

STUDY GUIDE QUESTIONS

1. The story hinges on the relationship between Bee and Sydelle, seventy years apart in age and light years apart in experience. What do they see in each other? How does the relationship develop?

2. Nate envisions a community that is ruled by its residents but avoids "the tragedy of the commons"—that a shared resource degrades when individuals act in their own self-interest. Do you think such a community could be created? Would you want to live there?

3. The Friends of White Bear Ranch believe they are working for the public good. They don't seem to know that their leader, Katie Morrison, uses dubious methods. Would they continue to follow her if they truly understood her manipulations? Should they?

4. Bee's doubts about her boss's motives grow over the four-month course of the novel. So do yours. What pushes Bee over the edge, causing her to finally quit her job?

5. Sydelle knows that in a changing environment, the future of her ranch is uncertain. She wants to leave the land to her son to figure what comes next. Bee disagrees. What do you think should happen to the desert?

6. Aided by Sydelle's moral and financial support, Bee decides to finish her education and set off on her own. What's the significance of her changing her name?

Sibylline Press is proud to publish the brilliant work of women authors over 50. We are a woman-owned publishing company and, like our authors, represent women of a certain age.